A LITTLE EXISTENCE

EDWARD ALEX SMITH

iUniverse LLC
Bloomington

A LITTLE EXISTENCE

iUniverse books may be ordered through booksellers or by contacting:

iUniverse
1663 Liberty Drive
Bloomington, IN 47403
www.iuniverse.com
1-800-Authors (1-800-288-4677)

ISBN: 978-1-4917-2290-9 (sc)
ISBN: 978-1-4917-2291-6 (e)

Printed in the United States of America.

iUniverse rev. date: 02/07/2014

CHAPTER I

——∘∘⊷◉⊶∘∘——

An Early Ending

(Friday Night, Midnight, September 4th)

All I can hear is the sound of my best friends suffering as quietly as they can. Two of them had been shot and the rest of us had almost been beaten to death. We were dragging each other by our collars and damp shirts. We had just barely escaped onto the train tracks with a burning building behind us calling the echoed sirens. We just kept running, holding on to each other. We had been set up by someone we used to trust.

In my mind I go back a few months when we were all a family, him and I were brothers. We were leaving a bar, a bar that the rest of the town had heard countless stories about, and a woman was watching me leave. I was with everybody, but she was only looking at me. From the distance I could see the concern, she was wondering why somebody at my age was hanging around with a group of adults showing off their money with clothes and jewelry, and all getting into their nice cars. The entire town was watching us and they knew who we were, and they knew what we were doing. We kept this dying town alive, but by the end, it fell. My name is Alex, and in one year, I am going to die.

"Most knowledge of much is none, for this beginning is the end, as the end is the beginning."

It was early September and I was in the worst state of my mind than I had ever been in. We were all very paranoid

1

and worried about the events that just taken place prior, our dear friend William Daniel's death. The phone was ringing off the hook and everybody was sitting on the edge of their seats, because that night was supposed to be the end for everything, one last simple thing and the end of this so called 'war'. We were reviewing what exactly had to be done and made sure that we had everything planned right. Ritz Sanko, sitting next to me was one of them, I always thought that was such a strange name. He was also a good friend of mine, and one hell of a good drug dealer, he could turn mud into gold. I dragged him into all of this ironically due to his overdose at the very beginning. He stood taller than most, and wore clothes twice his size, but he pulled it off.

I couldn't remember all the people there exactly. All the new faces crowding in the same small room Costa had called his new home. I kept my head down in anger, because I didn't trust a single one of them. This was a war amongst ourselves now and not some typical gang war fighting over territory or color. Just a town filled with people with something to prove.

I couldn't stop observing everyone, my eyes wondered the room as it filled with smoke and the ashtrays were filled with half put out cigarettes, everybody was fidgeting with something and there was tension in the air. I remember my friend Kenny not acting like himself either, which wasn't like him at all, but yet nobody was acting normal.

The leader and tallest of the crowd turned and said to me, "Kid if you mess this up, we will all deny we had anything to do with you, and you'll be on your own." How reassuring, a natural conversation with our so-called 'leader'. He was just a young man with a powerful father and a lot of money.

This was Costa, and no, I did not feel to say anything back. But right away I had a funny feeling about it, he was up to something. Only seconds later Chelsea had walked through the front door. She had this way about herself that everybody could see. At least she always grabbed my attention. She was small, but fierce, and as beautiful as her loyalty.

She glowed with a great presence. One of the originals along with Ritz Sanko, Kenny and the others including myself from the very beginning, and was still here, after everything. She was small for her age, but she packed a punch and her looks could fool almost anybody.

"You're late." Costa mumbled under his breath to her.

"I didn't get the missed call notification until after I left the hospital, relax." She replied taking her coat and bag off. The hospital provided no service to her cell phone.

"You knew tonight was important, it better not be because of you, Alex fucks this whole thing up."

"What the hell is that supposed to mean?" She asked. Wondering why I was the one to blame. The night was as young as me and I was already getting angry.

"Hey wait a second!" I finally yelled. "Why is this all on me? You're the one sending us to do your fuckin' dirty work! I don't know why you can't just do this yourself." I had to step in and say something, we had all been fighting for almost a month and Costa didn't like it too much when any of us spoke above him. He was spoiled, stubborn and unrealistic when it came to reasoning with him.

He and his big bugged eyed brother, Rant, gave me a real long dirty look, but there was something else to him, he was acting different. He was acting and waiting on his betrayal to me and my best friends. He was really wired and edgy about everything and I could tell he was just waiting for us to leave. Finally his look became a smile and he started laughing. His face rearranging and molding into the demon he truly was.

"You're hilarious kid, just last year you were all hopped up and ready to do anything I said, then I say something a little harsh to this bitch you love so much and you try to make a stand?"

"Hey!" Sanko yelled, cutting him off before he could say anything more and create disaster in this small room.

"That's enough! Let's do what we came here to do, shut up and sit down!" He screamed.

"Aren't you always the peace keeper, eh Ritz?" He sarcastically mentioned without evening looking at him.

Nobody spoke for a second. Costa sat down and picked up a deck of cards, and his way to blow off some steam, he snapped them all over the floor. His attitude was intended for his own perfection, in his mind anything he did would never be judged or mocked. He was so full of himself. He had always been a little odd, but tonight, he couldn't sit still to save his own life.

"Okay I'm sorry. So Chelsea, why were you at the hospital?" He said without a care in the world.

"You forget that Andrew was in there? I went to go see him, but they told me his visiting hours were up and I had to leave," She started to dig threw her purse and pulled out something for him. "But I did find this in the gift shop for him."

She smiled and threw a book on the table and I grabbed it and looked at the title. It was a book about World War II, if anything could cheer him up it was anything concerning any war in history. He was a military fanatic, he was a solider and he was my best friend.

That feeling I had earlier didn't get any easier, my heart started pounding and I began to feel sick to my stomach, and nervous like the first time in seven months. "Well, are you guys ready to go, or what?" Costa asked.

I just wanted to get it over with so I got up with Sanko, Chelsea and Kenny not saying a word and headed straight for the door, Kenny stopped us and gave me a sheet of paper that was folded up with fancy handwriting all over it, without Costa noticing. He shook my hand and said "Don't forget about old Kenny Pollock when that book of yours gets published, eh?"

I snuck the piece of paper in my coat pocket. "I won't, but I thought you were coming with us?"

"Oh, I'll be around watching you guys in case something happens. Don't worry Alex, I got your back."

"You always did, and it's good to know." By then Costa felt like he had to step in and push me and the others out the door and very bluntly said, "I'll call Carmine and let him know you're leaving now." While slamming the door.

"That guy is a fuckin' jerk. God, I can't stand him." Chelsea snapped.

"I think he's just nervous about all this."

"Yeah well, maybe he should do it himself. He has a lot of nerve yelling at me like that." She walked away muttering something else about him I couldn't hear.

Like always, I was the optimist and tried to defend him. Maybe I was skeptical and hoped that he had our best intentions. That made me wonder what would have happened if I had never met Costa, and how different things would be. My life would probably make sense. We all had lots of money now and we all had the right people behind us, but also a whole new list of problems. Because with Costa as the leader everything was falling apart, it seemed like the only thing holding everything together was us, just a small handful of us that didn't play games, and kept our word no matter what happened. We were loyal and gave hope that no matter how bad things were, there were still people that cared. We kept this dying town alive.

I was already with Chelsea and Sanko, ready to go. Andrew was in the hospital and the last guy we were supposed to meet was always known as the 'lookout guy', Carmine. I thought it was only going to be us three, but fate stepped in with a private number phone call to my cell phone.

It was Andrew. "Hey you better not be doing that shit without me! I'm on my way!" He said. Chelsea ripped the phone out of my hand relieved to hear his voice. "I was just at the hospital! Where are you?"

"I'm on my way to the place, where are you guys?"

"Were heading the same way, can we meet you there?" She asked.

"Yeah but wait a second, did you just leave Costa's?"

"Yeah we did, we're just outside his place."

"Alright wait there! I'll be there in a few, put Alex back on."

Chelsea put her hand over the phone and turned to me, "He wants us to wait here, and he wants to talk to you." Sanko looked at Chelsea and almost started laughing, "Then give him the damn phone!"

Chelsea handed me the phone, and started arguing with Ritz in the background. "Yeah we're gonna wait for you, aren't you supposed to be in a nice warm hospital bed anyways? We heard you were in and out of consciences."

"Fuck that shit, I ran right out of there, so they're probably looking for me, but shit I have to go. I'm on a payphone, and I'm still in my hospital pants and this fuckin' store clerk is looking right at me." Andrew arrogantly yelled, probably pointing right in his direction. Andrew was the kind of person that would fight anybody at any time.

I felt a little better knowing my best friend was on his way. "You sure you're up for this?"

"Damn straight I am, and I know you need my help anyways."

"Alright we'll meet you down the road from Costa's place, and after all this, we're all gonna talk."

"Alright, I'll see you there!" He slammed the phone down.

When he hung up, for some reason I kept the phone by my ear and I felt even weaker than before, I had realized that what we were doing was dangerous and one of us could seriously get hurt, or even die. I kept telling myself that after that night, we would all move on and forward from all of this. Enough was enough, and I was sick of being frustrated all the time.

Chelsea could see that something was wrong and asked me.

"What's the matter?" She looked concerned. Her eyes wandered into mine.

It had hit me then. It didn't matter anymore about the money, or the names we had made for ourselves, it all had to end sometime, and I knew it was going to be in the same night that I realized all of this, how ironic.

I shook it off like a bad gut feeling, and put the phone back in my pocket figuring I had one more chance.

"Nothing, but a lot has changed lately, hasn't it?" I had to ask to buy myself some confidence, but if I knew Chelsea, she was going to react the same way as me. She went quiet for a second then just simply told me, "Yeah, it has." Despite her social strength, she had a heart softer than mine.

We both looked at Sanko but he didn't care, his thing was always about money. He was distracted and eager to go, probably counting all the money in his head. The moment ended and the both of us stepped back into reality, ready for the worst.

Kenny's letter was still taunting me in my coat pocket, as we walked down the street to meet Andrew. I wanted to read it, but by then I couldn't remember anything, not even how we all met up, everything past that point was a blank page, like white fuzz. As we were walking it felt like my subconscious was being clouded, and I blacked out.

I saw everything that happened to us in the last few weeks flash before my eyes: Willie's death, all the shooting, the money, the drugs, the tears, how much we all changed, and Eva, the love of my life.

It happened so fast that the next thing I remembered was being dragged by Carmine the next morning. Covered in blood with the others, I started freaking out. I had walked into the darkness and was in shock.

"What the fuck happened? Where the hell did you come from?" Finally, we all hit the ground tired, bloody, hurt and confused.

We had run all through the night and the sun was just coming out. My favorite time of the day just became my worst, the tempting orange sky and the sun rising. We were all banged up pretty bad, it was time to stop running. The loss of blood was our resignation.

When I hit the ground I felt a feeling of guilt spill through my backbone, I was in a state of emergency and I still didn't know what had happened. I looked back and forth zoning in and out of conversations, dull and memorized by the moment in stillness. Finally my vision focused back along with my hearing, catching the end of the conversation.

"How long you think before they get here?" Sanko asked me out of breath and hardly moving.

"Who?" I was still confused.

"The cops, man." The words were becoming more and more structured.

"I couldn't tell you, but soon, I would think." The second I said that, I knew we had failed, I really thought it was the end for us. I started having faint visions of somebody's dark face kicking me while I was down and us all screaming for help.

"I can hear the sirens coming, man. It's a pretty scary sound if you think about it." He finished.

A brief moment fell between them and me that morning, everything had gone so wrong, the cops were coming and they knew exactly who they were coming for, and why.

My memories were haunting me. I couldn't see straight and my hands were shaking, and we all just sat there, bleeding all over the walls and ground, waiting for a miracle.

"Hey, do you think we can still run?"

"Not a chance." Our wounds were stiffening.

Andrew had a crowbar tightened in his hands hitting his head off the dirty wall we sat against, and was sitting right next to me trying to be tough like always, but when he tried to laugh he started spitting out blood.

"Hey, isn't this that same building?" He asked, referring to something we all knew. I looked behind myself and saw the mark I had spray painted so many months ago, my signature tattooed onto the wall.

"Yeah, it is." I could barely say to Andrew. I was so still surprised to see him but I wish he had stayed in the hospital.

"That's kind of funny man." He finished, he always was a tough one, one year younger than us, but when he wasn't training he made everything a contest and never liked to talk about anything negative. He just liked to have fun. We should have been more like him.

Carmine, who supposed to be on lookout, remained silent. I think he was angry that he had fallen into this trap with us. I felt guilty bringing him into all this because he never liked to be a part of anybody other than us directly. He hated the others, like Costa. He could always see right through him, he was smart, dedicated to school and his knowledge for computers. I wouldn't have blamed him if he was upset with me, but I think he was enraged at Costa, like he knew it was him that set up this little charade. Nothing was making sense, I couldn't remember what had even happened, but it obvious that we didn't do this to each other. It was a giant mystery, but I felt even worse and freaked out at the fact of where we had ended up, this was it. So many thoughts raced through my head at once, a cold feeling shook my hands again. "I never thought we'd end up like this guys, I'm so sorry."

"We came into this with our eyes wide open, Alex. It's not your fault." That's all either of us could say, with both our minds and bodies exhausted, our eyes closing, we had comfortably given up. But this story dates back even further than just that early morning, almost seven months flew by us faster than ever, and that's where the story really begins.

CHAPTER II

Too Much Coffee

(Friday night, March 14th - 7 Months ago.)

In the beginning things were so much different. The only people I knew were my friends and family and barely had any problems to deal with. I was just a kid. The ones I would grow to love later were people I had only heard of through rumors and stories. Things were simple, and I was happy. However, the day I'll never forget was the day of that one party in particular. A small party that would make big changes to all of our lives. It was so cold out this winter that nobody would even want to walk to the nearest corner store because the winds were so bad. There was not a flake of snow on the ground, it barely fell from the sky but the chilling freeze could remind even a flame it was winter. The moment I stepped outside my lungs felt frozen from my burning first breath, it stung. This was a town for summer, and during winter everybody hibernated, yet finally, a party was set up for us to finally step out and enjoy each other's company. It was nothing special, just a standard drunken night for all the kids that everybody in town knew about. It was a popular spot, everybody would be there.

Ritz Sanko, Chelsea and Andrew were already there when I was on my way. I didn't have a cell phone at the time, so whenever I was out I had to use a payphone to call the others. Payphones worked easier for me, I was never bothered and everybody knew it was me calling.

I was getting a ride with an old family friend of my mother's named Nico. He was more involved with the Bikers Gang in town and her business. He was going to give me a ride to this party after he made a few stops and I still had to call Chelsea from a video store parking lot to get the exact address.

When she picked up the phone all I could hear was people yelling and screaming having a good time. Everyone was drunk and probably up on something else being sold there.

Even Ritz, along with two others, was upstairs puking and was not in the best of situations. He found himself almost unconscious. The night had escalated so quickly it was already over for some.

"What's going on over there Chelsea?" I asked.

"Sanko is done for the night, he's in the bathroom." She said laughing.

"What? No way! I'm gonna be there in just a couple of minutes."

"I hope so!" She exclaimed in a certain tone.

"You're like a machine woman, so brutal and tough."

"Oh you love it rough!" She sneered back.

"Yeah I do, you know I do."

"And you're like a fucking pervert." Chelsea and I had a different sense of humor. It was like we always went for the biggest insult as a joke towards each other.

"I think you've had enough to drink, better stop or else you're going to end up like Sanko." I said.

"Okay whatever, but you got fifteen minutes to get your ass over here!" Timing me.

"I'll try." I added, "Idiot." then hung up laughing.

I got back in the truck with Nico but he didn't start it right away. "Who were you just talking to?" He asked.

"My really good friend Chelsea, she's at that party." Nico nodded his head and smiled. "What do you mean by, *'good friend'* Alex?" Asking me while he played with his bushy eyebrows.

He started up the truck and pulled out of the video store parking lot, looking at me waiting for an answer, a silent laugh struck the both of us. A smirk stretched across our faces looking out our own windows.

"She's a friend, but everybody busts my balls about that, though. I've heard it all."

"Is she hot?"

"Yeah she is, but dude you're like thirty-five, so I don't know what to tell you."

"Yeah but, do you think she's hot?"

"I got a girl, and we're almost going on almost four years now." I was proud to talk about my girl, Eva.

"Oh really? What's her name? Does she look like Chelsea?"

I started laughing but didn't answer, "You've met her before, man." I thought, but he wouldn't ever remember.

"You know kid, you remind me of your father sometimes." It surprised me that Nico of all people knew my dad while I hardly even knew my own father.

"You know him?" I asked.

"Well I did, that was years and years ago. He's a good guy."

"Yeah, last time I saw my dad I could barely even tie my own shoes."

Everything went silent for a second as I watched the road go by. "How does it make you feel, like about your dad not being around?" Nico asked curiously, his heart was in the right place.

"I don't like talking about it, but I'll see him again soon, and when I do, then I'll answer your question."

We didn't say anything for another second again, then he pretended to cough blocking out his little giggle, then he slowed down at the house where the party was.

"He's got a good woman taking care of him still, right?"

"Who, my dad? Yeah, why?"

"I bet she looks like Chelsea."

"For fuck sakes!" I shouted opening the door.

"Hey I'm just messing with you kid! But take her easy in there will ya'?"

"Don't you mean take *IT* easy?"

"No, because if she is, take her twice! Ha!"

I slammed the door and yelled, "That's hilarious man, but that is never gonna happen!" Then he took off and I could still hear him laughing, and as the engine dulled and I realized everything was quiet.

I knew I was at the right house, I could recognize it and I had just heard all the yelling and partying on the phone, so I wondered if they were playing a trick on someone or myself.

I walked up to the front door, and just before I opened it, I looked behind me. The silence was explained while a single car crept up the road. I could see a few dark faces looking straight at me.

Slowly the car drove by and a teenager about my age stuck his arm out the window holding a gun when somebody yelled from the house, "Get down!" I jumped over the railing and ran up the wet, freezing grass, almost slipping to the back shed and from what I could see that teen shot up the place and all I could hear were people screaming for their lives. I got so scared I didn't know what to do, so

I waited until the gunfire ended. It seemed like it went on forever, then finally the echoes had stopped.

"Is everyone alright?!" I heard a girl cry out, and then the car drove off screeching the tires. I could hear the front door being kicked open from the inside and glass falling from all the windows. "Alex? Where are you?!"

"I'm out back, is everyone okay?"

The noise had returned under different circumstances. The gunshots blew out my eardrums. It was like all I could hear was the static from an old radio or television set.

Chelsea ran around to the back with a bunch of her friends and some of my own, all shocked at what had just happened.

"Everybody's fine but we gotta get Sanko the hell outta here, the cops will be here any second!" Thanks to his current condition he had no idea what was happening outside, so we were held responsible to help him.

But before I could get a word in, Willie, god rest his soul, caught my attention showing up just in the nick of time behind Chelsea, and waved us down to his car, calm but concerned.

Chelsea turned around and ran for the car and I went in for the house, everybody was scattering not knowing what to do, some people just stood in the front yard yelling how cool it was and explaining what just happened as if nobody had a clue to get out of there and they were repeating to themselves at what just happened.

"Somebody come and help me drag Sanko's sorry ass out the fucking door, please!" I yelled.

It was like nobody heard me, there was no answer, but then again the whole world seemed off course because not one of us knew what to think. It was a weird feeling, being so confused while others were excited to be alive.

The door was already coming off the wall and when I got in, there was no blood. The shooters must have only gone for the windows, to scare us.

I remember seeing Andrew just sitting there, almost like he didn't have a care in the world flipping around a quarter. "When the fuck did you get here dude?" He asked, with no weight on his shoulders.

"What? You want to crack open another beer and keep partying?!" I snapped. "Fuck Andrew, come on! Help me with that wasted prick Sanko downstairs."

"He's upstairs." I turned around and seen some little kid dressed up like he was some sort of rapper with a name like *Little Pop*, acting as if he king-of-it-all.

"Yeah, thanks." I said back angry.

Andrew got up from his seat, calmly and walked around the little punk and followed me up the stairs. The hallway was filled with different doors, and with my luck they were all shut so I had no idea where Sanko was. I checked the first door and there was nothing but a room filled with adults not having a clue of what just happened.

They were all drugged up sitting on the floor, laying down or just standing there looking at walls.

"Oh sorry." I said just as I was about to shut the door, but the one girl laying down, with those black and glazed eyes looked up at me and asked if I knew anything about 'the heart', as if it wasn't my own or hers, but I didn't pay too much attention because all I was worried about was getting busted.

"No, can't say that I do, but do you know where my friend is? He should be up here somewhere."

All she did was point back at the door I came through, so I waved my hand goodbye and checked the next door, and there was still nothing, Andrew was still waiting at the top of the stairs and somebody was running up them, I could hear the footsteps pounding on the stairs.

It was Willie, out of breath holding his knees.

"Hey, what's the deal? What are you, retarded? You can't hear those sirens? Forget your friend or I'm gonna leave without you. Come on and use your head, man!"

"You have to give me some time, just wait." I said frustrated.

His one hand moved to his chin, he stood up quick and looked around, thinking about it. "Alright, I'll pull up my car 'round the front, hurry up though will you? I don't want to be here when the cops get here, they'll pin it on me that all these underage kids were drinking!"

I nodded my head and went for the third door, Andrew ran for the next one and I found Sanko sitting down next to a toilet, holding his stomach. When I got in there he didn't even see or hear us, he just kept moving his head back and forth.

"Hey buddy were gonna get you outta here, can you walk? Can you even hear me?" He looked up at us, his mouth hanging open but he said nothing. There was no way he was going to stand up on his own, so quickly Andrew and I grabbed his arms and started to drag him out the bathroom. When we got to the stairs, he finally said something.

"No, no fuck the tub."

Andrew and I had to pause for a second and look at each other. We tried not to laugh but then we picked him up and put him on our shoulders and headed down the stairs. We kept asking him if he could walk or even speak, but still nothing.

"Man, did he put on some weight or something? The kid weighs a ton." Andrew struggled to say, as we had to take it step by step. I smiled but before I could say anything

I heard the sirens just around the corner getting closer and closer and faster.

"Shit! Come on, head for the front door!" Somebody yelled.

People started running out of what was left of the door and jumping out the broken windows, and we pretty much got pushed out the front door, yet right away, Willie started to flag us down right out front, Chelsea was in the back seat rolling down her window, "Hurry the fuck up!" and not even a foot away from the door Sanko decided to lunge himself to the ground, hitting his head and still not moving.

"Oh come on, get your ass in the car." I pleaded.

Chelsea moved to the other side of the seat and opened the door and helped pull Sanko in. Andrew jumped in the back and I was riding shotgun, but the moment after we pulled out we saw over four cop cars cruise their way into the yard, not even taking notice to us speeding away.

"That was so fuckin' close! God, I hate cops!" Willie shouted taking every turn in sight. "I have to make sure I lost them."

I looked over at him for a second and could see he was in a panic, which was not like him at all.

"Since when did the police get you so worked up? They usual try to avoid you." I asked ordinarily.

"Since they've all been dickheads and arresting anybody for any good report. They've all turned into fuckin' liars man."

"How the hell do you know something like that?"

"What, you didn't hear about cop-shop?" He asked surprisingly.

"No, what about it?"

"It's gonna be shut down by the end of the month, if they aren't doing their job. And if that's not the worst part, if they do get shutdown, they're gonna be replaced by the region, who are even bigger dicks." He pointed to the glove compartment.

"Open that. Now pull out the newspaper. I've been showing everybody."

I grabbed the paper and the first thing I noticed was a picture of the entire police force standing in front of their station, with a big bold black print, 'Local police not on duty', the entire page was about crime rates going up and how it seemed our own boys in blue weren't doing anything about it. I could tell the article had been passed around, it had little rips around the edges and looked like some coffee had been spilt on it.

"My god, are you serious? Chelsea you have to read this shit, it's true!"

She wasn't too happy either, while we were babbling on and on about the cops. Sanko was still in the back in the middle of severe alcohol poisoning was deep in some sort of overdose, almost as if somebody had slipped something devastating into his drink. What a nightmare tonight was becoming on the seconds dragged into the next.

"I'll read it later, we have a little more to worry about right now, don't you think?"

Willie looked at them from the rearview mirror and gave his famous look like he had an idea. "I got a friend that will look after him, he's a bit edgy but he'll get the job done."

We pulled up to an intersection with a red light, when Willie finally slowed down to keep things cool. "So everything's going to be okay."

I was curious. "What do you mean '*edgy*'?"

"It means I'm gonna get in trouble for bringing your friend to his place."

"Where are we going then?" I asked, and thought nothing of it at the time, but this is how it all started, when Willie said that one name, *Costa*.

I thought to myself for a second wondering if it was the same Costa he was talking about, a young man that everybody in town knew about.

"You don't mean, that asshole '*holier-than-thou*' Costa? Do you?"

"Yeah, if that's what people call him."

The red light in the intersection turned green and we drove off towards the richer side of town. I was in a panic and scared to even go near Costa's house at the time, because the last thing I heard about him was that he's been out making a name for himself ever since I heard this rumor that this other big named drug dealer had his breakdown, and was sent to rehab. Every town has it's people with high reputations, and everybody always talked about them. The one was Costa, rumored to be the son of some wealthy, mafia connected madman, and then Shawn. They hated each other with a burning passion.

Shawn had a name for himself that he was a real psycho and apparently the most fearless person in our area.

"What's gonna happen when Shawn comes back and takes a look at Costa, he'd get pissed." I said to Willie as I was thinking about it.

"Shawn Taylor isn't anything going to do a god damn thing, except talk shit. You watch too many movies man." "I heard he had that breakdown, but I doubt he's going to come back a reformed saint. Knowing him, he'll probably go even crazier." Shawn was always the feared bully in town. He graduated from High school years before I even attended, and then he got into the drugs, badly. Things were tense around town, but they seemed to ease up whenever Shawn went to jail. But every time he came back, the people knew, and he didn't care what people thought. His 'breakdown' was a result of him withdrawing from his heroin addiction.

Willie then looked at me with eyes wide open, his lips moved like he was going to laugh.

"Don't say anything to Costa about him though, or you'll have to hear about him all night."

He pulled into a driveway and took his seat belt off, "But don't worry about it man, Costa's one of my best friends, he's a good guy and he's gonna take care of your friend."

He told us to stay put in his car until he came back out. Sanko still hadn't moved and Chelsea was watching over him like a doctor. She kept repeating to him "You'll be okay, everything's okay." while brushing his hair and rubbing his arm. He seemed to be half dead. He had white chunks of something at the corners of his lips and looked dehydrated.

In the back of that car I could tell he didn't have a clue what was going on, and neither did I because something was more than wrong with Sanko. My heart started pumping hard and I was shaking, waiting for Willie to signal us to drag him inside, but instead, he and Costa came out walking for the car and I could already see that Costa was angry. He walked fast and hard towards the car shouting at Willie.

He opened the back door and pulled Andrew right out of the car then grabbed Sanko's arms while Willie helped carry him to the front door then waved for us to come inside. I opened the door slowly and the night's cold air hit me like a sack of bricks.

I could still hear the sound of faded sirens, people all over were still walking in small groups from the party, and the gunshots kept playing in my head over and over again.

I walked towards the house when I wanted to turn back, Chelsea followed right behind Andrew and I.

"It's so cold out here, let's get inside and explain this whole thing." She said.

The front door was still open and I heard Costa continuing to yell at Willie, so I wasn't so sure about moving far from the front door once I was inside. In all honestly I wanted to hear what was being said, not a lot happened in my life, so I was always waiting for something, anything. I could feel something was about to happen though, something big.

This moment had become the end of my normal life. My personality, soul and hobbies were all about to change, for the better but mostly for the worse.

CHAPTER III

The Beginning of the End

(11:06pm)

"Have you lost your fucking mind?" Costa snapped at Will. The air could not catch its own breath.

"What was I supposed to do? Leave the kid there to die?"

"I don't give a shit if this kid died or what you could have done, but you brought him here! Do I look like a fucking doctor?"

"I know you can help him, Costa! Call somebody!" He begged.

I watched them argue too what felt like endless hours, only to be the slowest twenty minutes of my life. My friend was sick and needed help, and his three best friends were standing not ten feet away from him listening to a man decide his fate, life or death.

I felt as if I were going insane, and stupid little messages from television kept racing back into my head like, *'It COULD happen to you!'* or health commercials showing teenagers having overdoses. I didn't know what to think, I just stood still wondering if time would run out and not give us a second chance. I even considered performing CPR on Sanko myself, I was desperate. I had even considered taking him to the hospital, but it just came natural not too, it was almost a thing of honor and strength. Even at our age it seemed weak to call the authorities.

"What's in it for me if I help you and this kid out?" Costa asked, and the whole room went quiet. He caught us all at our weakest point knowing that we would do anything for him to save our friends life. I looked at Willie, and again, he gave me that famous look for an idea, and then spoke for me to Costa.

"Just take care of the kid, and I'm sure Alex could help you out with something."

"Like what?!" He yelled in return.

"He was the only one standing outside when this party got shot-up, and probably saw the vehicle."

Costa seemed very interested in this, he was probably thinking how to profit from this. So then asked me to tell the entire story, and what the shooter's car looked like.

"A white, old piece of shit sports car." I said.

I don't know what the key word was, but something caught his attention and quickly he said, "Ryan Lingerie, that fucking Italian." I had no idea what to say, but Willie snapped his fingers at me and pointed into the other room for me to follow.

We walked into a small room with only chairs and a table. This room was obvious for family dinners. He shut the door and took a seat. I was still standing, speechless.

"We all know your mother, kid. Have you ever done anything dangerous before?" he asked, knocking down his pitch a few notches.

"I've seen enough things in my life and done some myself I'm not proud of, you know that."

"Well tonight Costa's gonna want that favor from you three, understand?"

"Are you positive you can help Sanko? I think somebody slipped something into his drink." I panicked.

"He'll be fine Alex, but I'm gonna call my friend over here, you wait for him and do whatever Costa tells you to do, okay?"

"Yeah, I understand. I just don't want the kid to choke on his own puke or something, I mean look at him!"

Willie started to dial a number on his cell phone so I left the room, the second I shut the door I saw Costa was standing right behind me. "You're going to steal his car." He said with pride.

I turned around real quick and was a little disordered at first, but this was the favor he wanted from me.

"You mean *Ryan's*?" I asked.

"Yeah, that guy lives around here, and you three are gonna go steal his car." He repeated.

Chelsea and Andrew were still quiet and patient waiting by the front door, listening to every word we were saying, they seemed surprised at me when I considered taking the request. I also knew it would not require three people to steal one car.

"We'll do anything, where are we bringing the car once were in it?" Andrew asked. Costa looked at him with just as much of a surprise, "The quiet one finally speaks!"

You would think this guy wanted to have a coffee with his small chat, he didn't care about Sanko, and he didn't care that we were running out of time.

"Where is the car, and where are we bringing it?"

"Just bring it back here in the morning, any of you know how to drive?"

"I do." I lied.

"Better yet, do you know how to hot wire a car? It's not like the keys will be waiting for you in the ignition."

I didn't know what to say, I never thought that far into the plan, but I was in a panic and told him I knew how to, just so he would finally help Sanko.

I knew Costa didn't believe me but before he could say anything, that friend of Willie's squealed into the driveway, Tommy.

Costa looked out his front window with a big smile, "Regardless if you do or not, he does. And he's going with you."

Tommy opened the door with a big entrance. You could tell this guy had everything a man wanted, his style was expensive. His watch alone looked as if it were worth over two thousand dollars. His car sparkled with the words 'brand new and fully loaded'.

"Which one of you is Alex?" he said with a big smile on his face, just before I could say anything Willie came out of the other room and pulled Tommy aside.

I couldn't hear much other than he was explaining the situation to him, they were the ones talking in the room. It was as if they were used to this sort of thing. I just stood there, impatient now trying to stay calm and controlled.

Then Willie pointed over to Sanko, "That's him, he has been my friend for years."

"Jesus Christ! Is that kid dead?"

"He isn't dead, but he will be if we don't help each other out here."

"Fuck me, say it isn't so. That kid is gonna have one bad hangover."

I watched Costa walk over to the two of them and start whispering as well, then in the middle of all of it, Costa looked over at me and I barely heard him say, "Maybe the kid will come back someday." They could use me, but they only considered to help because I was friends with Will, and this debt would have to be repaid.

At the time, I didn't know or care what they were talking about, I just wanted to leave as soon as possible. So to keep time from going slow I went outside for a cigarette.

I hardly smoked cigarettes at all anymore, so when I got outside and saw that I had none, I called Andrew and Chelsea out to follow.

"Do you have any smokes, Chelsea?"

"Do you have a lighter?" She asked, bluntly.

"Yeah I do."

The second I lit the cigarette, I felt my nerves run through my entire body and I sat on the stairs leading up to the front door, I never noticed how much my hands were shaking until I put the cigarette to my mouth.

I started to breathe in and out slowly, and caught myself back on edge.

"This is so fucked up, I feel like I'm in a movie." I said rubbing my face up and down and through my hair.

I don't know if I said that because I was in a panic or because I seriously could not believe how these guys talked to each other. I felt so out of place, unknown to everything. I felt like I had been missing out on what I loved my entire life, and I didn't even know it.

I began talking to my best friends and I started to feel better. It was common knowledge that Andrew didn't have a single scared bone in his body, but I never liked seeing Chelsea involved in anything like this, although I knew she could take care of herself. My plan was to send both of them home and I would take care of it myself, I didn't want them around because it was not necessary to begin with. Plus they were still a little drunk from the party and it was too overwhelming for all of us to have to deal with it at the same time.

"Hey, don't smoke all that! It's my last one!" Chelsea shouted.

"Here," I handed Chelsea the cigarette and stood up, brushed myself off and followed my cue.

"You guys should get out of here, I'll call you in the morning."

"But I thought we were coming with you?"

"No, please let me take care of this myself. It doesn't take three extra people to steal a car."

I could tell that Chelsea was considering going home, but the booze took over asking me a million times if I was sure.

"Andrew, what do you think?" She asked.

"I think that guy didn't want us all to go together for this anyway. He seemed to favor Alex."

"Alright, you got it but don't get caught, and be careful! It's been a rough night already."

"Thanks, Chelsea."

"Well, good luck man." Andrew seemed a little disappointed he wasn't coming along.

We finished the only cigarette and they headed off for home, I stayed on the front porch waiting for somebody to come out, I was nervous. "Hey kid, where'd your friends go?" Tommy asked.

"I told them to leave." I said. "Good. Threes a crowd, let's go."

"Wait up!" Costa shouted from inside the house. "You bring that car back here, understand? First thing tomorrow morning, were going to have a little chat you and I."

I nodded my head trying not to shiver and walked for Tommy's car. Anybody could see that Tommy's heart was pumped for chaos and revenge, as mine was racing to get it over and done with.

He started up the car right away and flew out of the driveway, "Welcome to our twisted sense of humor, kid," he reached in his pocket and pulled out a pack of cigarettes, "It's Alex, right?"

"Yeah."

"Well Alex, you smoke?" as he threw the pack at me.

"Yeah."

"Don't talk much?"

"Ah, I'm just nervous man."

"Don't worry about it, the only guy whose gotta worry is Ryan."

"Good way to put it, I guess? But why are we even stealing this car? Who benefits?"

"Listen, everybody hates that kid and it was only a matter of time before somebody put him in his place. I'm glad it's going to be us. It's the little things that add up, it's all a matter of respect."

"I don't understand what you're trying to tell me."

"Don't worry about it, kid. You're going to learn a lot in the next few weeks."

"I hope so. I don't mind doing this with you because one of those bullets he fired could've hit me, I was standing right there." I said.

"Just do yourself a favor from now on and stay away from the east side of town. Most of the guys over there are fuckin' losers and drug addicts."

"I almost never go past the canal, it was just for that party. I don't even know whose house it was."

"Ha! No wonder why the place got shot up."

We drove into the very side of town were verbally bashing, slowly creeping up side of the road. When we arrived at the house, all the lights were off and the house was a dump, and the car was parked on the road, right out in the open. "Do you see what I mean? They're fucking idiots, all of them! We barely even had to look."

Tommy parked the car about four houses down and turned the inside light on, "Get out and keep an eye out for me alright? This should only take a couple of minutes."

Until we were both right there into the moment, I didn't realize that these guys were dead serious, he didn't even hesitate or give me a second to answer him. I was just told what to do.

He turned everything off and ran for the car, I watched him try to unlock the door, and then it just popped open. "The thing isn't even locked." He mouthed out to me in the street.

I wanted to laugh but instead I sat inside the car freezing stiff into the seat, and for some reason every time I was nervous or anxious while I was cold my body would shiver a hundred times worse. I turned around a few times getting a good look at the street behind me to see if anybody was coming. I was biting my nails when I heard the car start, twice.

"What a piece of shit." I thought, and then I did laugh. Tommy pulled the car around and picked me up.

"What about your car?" I asked.

"I have somebody coming to get pick it up now. Look how I got this piece of junk started." When I looked there was a screwdriver jammed in the ignition.

"I'm surprised nobody heard you."

"He's probably inside, in a coma from stealing his mother's sleeping pills."

"You really don't like this guy, do you?"

"In time, you'll learn to hate all of these degenerates."

There we were, having a simple conversation in a stolen car, and right then and there I started to feel something I was going feel for the next seven months: Power, control, fearlessness. The fear had become my friend, welcoming me into the dangerous world I would soon regret.

"So where you going, kid?"

"Home."

"You got your own place?"

"No, I live with my mom and my sister."

"Alright well, where exactly do you live?"

I told Tommy the address and he took me home, for a small town it didn't take more than ten minutes, and when I got out of the car I walked up the yard and turned around to say something, Tommy was on his cell talking to Costa and drove off.

In a way, I never wanted the night to end, the adrenaline in my blood wasn't pumping anymore and I felt like I had some fun, and I was excited to see what was in store for tomorrow.

When I walked in the door, I went to the house phone and saw that my girlfriend, Eva of four years, called a couple of times with a nice long message waiting for me on the machine.

"Hey baby, I guess I just missed you today, were you by chance at that party? The cops were all over the place! Anyways, I'm worried, give me a call when you get this! I'm home all night, I love you!"

I never called back, because my sister Meghan was in the living room watching television, and then she called me over.

"How was the party?"

"Didn't get a chance to go, cops were everywhere." I lied.

"Yeah I heard, how'd you get home?" I had to think of something quick, it wasn't for her ears to hear what really happened.

"I walked."

"Oh, well I'm going to bed, turn out all the lights." She yawned, turning everything off, wrapping herself in a quilted blanket.

"Goodnight, Meghan."

"Oh yeah, and Eva kept calling. I told her you'd call her first thing tomorrow morning."

Meghan and I are fraternal twins born just a few minutes away from each other. We always understood each other, we were like best friends, but if she ever found out about anything I was doing anything remotely dangerous, I'd never hear the end of it. She worried like a mother.

I popped a few pills and leaned against the wall, just realizing I had stolen a car and enjoyed it. The pills were starting to kick in to help me sleep and to drift away from the excitement but when I shut my eyes, it was morning already.

CHAPTER IV

——∘⊷❂⊶∘——

A Twisted Explanation

(Saturday, 9:10am, March 15h - 7 Months left.)

"Wake up." I thought I was dreaming, I thought I had just fallen asleep, but I kept hearing my sister's voice keep telling me to get up.

"Some guy is here for you, Alex." She said, "Wake up!" I was still a little drowsy from the pills.

When I finally came to I noticed she was fully dressed and that I had slept in, and as much as I wanted to keep sleeping, a quick thought of Ritz Sanko raced through my head and I quickly got up and out of bed.

As I threw on any piece of clothing I could find on the floor, "How long has he been here?" I asked.

My sister, most of the time, didn't like to be asked more than one question when she was in her certain, impatient mood.

"I don't know!"

"He didn't give you a name?"

"I didn't ask him, Alex!"

On that note I raced downstairs not even considering to call Eva back. I came to see Tommy making himself at home, looking at the only family portrait we had.

"Hey kid, you used to be gothic?" he said with an odd tone, putting his finger on the photo. I looked at it too still fitting my shirt on.

"Good morning to you too, and no, it was a mix of styles. Actually for a little while people were calling me Mr. Black."

"Well Mr. Black, you look gothic."

"You should never judge a book by its cover." I said shaking my finger at him.

He looked at me with a sense of confusion, his eyebrow lifted.

"Don't you want to know about your friend, Ritz?"

"How is he?" I needed to know.

"He's fine, come on we're going for a ride."

I looked out the front window and saw his car in the driveway, "I see you got your car back?"

"Yep, I got her back about hour after I got home."

"What did you do with Ryan's car?"

"What do you think I did with it? I took it to Costa's."

"What do we do with it next?"

"Come on, get in the car. We're about to find out."

I wanted to ask more questions as we headed for the car, but last night's feeling of power faded as I slept, I felt like I was at the bottom of the barrel again. So I listened and followed.

"I don't know why you were freaking out, Alex. Your friend only had alcohol poisoning."

"Really? I thought he was overdosing. Normally he can polish off a quart of vodka to himself."

"Alcohol poisoning can still kill you, but after a couple of hours he was fine." Tommy laughed.

"What did you guys have to do?"

"We had to get his stomach pumped, and then we just left him on his side and let him sleep it off."

I was relieved to hear that Ritz was okay. The events of the night prior happened so fast that I didn't have time to think. Within a matter of minutes between getting shot at and dragging him out to the car I guessed that taking him to Costa's was the most logical thing to do. As I stepped out into the daylight with Tommy, I noticed the shine to his car, and it made it look even more expensive. He took out his keys and unlocked it from a distance and pointed to the passenger seat.

It was little things like future reference to befriending these guys that made me smile, somehow I knew we were going to become friends, and I would possibly work for them and regain that feeling of power. It was only that one time and I was already becoming obsessed.

We only had some small talk on the way to Costa's and when we got there, again, Costa was yelling and screaming from inside.

"Oh, what now? The fun never stops." Tommy said to himself fed up and tired. The screams were brutal and ruthless, it looked like Costa hadn't slept all night. He was on the phone screaming at somebody.

"Oh yeah? And who is going to believe you over me? The cops? You fucking degenerate drug addict. You're going right back to jail!"

"Costa, what the hell is going on? Who are you talking to?" Tommy asked.

"Just wait until he finds out, he just walked in." Holding his finger out to Tommy, signaling him to wait a minute.

"Wait until I find out what? Costa!" Demanding he answer him.

"Yeah, whatever you say. I'll see you soon." Costa hung up and threw his cordless phone across the room.

"What the hell was all that about?"

"You really want to know? Shawn beat the shit out of your sister last night!"

"Jesus Christ, how bad? Where is she?"

The entire time they argued I watched Tommy pace himself back and forth, it was explained that his sister went to Shawn as a last resort for cocaine in the middle of the night. After a few lines they began fighting over something meaningless and ended up putting Tommy's sister in the hospital.

"She called me at three o'clock this morning, crying and I could barely understand her. Apparently he hit her so hard she has stitches and staples in her jaw." Cocaine, what an ugly drug.

"Why the fuck didn't she call me?" Tommy screamed pulling his hair. I could see it in his eyes he was getting furious with anger. He wanted to kill Shawn.

"I don't know, but it seems I'm here to solve everybody's problems. Like this kid and his sick friend last night." He pointed at me very rudely. "Do I look like everybody's fucking therapist?"

I finally stepped in. "Where is Sanko, anyway? I heard he was okay."

"What was your name again, kid?"

"Alex."

"He's out back, Alex." He said making me a feel a better sense of relief. I waited in silence until I received the queue to walk to the back door. I was interested to see what Tommy and Costa were going to do.

"That son of a bitch is lucky I'm not over there right now kicking his fucking teeth in!"

"Relax man, I know it's bad, but I have an idea." I could tell Costa had been thinking about something for the last little awhile.

"What kind of idea, man?"

It was at this time that I realized that these had two had dealt this sort of thing before, and on more than one occasion. Tommy was a man of action, he would not just sit back and let his only sister get beat down by anybody, let alone a man with eyes bigger than his stomach.

"We have his best friend's car."

"I see where this is going." Tommy smiled.

It was beginning to dawn on me that Costa had something planned from the very start. They weren't your typical guys, they were strategic, and organizing a plan to meddle in Shawn's affairs. My mind was elsewhere with Ritz Sanko so I couldn't focus entirely, but I admired their determination and Tommy's patience with everything. He kept calm after listening to reason and realized he could do even more damage without even using his fists. A part of me knew if the opportunity presented itself, he would still take the chance for one good punch. I didn't blame him.

Costa could see that I was eager to see Sanko.

"Kid, it's through the living room to your right." The last thing I expected was a compliment, I felt like he didn't want my presence there.

"Thanks." I wondered, what a strange person.

"You wait out there for me, understand?" Ordering me around like my own mother.

"Right." I said to myself.

Maybe I was just paranoid, but on the way out I heard him mention something about a gun. Somehow I knew I was going to be involved in whatever he had planned. "By the end of the day, you'll feel much better." He said to Tommy.

Outside there was a deck with a half frozen hot tub, a barbeque, an overly nice glass table with endless cigarettes put out in the wet ashtrays, and Sanko just looking over the railing, starring off at the yard having a cigarette.

"Sanko!" He turned around, saw me and his face lit up like a kid in a candy store.

"Holy shit man, you guys saved me last night!" We came into each other with a welcoming handshake that became a hug.

"How are you feeling buddy?" I asked grabbing his shoulders looking at him and down.

"Like shit, hung over, somebody slipped me something in my drink last night."

"Well you look good. Better than last night anyways."

"Yeah thanks again, man." I couldn't help but to start laughing.

"So let me guess, you drank somebody else's drink that had something in it?" He laughed too.

"Yeah man, any bit longer and I would have been somebody's date for the night."

It was an honest and stupid mistake, a pointless misunderstanding that could've killed one of my best friends.

"At least you didn't choke on your own vomit or something." I tried to justify to myself.

"I'm just happy to be out of that fucking bathroom. Man, my head was spinning." He laughed.

"Yeah Chelsea told me you were hitting the booze hard from the moment you got there."

"Whiskey and wine buddy, whiskey and wine. They do not go well together. Not at all."

"Especially when you chug booze the way you do! Consider it food for thought for next time, eh?" The worst was over it seemed, Ritz Sanko was better and his sense of humor was still intact.

Tommy and Costa came out the back door interrupting us, with an idea. For the first time I had seen Costa with a big smile on his face.

"I love these ideas I get! You know at first kid, I didn't know what to do with you, but I swear you and your friend here are a blessing in disguise." He began to ramble on and on, like dialogue from a movie filled with riddles.

"How so?" I asked.

"It's almost as if things happen for a reason."

"Just get to the point." Tommy added.

"That piece of shit car that shot at you and your friends last night, just so happens to be Shawn's best friend's."

"Ryan's." I said. We had already acknowledged so.

Sanko held his head. "Wait, what the hell did I miss last night?"

It was rushed on us so fast on what we had to do. We didn't know how or what exactly we were doing in Costa's process of explanation, but I was more than ready and very excited.

"We can do a lot of things with that car." Costa stated like a football coach.

"It's almost like wearing a mask." Tommy slid in. It was easy to spot that whatever it was they were trying to sell, they were trying to comfort me along. Yet, somehow I knew this was going to be a long day to remember, and I was wide awake and eager for him to just get to the point.

"If we want to hurt Shawn, we have to make sure he has nothing or nobody to run too."

"So, what does that have to do with this car?" I asked confused.

"We are going to frame them. We're going to make it look like Shawn and Ryan robbed the wrong person at gun point."

"Gun point?" My eyes widened. "They have guns?" I thought.

"Yeah, and you're going to use one." He said rolling eyes in disbelief. He looked at Tommy and squinted his face together like I was insane to think otherwise.

I looked at Tommy. "Relax, nobody is going to get shot." He reassured me.

Then I looked over at Costa.

"Costa, are you serious? Why can't you two do this?"

"Because, I need to know if I can trust you, kid." His tone darkened as he leaned his face toward mine.

"Last night wasn't enough?" Referring to the grand theft auto I committed.

"You ask too many fucking questions, kid." Costa snapped.

"This is for me anyways, Alex." Tommy mentioned to me.

It was really confusing still, but I knew Tommy would direct me most of the way, so all I had to do was follow instructions. His offensive anger would be his victory, he knew it himself. With him, I felt safe. He was just one of those people that you look at it, even without knowing him from a distance but just know that he isn't a regular person. He was a clean slate, a well-minded polite man, but I could see the real darkness in his eye. He had a talent with people, good and bad, he was smart. He and Costa made a good team with both their knowledge and connections throughout this small town. The pressure had been building with Shawn, and it was only right to finally put an end to all of it. Tommy wouldn't be disrespected in such a manner and not do anything to retaliate. It was in his genes that something like this could not go unanswered, it was just his general nature.

The plan sounded bullet-proof, but it went even better than planned. I really liked that Tommy was saving Shawn for last, probably just to stick every bit of revenge back in his face to choke on. Everything we were about to do was going to cut off any chance of a reason to stay in this town. Tommy was going to make his point by putting his foot down and everything Shawn had. His friends, his drugs, any sort of respect Shawn had would be carved down into nothing. We were going to stage his actions so that people and the police would come looking for him, forcing him to run. Since everybody knew everybody in town, Costa drew his attention on deciding who the unlucky drug dealer would be to get robbed by us, as Shawn and Ryan. He needed it to be someone who would recognize the car right away and immediately put the blame on Costa.

"Not only do we solve one problem, but we get a lot of money out of it too. We obviously can't give back whatever we're going to steal. So we might as well just sell it."

"I could get rid of it for you?" Sanko suggested.

Sanko becoming the nickel and dime drug dealer for Costa's insane crowd of money makers made him happier than ever. He really loved making money and was dedicated by any means necessary to do so.

"If you do well, Sanko, I can hook you up with whatever you want at a good price." Costa agreed.

"I'm in. Say no more." He laughed.

A discussion would take place between the two of them while Tommy and I took care of everything else. We ran over the plan again and again and Costa mentioned that he was going to find me one of his old cell phones and even throw me some cash for doing this for him. He really liked me off the bat because he knew I was eager. He even apologized for being such a hot head earlier. Throughout the couple of hours of waiting, Costa had finally pin-pointed where would we be heading, and who we would be stealing from. This was our action to move, and when he hung up his phone he just lifted his head up simply.

"Alright guys. You've only got one shot at this, I set it all up." A third party had acknowledged Costa's plan and arranged for a young man named Dalton to deliver a small fortune of different amounts of several narcotics and marijuana.

"Come on Alex, follow me, the cars out back."

While I followed Tommy to the car, I sort of forgot what it was we were doing for a second. Even though I was excited I knew my heart would start racing and get that odd feeling in my stomach when we got there.

It was like having a close friend die, you know what happens but it doesn't hit you right away for a little while. This was the first time I was ever going hold a gun, and that in itself didn't faze me. My mind wasn't like others. I watched a lot of movies and played a lot of video games to think it's just going to be cool. I wanted the whole world to see what I was going to do, maybe for that extra boost of confidence, but that's not the way it is in the real world.

I stepped back into reality and caught up to Tommy. I helped him rip off the cover to Ryan's dirty car, with one last question. "Wouldn't this car be reported by now?"

Tommy smiled, "Doesn't it make you want to shit yourself with excitement? Relax, everything's going to be alright, now get in."

The daylight showed how much of a piece of junk this car was, unlike Tommy's gorgeous exotic.

The seats felt like they were made of old dirty towels and down by my feet I could see nasty old fast food french-fries. It was just disgusting.

"Let's hope this thing starts today." He tried to start the car a few times but then his cell phone began to ring, he took it out of his pocket and threw it to me. The screwdriver was makeshift at best, it was going to be hard to start a second time.

"Answer that will yah?" I flipped the phone open.

"Hello?"

"Who's this?" A voice questioned.

"This is, Alex?"

"Oh! That new kid! I've heard about you, my name's Kenny!" I immediately got the idea that Tommy had told people what we had done the night before. I was a little puzzled about the 'new kid'.

Kenny was very much a bright spirit, but in the background of the conversation all I could hear was Tommy yelling at the car to start.

"As in, Kenny Pollock?" I had heard the name around town several times.

"That's me! Hey listen buddy, are you with Tommy right now? Can you put him on the phone? It's really important."

The car started, finally.

"Tommy, the phone is for you, it's Kenny."

He took the phone and kept his conversation short, something about the next day.

We pulled away from Costa's and headed for the outskirts of town, the best place for this set-up. Not one witness to worry about. It was all dirt roads and one big forest surrounds you for a few miles with left and right turns all around. The main road that leads to it was about a mile long with a few fields until you saw all the trees.

It was a road off the highway with those real long bends with only one house every so often, with very high priced properties, and with peace and quiet all year round.

"Hey kid, I know what you're thinking, you're thinking we're messing with the dangerous side of town, but we've been doing this shit for years." He said out of the silence.

"Are you guys, like a gang or something?" Right away Tommy started laughing.

"A gang? No, kid I told you last night, its east and west, just a group of friends against another."

"That's sort of childish."

"In a way," He agreed. "But the east has its aggression, anger and the muscle."

"Then what do we west boys have?"

"Money and the power of being smart, we never wanted this, but after a while people break away. No matter where you go, you're going to deal with bullshit, so might as well make money while you're at it." He replied as he drove, hardly paying attention to the road.

"I guess so."

"You should *know* so. It's not about whose right or wrong, it's about doing what makes you happy and doing the right thing for yourself. I see fit doing this kind of thing."

"So it's all about the money?"

"No." he simply said.

This is where the story really began, and it started to make some sense. It went quiet for a minute, giving me time to think about a war between the east and west sides of town. It was a line divided by a canal and one bridge.

It was true that the east side was more troubled, and had less money and nobody had a job, nor did they want one. But the west, our side, wasn't perfect either. Tommy was trying to tell me that no matter who you are, you're going to have to deal with somebody that doesn't like you, and he figured he could use it to his advantage. "No matter who you are, somebody isn't going to like you. So why bother being anybody else but yourself?" This group of people was different from us, we didn't like them, and they didn't like us. It was because of the area was just rough with the architecture. It all just sort of fell into place for this pointless and endless battle to start. The tranny of one's opinion makes another stubborn man smash their heads together.

Most of the people found every excuse not to do something with their lives and always complained and had something terrible to say about their own family members and friends. They blamed everything and everyone else for their own failures and not even taking notice to the less fortune that were disabled and had no choice in the matter. It was a mistake to underestimate their endurance and anger, though.

It was more pathetic then I ever found it scary over there. Everyone on that side was known as drug addicts or dealers, pushers, fighters, junkies, thieves, scoundrels, you name it. They all knew each other in that somewhat civilized place people called home.

If they wanted, they could all charge at anyone as one force and kill them all in a matter of seconds, maybe that's why we fought back. Both sides just hated each other for our flaws. It was obvious they thought we were all stuck-up.

Tommy did say, "We never wanted this." and a couple parties I've gone to on that side made me sick to my stomach by just observing. People would fight for no reason, or start unwanted drama on another's behalf for their own entertainment. Our differences created hatred for one another.

It was bullshit, it made me mad thinking about my own personal problems on that side. So I was ready to take whatever was coming at me.

"Shit, there he is!" Tommy shouted, he started to speed up and told me to put the mask on and handed me a handgun like it was nothing on his conscience. I was right, the second he handed me the gun I felt tension like never before. I checked the barrel and there wasn't a single bullet in it.

"It's not loaded."

"That's the point, we're only scaring him."

"Is yours loaded?" I asked hastily.

"Yep."

I swallowed what was left of myself. I had to live for the moment, no sign of weakness, nothing. Dalton had to believe that these guns were loaded and we were ready to kill him if he didn't hand over the goods. We were supposed to act as crazy as the man we were framing.

When Tommy drove next to him on the opposite side of the road, right away Dalton looked over at us. We could read his lips say "Oh shit!" He started to speed up, seeing two men wearing black masks would cause the impulse. Driving in that piece of crap car made things a little difficult, he was getting away.

I started to panic. "We're gonna lose him!"

"Shut up kid, he's all mine, he isn't going anywhere!"

I started grinding my teeth, not sitting still. I wanted to just jump out of the car and forget this whole thing. I wanted out, I couldn't take it. It was the most unreal experience as he drove faster and faster.

The two cars were racing down this dirt road, heading straight, but the funny thing is, Dalton not once tried to cut us off, maybe because of the dirt road. Just then, Tommy stuck his gun out the window and he slowed right down, and pulled over.

My guess was he didn't want to get himself or his car shot.

"Yeah! He's all ours kid!" I could not believe we had stopped him so easily.

Our beat up car was still running and before I could even think of what to do, or how to do it,

Tommy already had his door open running for Dalton. He tried to get out but Tommy kicked his door shut and stuck his gun in his face, actually, almost right down his throat.

"Open up the fucking trunk!"

"What the fuck! Ryan? Don't shoot, don't shoot!" He struggled to say.

"I'm not going to tell you again, open the fucking trunk!" He was screaming as hard and as loud as he could.

I raced out the door almost dropping my gun and went to the other side.

"Get out of the car, and open it, you want to die or you do you want to live?"

For some reason I felt a little stupid, what I said didn't make a bit of a difference. I wanted to be more like Tommy, but I still didn't show a sign of weakness, or let him know that was I terrified myself.

I tried to say something a little more convincing, and it came out, "it's a damned easy question!"

Dalton was so scared though when he opened the trunk he didn't move afterwards. He was speechless with his mouth wide open. I guess it doesn't matter what you say when you're the one with the gun, with an intimidating walk crunching on the stones. "Are you guys kidding me? Is that you Shawn?"

Tommy grabbed a bag out of the trunk, checked it out and headed back to the car. "Shut the fuck up!"

I looked back at Dalton, and got a good look at him, I felt kind of bad for him.

"Give me your phone!" I yelled.

"What?"

"Give me your fucking cell phone!"

"Okay! Okay! Jesus Christ!"

He handed it to me and I smashed into pieces and I just simply just walked away back to the car, nervous and in a slow-motion feel. I felt my leg twitch and almost buckled to the ground.

We squealed away and made him look at the car once more, and he got a real good look at it as we watched him from the rearview mirror. He was convinced that it was both Shawn and Ryan, giving us the upper hand to frame them and write his own resignation to leave this town once and for all.

A few seconds later, flying down a dirt road we just realized what we had done, and it felt great. I was laughing.

"That was fucking awesome! You did so good kid! What did you smash?"

"His phone." I yelled in a more calm excitement.

"What? I didn't even think of that! Wow kid, you're even more clever than me!"

We both ripped off our masks and drove away back into town. Tommy picked up his phone and called Costa for somebody to pick us up. "Mission accomplished, Costa, you should have seen the new kid, he was so god damn relentless! There is no way that could have gone any smoother." As he went on, I kept smiling.

Tommy could not get over the excitement, he kept bouncing up and down in his seat hitting the steering wheel, screaming and laughing the whole way back.

Even for somebody that seemed used to this lifestyle, his blood was pumping at the same pace as mine. A gun can make anybody feel tough, especially when the victim doesn't know who you are.

We dropped the car off in some parking lot near downtown. It was a restaurant called Lucy's. Costa was already waiting there. I expected to hear the words of some kind of congratulations, but not today, not from Costa at least. He seemed very impatient and took the bag with no surprise, the usual business of their twisted sense of humor.

CHAPTER V

—◦◦◦❯❮◦◦◦—

Trying to Fit into this Regret

(Saturday afternoon, March 15th.)

I wasn't scared at all, I felt invincible, even the long last of the cold air didn't faze me. However Costa's unhappiness always brought people down because he was the one we all had to listen too, but at least we didn't have to call him boss. At the point while he was ranting again I wasn't paying much attention to him. I was too busy thinking about what exactly I had just done.

Was I doing this all just to fit in with a crew that made a high name for themselves? Would I regret everything I had done? It was like a tattoo you were considering to have on your body the rest of your life, the result would come in time.

It was obvious that Dalton wouldn't have called and told the cops that he just got robbed at gunpoint over a trunk filled with drugs. It was Costa's phone that caught me off guard. It had this high-pitched ring to it that nobody could miss. He flicked his cigarette out of sight as he flipped open his phone.

"They're with me right now." Were we a scapegoat?

"Today is a new day for you, brother."

Tommy had this tired look in his eyes, already over the excitement of not only 10 minutes ago. He was frustrated and just waiting for the words to come out of Costa's mouth.

He knew we were going to have to go back out. He could finally get his recompense on Shawn for what he did to his sister.

"I'm going to beat that motherfucker to an inch of his life, I swear to god."

Instead of the reaction I was expecting, Costa seemed somewhat concerned.

"It's the middle of the afternoon, you'll get busted for sure." He said like he already knew what Tommy was capable of doing, that without caring, Tommy could kill somebody out in public.

"Maybe, but he won't see it coming, especially from this little guy."

Pointing at me, he was setting me up to take down the biggest and craziest guy that I had ever heard of at the time. It was madness. At the time I wasn't even sure what he meant, but I already felt like this was way out of my league.

"You're going to kill two birds with one stone."

"Alex and I will take care of this." Knowing fully of Costa's reaction, he looked over at me and smiled.

"I guess stranger things have happened." Costa said rolling his eyes in sarcasm.

I took a lot of offence to that, but I knew better than to start running my mouth, but two birds with one stone? I never wanted to know what would have happened to me if I didn't succeed in intimating a man twice my size. Tommy has his own vendetta, so I knew the two of us together could probably do whatever was necessary if things were to get physical. "This'll show me that Alex is serious about working with us, and if Shawn is literally scared to death over a kid half his size, he would feel more inclined to stay away from the embarrassment." Anything Costa could say to insult me, he didn't mind throwing my way.

"So you want me to take out this drug dealer?" I asked, and it seemed to get on Costa's last nerve.

"Hey kid, in case you didn't clue in yet, Tommy is my best friend and it'll help me sleep better at night if you'd stop kissing his ass."

"Hey wait a second! Costa? Costa!"

Walking away making another call he didn't bother to listen to me. I was too shook up and nervous if I was the one getting up, he said so himself, *you never know*. Tommy ran up to Costa and stopped him.

"Come with us then, see for yourself, the kid's legit. He's a solid guy." Defending me, I felt a little better. I took a deep breath and pulled myself together for the second most dangerous thing I've done in all my life, all in a single day.

Costa was like a boss you didn't want, you'd work and push yourself as hard as you could but it still wasn't enough. It was as if there was a quota involved, a deadline. Ending the conversation Costa smirked at Tommy,

"Alright, let's see what the kid can do."

Thinking about what I was going to do never really entered my mind until I got there. I took everything a step at a time.

Getting into one of the most beautiful cars I've ever seen, Costa offered me a cigarette calmly. I was still angry at the fact he was considering me as just another scapegoat at his disposal, a threat to whatever kind of organization he ran and insulting me while I was standing right there, right in front of him. And then just to offer me a smoke like it was nothing?

I guess it was just business. Anybody would tell you that he had some trust in me, he only showed it in his odd smile, a liar's smile.

"No, thanks."

"Hey don't take him so seriously, he thought I was an undercover cop when he met me."

"Really?" He clearly had some issues with paranoia.

"Yeah, really, don't you remember that Costa?" Tommy added laughing.

"Hey if I would have known our Dad's played pool together it would have been a whole other story."

"I'm just saying."

"And I'm just saying that me and this kid's Dad don't play pool."

"I don't know my father." I said.

"Well maybe mine knows your mother." He said sarcastic, laughing with Tommy.

"Maybe." I said with an attitude.

The laughing stopped and they looked at each other brushing it off and started up.

"So you know what you're doing when you get there?"

The task was simple, sneak in through the back door while that "*Fat-Fuck*" was watching TV and scare him right out of town, and never to come back, he had 48 hours.

Tommy was coming in with me and lending a hand, but the thought came, what if he didn't listen? It would have been a mess if he refused to listen to me. I wasn't a very convincing muscle.

"Then make him listen, you still got that gun don't you?"

"Yeah, but, what do you mean? Kill him?" I swallowed my soul at this brief moment.

Before the next words even came out of his mouth, a thousand and one words raced through my head. This was too much for me in one day, it gave me a headache, but ending somebody's life? I wanted to jump out of that car right away, and I knew I would have never done it. I knew that just watching something like that would leave a brutal scar in my memories.

"Just because we've never killed anybody doesn't mean we won't."

"You're serious." Tommy and I both said at the same time.

"I'm kidding you idiot! Well, at least about the *'you kill him'* part." I purged my conscience back into its place, and laughed myself back into clarity. Since the idea of killing somebody was gone, the quickest idea came to mind and I knew exactly what had to be done if Shawn refused.

I didn't mention it, I wanted to look clever, but I did ask for Tommy's gun in place for mine. He checked the clip and handed me the gun. It was funny though because he was quick to hand over the *loaded* gun, he really did have faith in me, unlike Costa. I almost felt in place.

The rumors that fled around town about Shawn weren't much for reality. His house was a typical east side dump, not as bad as Ryan's, but the only difference was his yard was clean with just-cut grass.

I could only see his house from a distance. The cold and dead trees around us made the situation extra groggy. Parked on the opposite side of the road Tommy's mood began to change. His heart started to race as he looked towards Shawn house. Memories were floating through his mind about his sister the night before, he could only imagine the pain she was feeling.

"I want to put as many bullets in him as stitches he put in her." Tommy snapped.

"It's not worth a murder charge." Costa added, arguing.

If knew now that with the three of us here, Shawn stood no chance whatsoever for things to turn against our favor, "You guys really planned this out accordingly." I said.

The smirk of distrust left Costa's face, "Exactly." He turned around. "I could have been wrong about you."

"Just wait a couple minutes, I'll show you." I loved the feel of having power. I really did feel like nothing could stop me.

"Alright guys make this quick, get in and get out."

"What? You're not coming with us?" Tommy asked.

"Nope, somebody has to be a lookout? It's the middle of the afternoon." He repeated from earlier.

The smirk returned, sarcasm was his best game.

"You cheap bastard, you're buying the beer when we're done." Tommy said under his breath. He got out of his seat with force.

The approach to the house had the both of us speed walking, "Get in and get out." kept playing back over and over. I think I may have even said it out loud once or twice. The guns were both tucked into our pants and we snuck through his neighbor's backyard. The sun was out, we could see what was left of the snow melting away. The only thing between the house and us was a small, bent rusty fence, I grabbed the top of it to do an easy jump but it wobbled and it creaked and made the most annoying sound.

From inside Shawn's you could hear the sound of some old comedy show. It was the kind with a family based humor and a fake audience laughing in the background, laughing at things that weren't even funny. I remember thinking about this when coming up to the back door, grabbing my handgun, ready to kick it open.

"Not yet kid, you have to wait and make sure he's downstairs. Wait on my mark." He whispered.

Without a doubt, he blew my mind sneaking around to the only window on that side of the house. He knew exactly what he was doing. He then he came running back, already counting down from three with his fingers. "Now!" He kicked the door so hard that it was half hanging onto the frame itself. I passed by the ruined wreck and ran through a destroyed looking room of nothing but old shoes and chopped up entertainment stands. "Move it, kid!"

He was sitting in his living room watching that horrible sitcom. We rushed in while he did absolutely nothing but calmly rub his hands together, after picking out some gunk in his teeth. The speed of us rushing in almost made me fall through the doorway into the living room, but I caught myself on the frame. It was like he was expecting us.

A quick and easy assault turned into a silent stare down between the three of us, and just as I was about to say the first words I got a feel of the room around me. I had already forgotten that my gun was loaded and the robbery earlier. I started to feel less scared as every second flew by.

"Who's the new kid, Tommy?"

"What are you, all fucked up or something?"

He kept picking things out of his teeth, rubbing his disgusting hands on his pant leg. He seemed like he had taken some pills or sniffed something. His eyes were dull and tired. I saw no reaction in him, like he had been used to this, or he had just given up.

"I know what you did to my sister, you sick fuck." Tommy kept shouting."

"He looks young." Continuing on about me.

"Slim here is a bigger man now than you will ever be! You're fucking scum!"

Slim? I guess he called me that because I was a little skinnier then the rest of the guys. It was better than everyone calling me kid though, especially at that time.

"What the hell are you talking about, Tommy?" Getting back to the main topic, Shawn seemed confused about everything going on, did he not remember? Was he lying? Was he just too high to acknowledge what had even happened? Tommy walked over to him pulling out his pistol and kept striking him in the face with it. I could hear the metal hit his teeth. The sounds were clapping and echoing throughout the living room. Shawn barely moaned in pain, but it hurt.

"You like to hit fucking girls?! You beat my fucking sister? I'm going to fucking kill you!" Tommy screamed, and just kept constantly hitting him, over and over again. His face was bloody and looked to be uneven now.

"Go fuck yourself. You've already ruined me." Shawn coughed out at him.

"Shut the fuck up! Just shut the fuck up!" It was very clear to me at this point that he was so high off his own supply of garbage he couldn't clue in what was going on. The pain was muffled by drugs, he could not feel the pain even if he wanted too. Tommy threw his arm far into the air behind him and struck Shawn with a massive haymaker and then stuck the gun in his mouth. "I'm going to blow your fucking brains out you cocksucker!" He had courage and a lot of it to keep the room filled. With his other hand, he pulled hard on Shawn's hair and stuck his forehead to his. "You are going to leave, and never come back, or I will kill you, do you understand me?"

Just outside Costa was waiting for some sort of sign that Shawn got the message to skip town, so my earlier idea was at its time for its release. "Slim, get over here, and end this." Tommy said, queuing me.

Without hesitation this time, I walked up quickly and stuck my gun right his on his knee cap, almost bumping into Tommy. We were right in his face.

"Pack your shit, because if you don't leave tonight, you will die."

I was getting a closer look at his pupils, they were huge and glazed. It made me sick that people could live like this, and I started to feel angry, I felt like grinding my own teeth to nothing and ripping my own hair out. The frustration of how this guy lived and acted just made me so mad. Then the look he gave me when I told him to leave just made it worse. He reminded me of a clown with bad make-up, turning his face slowly not even looking at me in the eyes. He had crossed a line he should not have, and we were here to remind him of that.

"What are you going to do you bag of bones?" He couldn't have said it any slower.

My surroundings did not exist at this point. I really couldn't tell you what Tommy was doing, this moment was ours. It just smacked me in the face that I, a seventeen year old kid was holding a gun to a guy almost ten years older than me. I felt very unoriginal. Kids should never point guns at each other. Welcome to the new age of today, kill or be killed I guessed. Without any more hesitation I pulled the trigger and blew out Shawn's kneecap. The air pressure or something didn't make enough of the blood splatter onto my shirt. It was part of my plan to have lots of this psycho's blood sprayed onto me for proof. Proof that I had what it takes to be in this twisted world of Costa and Tommy's.

He didn't yell much. Fact is I think I wanted to scream more than him, out of anger, out of confusion. "What did I just do?" I thought to myself almost dropping the gun. I turned quickly to Tommy and his reaction was just as priceless as my own. His eyes slightly got wider but then his faint look of "it's just business" took over. I never squeezed something so hard in my life. I closed my own eyes so hard that it hurt to open them, the pain was so horrible.

Something about fitting in and being cool kept going through my head. Maybe he was used to this sort of thing, and maybe my first instinct of regret and of mistake was it. I couldn't tell, it was a mess, I was a mess.

The funny thing is how fast this entire thing went by, everything going through my mind was only a second compared to reality. When I looked up and saw the face of hate and anger in Shawn, the hate of my own past blew out his other knee. Not even a flinch inside me, but he screamed for his life this time.

We both tried to hold him down and cover his mouth. It was one of those awkward moments where it looks nothing like the movies and you look stupid bouncing around with somebody struggling to win. It didn't feel like this was happening. At a time like this, all anyone mainly focuses on is proving their own point and getting what they want done. I on the other hand was drifting off in my weird world thinking about what I had been doing all day. People can very well change overnight, and I was becoming this person. A monster to the eyes of a truly unique and special person, Eva. I should have realized I had everything I needed already, and not wanted more.

His breath was hot and musky as I held my hand down over his mouth. He started to spit all over my hand and as much as I wanted to wipe it off, I couldn't. Tommy kept hitting him over and over again telling him to shut up. I knew I'd be screaming too if my kneecaps were blown off.

Finally the screams turned into tears, he had given up. His blood was dripping all over the place, it was more blood then I ever expected, but there's always more blood than expected. I wondered if this man was ever going to walk again.

I took my warm, damp hand and rubbed it all over his knee then patted my white shirt for the proof I needed. I looked at him with a smirk and said,

"Now, do we understand each other?"

"I'll leave, and you have my word!" He was very convincing.

A calm finger touched my shoulder, signaling me to leave. "Let's go kid."

Get in, get out. Instead of taking the best way out, we both decided to walk right out the front door. The sun never looked so dull. Shawn's house was one of those places that had old garbage bags nailed to the window frame. You'd think that with all the drug money people made, they'd make their drug den at least look a little nicer. I had one hell of a power trip so I turned back and yelled through the door,

"And clean this place up will you?"

Whatever it was that took over me those last two days, I liked it. I loved not being stepped on. Doing this with Tommy would make anybody feel incredible, powerful, and cocky.

"Fuck being a scapegoat." I had said a few things that didn't make too much sense if you were there listening to me, and I kept saying a few things out loud that didn't really go with the mood. Random things were just popping into my head. Movies, books, newspapers, quotes, the realism of the whole matter and there messages of warning. I felt mad and upset wondering if I was comfortable with what I just did, but I heard a familiar voice in the back of my head,

"Don't be such a coward." Good old Tommy.

The day was coming to an end, the pink clouds were bleeding through the sky. We both saw Costa at the same time puffing on a cigarette faster than ever, sitting in his car nice and low so nobody could see him. The street was dead, not a single witness could see us walking away from a house covered in blood. I sat in the back seat and took off the shirt and threw it to Costa. Needless to say he was impressed, and he turned back to me with a huge smile.

"That's my boy! Come on! Let's go get you some new clothes." I ripped my shirt off.

"Don't feel bad Alex, that sick bastard sells drugs to little girls and minors, he parties with them and gives them alcohol. I'll let you use your imagination to figure out the rest." Tommy assured me.

"So what's next?"

"We should go torch that car." Costa suggested.

As day turned into dusk, we took Ryan's stolen car far out of town, in the middle of nowhere. We were in the middle of a field behind a broken down building what looked to be a school once. The walls left standing were covered in graffiti teenagers had left. We syphoned what gas was left all over the car itself and ignited it. The car burned away as we all we watched in awe. I found inner peace in myself and that day watching any evidence turn to ash. The three of us stood proud, and walked away as the flames finally died down. I was in.

CHAPTER VI

Love Sells

(Saturday night, almost midnight, March 15th)

Like a bad intro into a really good movie, I felt like things were starting to come together. The rest of the night turned out pretty well, Costa got all the details about everything, and the both of them ended up driving me around everywhere. If I needed something they took care of it. They even offered to get me hair cut or a tattoo, but we all ended up deciding to get me a brand new cell phone. These were the two coolest guys on the face of this earth and they wanted to hang out with me. I couldn't explain how grateful I was, although I wasn't excited as much I thought I should have been. Was I already used to this? I could not believe how fast I was adapting.

The both of them kept referring to my earlier act of madness as the 'miracle favor' and tonight had been all about me. We went and ate dinner, we probably laughed the entire time talking about everything possible. I was more a night person. It's the time to live. Daytime is the time to work, at least that's what I always said. Out the window I watched the sidewalks shine and I finally had the time to think about my girlfriend. Until these last two days we spent every single day together for almost four years, every single day. She and I were inseparable and each other's first loves. She taught me a lot as she learned from me. We had some good fights, laughs, cries, moments, silences, and most of all, her eyes always reminded me I was alive.

We both had a strange glowing gold halo that really looked as if it slowly moved around our pupils. With my new, beautiful cell phone, I called the most beautiful girl in the world. She wouldn't have known the number so she didn't know who was calling, but the second she heard my voice, "Hey!" she yelled with a great excitement.

"Can I come over?" I asked with a big smile myself.

"Yeah please? I miss you, where have you been?"

"I miss you too."

"Then come over!"

"I'm on my way, hold on a second."

I covered the phone, "Costa! Can you take me to my girlfriends place?"

"Are you fucking serious? We're going to see some strippers, and get some beers man!" Tommy yelled.

"They wouldn't let me in there, I'm not of age."

"We know people in there, they'll let you in." Costa whispered.

I thought that's what he was going to say, it figured he would. These guys didn't joke around. I didn't care, I just wanted to see Eva, my day was over and I missed her.

"Not tonight man, I have to see her."

"Let the kid go and see his woman."

"Suit yourself." Costa got a little bummed out. I put the phone back to my ear.

"I'll be there in a bit."

We couldn't wait to see each other, it was kind of pathetic. Most teenage love is pathetic, but it does in fact exist. I fooled around with my phone and got used to its gadgets and gave directions to her house. When I got there

I said my goodbyes but Costa grabbed my forearm and stared at me.

"You're a good kid, Alex."

"Thanks, you guys gonna give me a call soon?"

"You bet. First thing tomorrow morning." He said calm and simple.

For some reason, I remember her sidewalk glowing wet and cold, but the black tar seemed amazing because I knew Eva would be waiting at the end of it. She was the smile on my face all night. The car sped off and I could hear them howling away, I giggled a little bit looking down at the new outfit that I picked out with the guys. I could not wait to see Eva. Before I could knock on the door she was already running and ripped open her front door.

"Alex!" The grace of seeing her was ecstatic. It was time for me to feel like a kid again.

"You like my new outfit?"

"You look very sexy." She said looking me up and down. I smiled.

"So do you." Like always.

"So what did you do today?"

"Can we go inside? I have a lot to tell you."

I was a sucker for romance, but we both sounded desperate. She was excited to hear what I was doing while welcoming me in. Every time I've been in her house there were a few more details moved around or something new like a television or an entire living room set. She was always at my house because her father was kind of strict with everything she did, with me anyways.

I didn't tell her the brutal details involving the blood and so forth, she would lecture me for hours on end. I did let her know about Tommy and Costa, she didn't know much about them but she was proud that I wasn't hanging around with people like Andrew this whole time.

"What's wrong with Andrew?" I asked.

"He's just really quiet. You know me, I'm a very social person but I think he looks down on me."

"That's the most ridiculous thing I've ever heard, he's like my brother."

Unlike most couples in the town with no name, we didn't have the same crowd of friends. She wasn't judgmental toward my group or me but her friends were. I guess it kind of rubbed off on her.

When I thought about it, I haven't called Sanko, Andrew or Chelsea in a while. I wondered if they all knew about what exactly has been going on. This was a new lifestyle, an opportunity, and I thought we should have all taken it.

Even in the happiest moments of being with her, I was still thinking about business and all its fun. She could tell I wasn't telling her the entire truth. We literally knew each other inside and out. We couldn't hide anything from each other. I wondered all night if she was going to mention anything, but she never did, but we both knew that curiousness was in the air.

It wasn't awkward at all at this point. That night turned out to be one of the best nights of my life. I was very relaxed not worried about the past events. I knew the guys would take care of me if it came up to it.

Cops were not involved with our world, we weren't idiots or doing the wrong things, everything was kept to a street code I guess you could say.

Everybody knows never to rat out anybody, even if it's your worst enemy, even they know never to do something drastic without permission from the guy paying you. The thing is that every day is a new day and you never knew what to expect.

"Do you think we'll get married?" Eva asked completely off topic interrupting my thought. The night was quiet and we were both just listening to music while she flipped through some old magazines.

"I don't know how to answer that."

"You should purpose to me." I paused for a second, in disbelief.

"Wait, what?" I got up from laying on my back and gave her my full attention.

"Well this doesn't seem to cover what we have, just dating." She closed her magazine and sat closer to me as we shared the bed.

"Nothing will cover what we have," I grabbed both her hands. "But if that's what you want."

"Well, do you want too?"

"Of course I do."

"Surprise me then!" I couldn't put a word to describe how happy we were, it would be impossible. Everything just came to me naturally when it was about her.

"I will."

I didn't take this new discussion very seriously, which I should have. I didn't expect she did either but she kept on it almost the entire night, The more I thought about it, I knew I'd be hanging around with the others more and more and have less time to spend with Eva.

I was used to having her and never thought of the possibility of losing her. She loved me more than anything.

We had this fight once, our only big one. It was my sixteenth birthday and I made a joke about another girl flirting with me over my new bike's handlebars. Eva noticed this girl smiling at her with an attitude. I've known this girl almost my entire life so I wrongfully defended her point when Eva mentioned it.

We quickly broke into a ruthless fight.

"She's drunk!"

"So what? I know you Alex, you were flirting too!"

"I was not! You don't know what you're talking about!"

Everybody was listening to us in the other room, and frankly my party didn't turn out the greatest this year. My sister, Meghan had an argument with my mom earlier that day and the party was cancelled so the few people that didn't hear about the last minute news showed up anyways. There were seven different people that didn't really like each other all involved with different crowds of friends, some wanted to get so drunk they passed out and the others said and did nothing sipping on their root beer. If matters weren't already awkward enough.

I remember how furious my older brother and I were at Meghan for ruining that night. Then just to make it worse. I had to open my big mouth and say the most unnecessary and brutal things to Eva. The night was fueling on hate. She started to walk up the road and screamed that she'd walk all the way home and that it was over between the two of us.

I thought about my reputation in front of my group of friends, but right away I had already realized that I knew what I'd be missing. I chased after her, grabbed her and cried like a little baby.

I knew what the others were thinking, that I was a weak hearted fool that fell for Eva's dramatic scenes, but she was more than worth it.

"No, no please, please don't go." I don't remember the exact order of how I said it, but the point I made got across to Eva instantly. She looked at me like the first time she had met me. She looked like she was going to cry. Her eyes shined to the moonlight, I'll never forget that.

"I wasn't really going to walk home." She laughed, "You really do love me, don't you?"

"You know I do."

"Oh my god, I'm so sorry." We were wrapped around each other tighter than our own bond. I held her in the dark, relieved.

After that one little fight, everything was perfect with us. Everybody knew we were different and thought we were soul mates. My point on this story is that you should always know what you would lose before you get the chance to. This is because most of the time, it's better to regret something you did do then something you didn't do.

What if I did try to hold back the tears in front of that small crowd? We both knew we'd regret losing each other, even if it only lasted a couple hours. It was the best feeling to know that she and I were true.

This was us every day and night. I can't remember every detail of this one night in particular because it wasn't anything out of the ordinary. I have to set the record for how important this girl was and still is to me. Love sells.

Now back to the main story at hand. By the time we both went to bed I was locked in to a comfortable position, but I could not fall asleep. I was tired but restless. At about 3:30am I could hear my phone vibrate on Eva's nightstand. I could see the light reflecting off one of her mirrors. It figured, I had to have left it on her side.

"You've got to be kidding me." She was sound asleep and it would take a tornado to bust through the walls to get her up. I got out of bed very oddly and carefully, not making a sound or sudden movement, but her damn floors were so creaky and stiff I had to walk like a cartoon spy. Putting my feet down slowly and moving in a smooth motion.

"Don't eat them all." Eva was dreaming and half awake, trying to say something.

"What?" I asked softly.

"Don't eat all of them." She clapped her gums together and tossed over in the bed. It was nothing, she was kind of sleepwalking only she couldn't even stand up. I just smiled and didn't answer.

I flipped the phone open to see a text message from Tommy, "Make sure you're up bright and early, were coming to pick you up." It read. I sent him back just saying that I would be and that I was almost asleep. The real spelling from the text message was sloppy and drunk written, they must have just finished their night.

I was surprised to find out that they remembered the address. When they dropped me off they were already half in the bag and wasted on Costa's soon to be favorite whiskey.

Tommy got the message that I was going to be awake for this unknown reason.

Only a few hours later and the sun rose up halfway across the earth.

"Hey, I have to go." I didn't sleep all night. I would daze off into a half sleep with any little noise waking me back up. Every side of the pillow was warm.

I was shifting between watching Eva sleep and looking out the window staring at the cold, blue morning lift into an orange sunrise. I did realize that morning, that Eva did not move an inch that entire night. She was completely stuck in this gorgeous picture, she looked harmless, and happy.

"Why?" She asked. She wasn't used to me getting up at this time leaving for no reason.

"I just have to." She barely opened her eyes but knew were my hands were.

"I'll call you when I'm up."

"Okay." I said under my breath kissing her goodbye. She moved around until she was comfortable again, she fell asleep quickly.

When I left I could actually hear "*I love you.*" Play into my head, and I walked away knowing that the last things I said to her were more positive than negative.

The car pulled up in the mist of what was left of winter. The both of them already dressed up and ready, drinking their coffees.

"Come on, were going to go get some breakfast." Costa said popping his head out of the window, he seemed very happy.

I didn't say much except rearrange my jaw together from the dryness and earliness of the morning. I got in the car wrapped up in my small sweater looking at my cold air leaving my mouth. It woke me up a little bit seeing myself in such a panic, but I was just cold.

I wondered if that was why they woke me up, just to take me out to breakfast.

"It's 8:30 in the morning guys, I'm not really that hungry."

"Sure you are! Come on, I'm buying."

"You're in a good mood."

"I usually am in a good mood, you just caught me at a bad time." Even then I found that hard to believe.

"He's happy because our hacker got into Shawn's e-mail and got the entire scoop on what's what." Tommy told me.

"You, have a hacker?" I asked. I myself was a computer hacker so I wasn't too surprised, but did he work for them under the title as *'Our Hacker'*?

"Yeah we got all kinds of guys, drivers, hackers, enforcers, informers."

"Do they work *for* you?"

"Well, for Costa."

"I thought this type of thing was only in the movies?" Costa looked at me through the rearview mirror, his eyes were serious.

"Money talks kid."

At the beginning of all this I thought I just befriended two smart guys with some connections with the basics of this and that, but as the days went on it just kept getting more serious and too much to handle.

I looked forward to meeting the rest of the crew.

"So what did this hacker of yours find?"

"Shawn's been taken to an unauthorized, low-life 'duct tape' doctor, hiding from us and plans on leaving as soon as he's better."

"Well that's going to be awhile." I kind of laughed, couldn't get too far with two blown apart kneecaps.

"Yeah but there's bad news too."

"Great, I can't wait to hear this." By now, I was used to things going wrong.

"He talked to his friend's about you."

Right in front of Eva's house, I was told that my name was mentioned to all of Shawn's friends and crazy crack addicts. A kid named Slim was being hunted, along with Tommy and the others involved in yesterday's little endeavor. Now I didn't feel like such a jerk for telling him to clean up his house up. I knew how much trash they would be talking and what they would do if they found me.

"So, what do we do now?" I rubbed up my face and hair taking a deep breath.

If I could put a gun to him, he or one of his buddies could do the same to me. This was not a very good wake up call. I had already completely lost my appetite.

"You're worried aren't you? Don't, because we're going to take care of this. Everything is going to be alright."

"What if the cops are brought into this?"

"Are you fucking kidding me?" Tommy yelled, "Didn't we already go over this?"

This was something I was supposed to know already, driven and stuffed into my head, common sense for a kid in my position. I could remember Willie mentioning the cops were on a high alert and busting anyone that looked suspicious. My situation would make the front papers if I was caught, and give them the bust they needed, and wanted.

But I figured Tommy knew what he was talking about, they were smart at this game. I followed his advice and let time tell and the stress settle.

"Look around you Alex, you'd be caught by now, these cops have nothing better to do."

"True." In the most truthful look I've ever seen in Tommy. I knew it before he even told me.

"We're free."

Freedom had its way of hunting and betrayal, hatred yet denial, laughter with ambition. A mix of emotions separating happiness and anger. Everybody in the world had a different approach of their own freedom.

I didn't care, I just wanted what was mine. Eva.

CHAPTER VII

---∘∘◦🔘◦∘---

The Town with No Name

(Sunday afternoon, 1:30pm, March 16th)

I made it back home after going through some of the feedback of this town we all lived in. Everything was within the walls and border of something without a name. Everybody knows everybody and they all know what they're doing.

This was the type of town that even if you're alone in your home, with all the windows blocked off. All the doors locked and did something embarrassing or worth a story being told about. Somehow every last soul would know about it.

"We live in our own world, driven out of the madness of what goes on outside our own chaos." A small urban city outside and separate from the rest of society, we were alone in the world and even the police were getting thrown out.

Tommy had the coolest way of putting things together for me. Unlike everyone else I haven't lived here my entire life so a lot of this was new to me. It was pretty much divided into two sides, east and west. The line separating the two life styles was a long canal cut into three sections with bridges. These bridges caused a lot of tourist attention and general frustration for the locals. The bridges would lift over 100ft tall causing endless pictures to be taken over and over again just so a couple of boats could pass by, obviously interrupting everyone else's daily routine.

Sometimes you could understand the love for this, usually later on in the night when everything was peaceful, quiet and shockingly beautiful. Our town didn't light up like Las Vegas but it oddly shined with its own color. The reflections from the black water and the golden streetlights had a mysterious flow of memories, and they were everywhere.

Not many hobbies existed except drinking alcohol, smoking, fighting and causing pointless drama. Not a lot of people had the ambition or belief to make something of themselves anymore. However, few who did were very unique and worth being your friend, we were the ones making the difference while we watched everything happen. Tommy and Costa had big reputations and lived up to their records. Some people thought of them as the Hollywood, sunglasses wearing drug dealers with sarcasm to boot. They were cocky and ruthless, but that wasn't who they were. They just acted that way around groups of people, especially girls.

Tommy wasn't a fake, he just had his own way of dealing with people. Costa on the other hand didn't have much of a heart. His brother Rant looked nothing like him and yes, Rant was his real name.

That's the thing about this place, almost everybody had a weird name or they were given an odd nickname from one their own traits, perks or style.

I met a few of these people at breakfast. In person you could understand the names given to them like 'Tiny'. Tiny got this name because he was one of the enforcers mentioned earlier. He was actually one big guy, settling into his mid-thirties.

Without a doubt one of the toughest guys I've ever seen. He made my mom's boyfriend seem like nothing compared to this monster. When I first met him I was nervous that I'd say something out of line, but he gave me this quote and it means a lot coming from somebody like him.

"Outside I'm a grizzly bear, but inside I'm a teddy bear." I liked that, it meant that he was a man of his word and had heart of gold.

I was told a lot of stories about him taking out guys half his size, getting stabbed, beaten and broken. He also had a little girl that he loved with all his heart, showing me pictures of her in his wallet I started to wonder about his regret or if it was all bullshit.

I mean think about it, a group of friends sitting around for breakfast going on about how great this enforcer was. My brain told me to believe him, but how did he not feel regret over his daughter?

If I had kids, I wouldn't be in this type of business, the only I reason I was now was because I felt I needed a good story to be told, I had my entire life in front of me.

Maybe Tiny still just felt his youth. Rumors were everything in this town, people would come to you with their problems about how much they hate the current drama. Then they would all turn around and most likely talk their own towards you. Today was a day I walked around my house aimlessly thinking about all of this.

It was one of those days where you didn't realize how much you walked back and forth into the same rooms looking for something to do, only you weren't bored. It could have just been me but this happened to me a lot. I was so eager to move again and very curious as to what was going to happen next. I was also wondering if Chelsea and the others were up to date. I was alone and nobody was in the house so I could hear every last cracking sound in the walls and the giant wall clock ticking. It sounded slower from the lack of sleep and dragging my heavy eyelids.

Andrew once told me that he hated this town for not being able to do much, and it was true. Other than the friends you had and the stories being turned around and against yourself, everything would be useless here. In a way you were trapped living in this place you kind of wanted to be trapped in. So technically this war had started over pure nothingness.

Ritz Sanko saw it as the town that never sleeps. There's money here, money there, sniff this, smoke that, he's a one-minded person most of the time. It was his sense of humor was the ticket to our friendship.

Sanko being his nickname we always forgot his first name. I remember some girl standing outside of school asking, "Sanko, what's your last name?"

Other than the two crowds constantly fighting, everyone else was set back a few years. I mean they didn't have much common sense, but it led to the main reason why these kids were followers and not leaders.

I finally said to myself, "Who am I?" I wasn't very much of a leader, but I knew I wanted to start punching holes in my wall from the confusion. I felt as if I was betraying a lot of people who knew me as the innocent little Alex. Change didn't faze me and I could care less about what people thought about me. It's just that when you know something is going to change for better or worse, you hope and pray that the better is more worth it and that you don't let your loved ones down.

When I finally sat down to think I just started to notice how much my feet hurt. I could feel the car ride earlier bounce my feet up and down, like a sickness you don't remember until you get it again.

I felt beaten, confused and stuck, and just when I started to push myself to quitting this entire situation. That's when I heard a pounding on the front door. I knocked my head back into my chair.

"Give me a fucking break."

I slammed my hands against the chair and stomped the entire way down the stairs to see my sister waving her arms with a muffled and angry, "Hello!"

She never gave me a second to do something for her, it had to be done yesterday as far as she was concerned. Standing next to her was a guy I could have sworn I've seen before.

I unlocked the door, "Did you forget your keys?"

Sarcastically she said, "No Alex, I just wanted you to unlock the door."

"Who's this?" I asked, but my sister bumped into me stormed off holding at least five bags over her shoulder, muttering up the stairs.

"We talked on the phone, my name's Kenny."

He had a strong reputation for distributing cocaine. When he got caught his parents and law enforcement sent him endless miles away to a rehab center. He used to write to my sister and her friends all the time because he had a heart of gold and loved all of his friends. One thing about him was that he always gave somebody a handshake even if he didn't know who that person was, he was very welcoming.

I've only met him once prior so I had to ask if in fact it was Kenny Pollock.

"Yeah that's me buddy." I exclaimed.

"I remember you now! We met at Meghan's last New Year's Eve party."

"Oh I bet buddy." That didn't surprise me.

"You were pretty drunk." I said.

He reminded me of Tommy coming in with his introduction, when he shook my hand he tightened his grip and kept it shaking.

"I was so fucked up that night, I did Acid for my first time."

"That would explain the love for my wallpaper."

"You my friend, you're going to own this town one day." Changing the subject instantly, while being polite.

"Yeah, if I don't fucking die first." As long as something you said was remotely humorous, you could count on Kenny to laugh.

"I've heard a lot about you, you've made a big difference in the last couple of days."

"So there are rumors about me?" I made the impression that I was mad at this, but I almost couldn't hide the smile that somebody in his position was giving me a compliment.

Who I was turning out to be was somebody who fit into this business, people liked me and stories were being told of my actions.

"No rumor, the things said between the guys stays with the guys."

"I should have known that already."

I had already forgotten that I was given a cell phone so when it vibrated in my pocket it kind of scared me, I remember telling myself I had to stop being so jumpy, Kenny found it hilarious, "Got a snake in your pants?"

"I'm new at this." I said smiling having a laugh with my new friend. It was Chelsea calling.

"Hold a second, I have to take this."

"Take your time buddy." Admiring the photos like Tommy did.

I flipped open the phone, "Hello?" but the phone was still ringing right in my ear.

"You have to press the talk button, Alex." I put my index finger up signaling him to be quiet.

"Hello?"

"Where the hell have you been?"

"How did you get my number?"

"I'm at Costa's house! Looking for you! So he told me to call you and gave me your number."

"I've been everywhere, I've got some stories for you." Being cocky.

"Well I've got a pretty good idea what you've been up too. Eva is looking for you too, you know, she even called *me*."

"She is?" I prayed right there and then that she didn't hear about what I've been doing. I wanted to ask Chelsea if she knew but I didn't want to risk it for Chelsea to find out everything either.

"She's worried about you Alex, get over here please."

"I'm on my way, if she calls you though, Chelsea please don't pick it up."

"Why?" She had a real odd tone when she asked me that.

"Matter of fact turn your phone off."

"Okay?"

"Thanks."

"Whatever." She didn't seem very happy with me.

I shut the phone and Kenny didn't really move from his spot. When I turned my back to him I thought he went upstairs to see my sister, but since he was still standing there I thought we could use his truck to get over back to Costa's.

"Can we go for a ride over to Costa's for a second?"

"Yeah sure, I was only dropping your sister off anyways."

"So you know Costa then?"

"Of course I do, Willie, Costa, Tommy and Marc, they're like my brothers man."

"I haven't met this Marc guy, yet."

"I wouldn't doubt it if he was there right now."

I grabbed the railing leading upstairs and yelled to Meghan, "Tell Mom I'm going out for a bit."

"Yeah, whatever!" I looked over at Kenny and had a face of disgust for that damn word, 'whatever'.

He just smiled, "You good?"

"Yeah, let's go."

I stepped outside into a blistering yellow reflection off what was left of the snow, I had to keep my head down it was so bright. I remember walking feeling like an idiot tightening my eye lids closer, looking down, it seemed like a struggle against absolutely nothing. I needed to get some sleep.

"Fuck is it ever bright out here." I looked shifting my eyes from down to my right seeing Kenny actually blocked the sun with his hands against his head. Why I think about these types of things is truly beyond my own imagination, but in a strange way it kind of reminded me that I was alive.

I was a different kid from everybody else, if I could speak the words that constantly went through my mind then I would put them down on paper. The town with no name didn't have a kid like me, maybe that's why these super-cool guys were letting me into their crew. I wasn't smart, tough or even that good looking. All I had was my writings and computer skills. I was a shy kid who only had my three best friends. People have said that I'm oddly clever and had a great sense of humor. Come to think of it, that mainly was the parents of those three best friends, Chelsea, Sanko and Andrew.

I liked the fact that Chelsea would get mad at me sometimes, because the others and I wouldn't. Chelsea and I never actually got into a fight, but that's because we really understood each other. The day we met was something else then most friendships. I'd be lying if I said I never had a crush on her. I was nuts about her for a short time, but it quickly blew over for Eva. The sad part is she knew it too.

We were the youth, we basically already made all the decisions by default. That could be one other reason we fit so well with Costa and the others. Then I turned to Pollock and asked.

"How old are you anyways?"

"Nineteen, in a couple of days, you?"

"Seventeen."

"You look twenty."

"Yeah, I get that one a lot." I never really did get told that, but I had to say something when I realized that he was pretty short for his age. He almost had to climb into his truck. He was stocky and stubby for his small size.

It really amazed me some of the vehicles they were driving, sports cars, exotics and brand new trucks? I knew people in their thirties and forties who barely had enough cash to scrap together a bicycle. How much money was being thrown around with these guys? How long have they been doing this sort of thing, and what types of things were they doing with all this money involved?

Some of them had legit jobs that paid very well, and why not? They were smart.

"So how do you know Costa?" I asked.

"Before I went into rehab I used to sell coke for him."

"Now what do you do for him?"

"I sell coke for him."

"Uh huh." I couldn't tell if he was serious or not. He stared at the road the entire time we drove, and he didn't hesitate to answer any my questions, he was a straight shooter.

"You don't feel obligated to work for him do you, Alex?"

"Obligated?"

"Well, I heard it's because you're the only one that set eyes on that getaway car." Meaning Ryan's, the one we had just set ablaze.

"At first it was, but I'm starting to enjoy this type of thing."

"So you're coming with me tonight then?" He said with a big smile.

"Why doesn't this surprise me?" I couldn't even get an hour to myself anymore, but it wasn't like I had something better to do.

"It's not business, it's personal."

"Then why would I tag along?"

This was probably the key information of our town. We didn't have any main enemies to fight against. Even though we have the east and the west, this was a battle going on long before I was even born. Tommy did mention to me prior to this situation that they were not titled as anything, not a family, not a gang, more along the lines of friends. The struggle we fought and still fight for was ourselves.

Everyone around you would sell you out over absolutely nothing. Their way of attention and satisfaction was to repeat something they swore to you they wouldn't. It was ridiculous how your own best friend would twist a story he or she heard just for being the top conversationalist.

This isn't a story about guns, drama or two sides fighting. Our problems were in our own backyard. There are countless so-called friends spreading rumors and lies, and before you know it, the entire town knew a false stretched story of something so simple.

"To show people that you're crazy, man!" I couldn't think of anything to say back to this, considering I just did work for Costa the last couple of days, doing all sorts of crazy things.

"You're new at this game are you not?" he asked.

"Yeah, it's all pretty new."

"Well then?"

"Well then, what?"

"You have to make your first impression to last a lifetime with these goons."

"These goons?" What a character.

I figured my first impression was Shawn's entire kneecap thing, or Ryan's stolen car, or Dalton's gunpoint robbery, but I guess not. Around here if you were working, you had to *'be there to understand it'*. I didn't want to just speak my mind in anger towards Kenny, I just met him. He reminded me a lot of Tommy, and already his judgment and opinion meant a lot to me.

In my head I had already agreed to go, but Kenny did not give enough details of what exactly his personal business was. I started a theory that some of these guys abused the favor system to aid their personal vendettas.

"Well what do you want me to do?"

"Nothing too much, were going to the bar tonight."

"Yeah, and?"

"Then, we are going to beat the shit out of Ryan."

"What the hell? How is that personal?" I was so damn confused.

"Every day that guy is running around stealing shit off of people, and why people don't kick ass every single day is beyond me!" He started to yell a little bit, I could tell he was going to start ranting and raving about this kid.

"That guy sold his toaster and computer for crack, man! He stole my two thousand dollar bike, my movies, even my dinner!" I started laughing hysterically, and it was true. Ryan didn't really have much of a brain, I just never put it together that it was the same Ryan we stole his car from.

"He stole your dinner?" I asked, continuing to laugh.

"Right off of my plate, that piece of no good-"

"Where were you when this happened?"

I tried so hard to stop, but Kenny was too serious for me. I couldn't believe this story. I'd be angrier if he took my bike, but I guess it was the point behind the story Ryan's dignity.

"This was about two years ago, he came to my parent's house looking for some blow. So when I went upstairs to weigh it up. I came back down and he's gone, and so were my tacos! I couldn't fucking believe it!"

"What about your bike?" I asked still cracking up.

"That was about last week, I didn't know who took it until Tommy told me he saw it there."

"I was with him that night." I mentioned.

"Yeah I know."

Here we go again, a simple job this time. I just have to basically watch Kenny Pollock beat up some junkie to get his stuff back, if he didn't sell it already.

We talked back and forth about this town we lived in. It seemed as much as I knew already I didn't know nearly enough, yet nobody did. However, I did put together that Costa himself was fed up with the lack of loyalty and respect this town had. His main goal was to put together the perfect crew, a crew that would never betray each other, no one would go their separate ways and would stay together for the sake of friendship and not money.

Unfortunately, in today's world this does not exist. Change is always around us, people go with the times and it could just be me, but I find it very pathetic. Costa's dream was a dream, and nothing more.

When we pulled into his driveway I suddenly remembered about Chelsea and Eva, and got that old nervous feeling back in my stomach, the numb bottom teeth feeling.

I got out of the truck instantly and saw Chelsea waiting for me on the front porch. Before she even noticed me she yelled, "Pollock!"

I couldn't help but notice the love between these two. Anybody would be able to tell you that they haven't seen each other in a while, so they were excited to see each other.

"You two know each other?" I asked. How much did everybody else know that I didn't? I felt like I was in a deep hole living outside of the news feed. I was out of date and had to keep up with everybody. So this entire time I thought I was the only one involved with these guys, what a goddamn surprise this was still turning out to be. I could not help but feel jealous, but I knew it was better to have good friends with me fully aware of everything.

CHAPTER VIII

--∘∘-◦❮◉❯◦-∘∘--

Concrete & Cocaine

Sunday afternoon, 2:30pm, March 16th

So everyone up to this point was not very impressed with me as much as I thought I was with myself. Perhaps 'impressed' isn't the word any of us were looking for. I felt that I needed some comfort considering it my first time living a style like this. I didn't allow it to get to my head, bitching and moaning over something they didn't care about it would be an obvious sign of weakness. I kept my mouth shut, observing.

"How long have we known each other Chelsea?" Kenny asked, stressing how good of friends they were.

"It would be one year last New Year's." She always had a memory like a calendar.

"New Years, fuck." He said grabbing his head going off about some of the regrets.

I paused a bit, because a few months prior to that, I had just met her and we were even closer than we were now. I did not see her at this New Year's party, and my sister and I were the ones who threw the party in the first place.

"Where were you Chelsea? I didn't see you."

"I wasn't at your party, me and Pollock stole his Dad's truck that night."

"And did what?" I was so disrupted by this, because until this moment I could have sworn Chelsea was an angel, she never did anything wrong.

"Man, all over the place, we went at least ten feet high when we flew over those fucking train tracks."

The train tracks were subjected to a ramp on every intersection, which were the only connections over any road around here. A lot of times I thought we would catch some air, but we weren't nearly going fast enough any of the times.

It was weird to think that my sweet, innocent girl actually had some secrets of her own. I thought I knew everything about her, top to bottom, inside and out.

"I'm not ever driving drunk ever again, how we didn't get busted is still a mystery."

I figured I'd let it go, after all she wasn't my girlfriend and I could feel some jealously. I had a lot more problems in the back of my own head to deal with. I could hear Costa's voice in the other room talking on the phone. He was slurring his words and sounded piss drunk, and it wasn't even two o'clock yet.

"Where's the phone? I have to call Eva."

"It's just over there, around that corner and keep going straight." Kenny pointed.

For some reason I had this feeling that I had to hear what exactly Costa was saying, not just the muffled sound of a conversation blocked by a wall. For not even a split second could I feel that guilt and resistance not to pick up that phone, but I was starting not to care about anyone except myself.

Something was giving me this lust for power.

I felt like I was playing a video game, getting millions of points just for being tough, it's very hard to explain. My mind was constantly thinking and running about the surroundings and current objectives. I felt nosey and couldn't decide for sure whether or not to pick it up. I was so far off thinking about this that I zoned out not really thinking of the phone. I had to kind of remind myself what I was doing.

Slowly I picked up the cordless phone. I put my hand over the microphone and slowly clicked the on button. Nobody was talking and the first thing to mind was that they heard me pick it up.

"Are you there?" I heard a clear voice say.

"I am, I am, I'm just thinking about this." The booze was talking and not Costa.

"It would be a wise decision."

"But you benefit more than I do."

"You're my son, if I benefit, then we both do. If somebody offers you a hand, grab it."

Costa's father really was involved, there was a boss to my new boss. How deep did this damn hole go? I will admit that his father was a lot nicer, smarter and richer, and I really liked his quote about grabbing the offered hand. I guess he meant that no matter what, Costa was going to be okay. It all made sense now, the money, the cars, the power, Costa being in the position to call "leader". It wasn't him, he was a front man for his father, the real fear.

But he was so stubborn that he argued the fact that whatever it was the benefit was over. The only thing I got out of the conversation was that Costa was one selfish guy. Then again it could have just been the booze.

"So how's the new kid?"

"He's alright, he does well."

"I'd like to meet him."

Without a doubt they were talking about me, word was getting out about me, at least he was impressed. I felt important again. I almost started laughing at myself but it turned into a little smirk shifting to the side putting myself at ease, god I hate the way I think. When I heard them hang up I did the same thing then flipped open my cell to finally call Eva.

Dialing the number got to be a major decision for me. I didn't know how to lie. I couldn't decide whether to just tell her the truth right off the bat, or don't even mention anything. How was I going to tell if she was playing a game, and was just waiting for me to tell her?

Her father picked up the phone. "Is Eva home?"

"Yeah, is this Alex?"

"Yeah."

"How's it going?"

He never started a conversation with me, but for some reason today he did. Frustrated I answered, "Really good." I had to sound like I was enjoying this conversation.

"That's good."

There was a short pause between this, "How are you Patrick?" even he could tell I wasn't enjoying it anymore.

"Just ah, bought some property up on Delhigh, and might build us a house."

"That's cool." Nodding my head.

"Hold on I'll go get Eva for you. Eva! Eva!"

"Finally." I sighed.

Do you ever wait and wait and try to be patient on the phone, and you wait for that weird crackling sound you hear on the other end from them picking it up? That has to be one of the best sounds in the world.

"Hey."

"Chelsea just told me you were looking for me, what's up?"

"Yeah," She froze. "Do you want to come over?" Something was wrong.

"Of course I do, yeah I can be there in a few hours."

"No, can you come now?"

"Right this second?"

"Please?"

"Are you serious? I don't think I can Eva."

"Why, what are you doing?" She knew it, I could tell.

Now here comes the part where I either tell her, lie, or don't at all, but I didn't want to tell anyone. After all I did shoot someone. I should have put it together that sooner or later she would figure it out, this was a small town with only a few big names.

"I might be going out with Tommy later, I saw you last night."

"Yeah and you left nice and early." She was not happy.

"I can't fight with you right now, I'll you see later, I love you."

"Bye!"

Eva had a way of being very dramatic at times. The few times she never said I love you really bothered me, I hated it. Our lives could change in a split second. I could die or she could, the world is a surprise bag. Normally by now, I would have called her back and we'd argue some more, but not this time. I was busy.

I stepped out to see Kenny's arm wrapped around Chelsea with them both looking at me. Chelsea hinted her eyes at Kenny when I looked at her, and we both smiled. That's who he was though, it didn't matter how many times a girl would turn him down, and nothing would stop him. He tried over and over again with those stupid pick-up lines.

"Want to come over for some sex and pizza? What you don't like pizza?"

"I lost my teddy bear, can you sleep with me?"

"If I had a nickel for every time I saw somebody as beautiful as you, I'd have five cents."

My favorite one was "I'd hate to see you leave, but love to watch you walk away." I never said them though. I didn't have to. He was allowed, it was just his character.

"So how'd it go with Eva?" Chelsea asked, seeming a little too much concerned. I guess she was trying to hold off the laugh that Kenny didn't have a chance in hell. The subject had been changed.

"She's pissed." As the conversation continued between Chelsea and me, I noticed Kenny spotted somebody approaching the house. From the angle I was standing at I couldn't see who it was.

When he opened the door he reminded me of Tiny, "another enforcer" was my first opinion, he was strapped with tattoos and stood like a mammoth on steroids. He was the darker side of Tiny, and his name was Marc Strains.

"Marc! It's been too long, man!" his greeting with Kenny was, odd. Marc looked like a giant standing clear over Pollock.

"Yes it has, we working today or what?"

"Damn right, have you met the new kid?"

"A new kid, where?"

I was standing but five feet away.

"This guy!" he pointed.

"What the hell, he really is a kid." Just before our introduction a door was ripped open from behind me. A bottle of whiskey was spilling out from his back pocket, Costa.

"Is that my man, Marc?"

"Costa, you're fucking drunk again man." He replied unhappy and not surprised.

"Shut up! Have you met my little buddy here?" smacking my shoulder.

"Yeah by the way, I'm Alex."

91

"Marc."

If I were in his position right there and then, I would have just said, "Well you've obviously heard my name, Marc." He seemed a little dumb, but muscle was his best strength, literally. You could tell he wasn't from around this area, he looked like he came from a major city. His handshake was brief but powerful. He didn't talk much unless he was spoken to, and he was always hungry.

"You got anything to eat in this dump?" Costa's reaction was five seconds pointing at him and barley let out, "Help yourself, your house, is my house." He wasn't the typical drunk, dancing around trying to stand up straight or say anything out of line. He kept his head up and could hold his drink. In a way he was still Costa, but only with bad grammar and slightly off his already horrible judgment.

From inside the kitchen I could hear them laughing and throwing food around. They were talking about money and stories, like how the one time Kenny fought some kid at a party, or when Marc hustled another for twice the amount he owed him. They all had a strong friendship that never looked back on something they might regret later in life. They joked about it instead, or in their minds, it never happened. At the time I respected the way they all thought, but we all do stupid things when we're young.

I stretched a little bit relaxing my body, rubbing my eyes yawning and waiting very impatiently, I tried to pass the hint but all Pollock was doing was still trying to get with Chelsea. I felt kind of stoned, burnt out waiting for a window of opportunity to get out of here. I just wanted to get it over with. I don't even think they knew I was standing there for a good ten minutes. I tried coughing, tapping my foot, you name it. In one ear I had Marc and Costa raiding the fridge, and in the other I had Kenny making an ass of himself, finally I just asked.

"Can we go?" I didn't even get a wink out of him.

"Pollock!" I yelled. He looked up at me, didn't even take heed how long I just waiting for him.

"Hey bro, what's up?"

"Can we go now?"

"Ah, yeah just hold on second, I'll be right back." I'm pretty sure he whispered something into Chelsea ear, and then walked off.

"One second."

"For fuck sakes."

Looking back at it now it is kind of funny, but he was always late, and made you wait. Kenny Pollock, what a guy. He never heard *how* you said something, he only heard *what* you were saying. But this gave me a second to sit down with Chelsea.

"He really likes you, eh?" I asked.

"Yeah he's nice and all but, not my type."

"He's for every other girl." I said while rolling my eyes in sarcasm.

This is the part of the conversation where you both know something should be said about something brought up a little earlier, just neither of you knows who's going to bring it up now. No silence this time, we got right to the point.

"So about these 'stories' you have for me." She said, her smile also let off, "I know already."

Instead of grabbing that hand she was offering, I played ball.

"I don't know. How did you know you could find me through Costa?" Starring her right down.

"You know this town, eyes and ears are everywhere, so tell me. I mean, it's pretty obvious."

"I know you've already heard Chelsea, I'm not stupid."

"I didn't hear *everything*."

"Who says I'm going to tell you *everything*?"

"Look, all I've heard is that you're getting mixed up with all of this." Putting her arms out and in every direction meaning everybody and everything they were into.

"What do you know about these guys?"

"A lot of them are drug dealers and cause problems for people."

"It's more complex than that Chelsea."

"You're stealing cars, Alex, *that's* complex."

It was like our different sense of humor, but this time somewhere in the back we were kind of mad at each other.

I couldn't bring myself to tell her about Shawn, that's if she didn't already know. This conversation was tricky. Keeping my spirits in action was a constant reminder and struggle to see what Chelsea was thinking. If anybody knew me it was her, if I was lying she'd be the first one to point it out.

"You don't have to worry about me. It's not what you think." Her eyes glazed and got wider, she was in a state of temporary shock calling me on my wits.

"You think I don't know?"

"What are you talking about?" She bit her lip shaking her head.

"You're so full of shit your eyes are brown!"

"Chelsea." I couldn't even look her in the eyes anymore, I was blown away by her outburst.

"Just call me when you're done with Pollock." She said, mocking his very name.

Speaking of the devil, out came Kenny snapping his fingers dancing down the little hallway eating a huge sandwich. I could see lettuce and tomato chunks hitting the floor. I stood up brushing myself off while there was nothing on me. I just needed something to distract myself, an action following an action.

"You ready to go?" I asked. He couldn't even speak his mouth was so full. He lifted his finger chewing his food then burped.

"Change of plans." Picked his teeth, "You're going with Marc and Willie."

"What happened to personal and not business?"

"Well I'm making it business." Right after he looked at Chelsea, it wasn't for our business, we weren't even gaining anything from this. It was so he could finish his attempt on Chelsea.

I turned around and looked at her still smiling back at me, laughing at Kenny trying to be the big guy. She knew what I was doing and accepted it. It felt really good to know that someone like her believed in you, and so quickly.

"Where's Will?" Marc yelled from the kitchen.

"He's on his way, porky!" Kenny could be obnoxious sometimes.

"You're gonna get smacked in the mouth talking like that you little shit."

"Yeah, you're hilarious!"

"Shut up Pollock."

You could hear it in Marc's voice that he was somewhat serious, but at the same time, it was their sense of humor. Kenny turned back to me leaving the conversation. "Anyways,"

"Marc and Willie are going with you." Repeating himself,

"Yeah you said that already."

"Just listen, Ryan is at the King's, all I'm asking is that you keep an eye out for these two."

"Then what do I do?"

"Call me."

Out of all things that have happened so far, I knew I wouldn't be coming back in time to see Eva.

"You're alright, kid." He tapped my shoulder, stretching his arm almost standing on his toes.

"You owe me one." I said.

"We'll go get a case or something later on."

He turned back and went into the kitchen, obviously to get more food. I started to walk back to the door but a dark coat stood in my way and I nearly bumped into it.

"Jesus!"

"Whoa man, look where you're going!"

"Fucking Christ man, you scared the hell out of me." I didn't even hear Willie open up the door, or his footsteps. That was the thing about him, he always just popped up out of nowhere. For a good friend he didn't come around half as much as everybody else. It would be months before you would ever see Willie again, then he'd just be there. That's what made his re-introductions that much better to see him again.

"Marc! Let's go!"

"I'm going with you." I said. I was trying to get his attention.

"Yeah I know, how are you doing kid?" Was anybody ever going to stop calling me kid?

"I'm good, I'm sure you've heard it all by now."

"I have. I'm only checking on you, making sure you're alright."

"I'm fine as long as I don't get arrested by the end of the day." I tried to make a joke about that, but his attention was mainly focused on Marc. The more I thought about it, the more I remembered Willie talking about him in the past.

"Marc! Come on man!" The jokes did not stop in the kitchen with those three, they were deaf to all else but their own kin it seemed. Eventually Willie had to go in there and yell at them. "Yeah, hey! You guys wanna shut up?"

"Hey look who it is!"

"What are you guys deaf or something?"

The argument went on for a brief couple of seconds. The next thing I remember was walking to the car and Willie grabbing me whispering. "Be strong kid." It got into a conversation that this wasn't going to be some simple high school fight. They were going to brutalize Ryan to 'set his mind straight'. I was about to get into the back seat when I heard Willie shout out that I was going to ride in the front. Marc looked up at Willie with a sigh, and we drove off.

In the interest of time, we pulled up in front of the rundown bar, Kings.

"So, where is this guy?" I asked.

"He's in there, undoubtedly playing pool."

"So what do I do?" I asked.

"You wait here until we come back, if we're not out in ten minutes you call Tommy." Marc interrupted.

"Wait a second, keep it down, I think that's him." Willie pointed.

We lowered ourselves into the seats, looking up at Ryan wearing this ugly orange jacket. It hung down almost to his knees undone, and dirty. He was shaking hands with a couple of people outside having a cigarette. Everyone at this bar was twice his age and they were all just as drunk as Costa.

"God, that's an ugly fucking coat." Marc muttered.

"I was thinking the same thing."

He pulled something out of his jacket to show this older guy who looked either like the bartender or a cook, hence his white apron around his waist.

"Is that a flare gun? The hell is he doing with a flare gun?"

"Beats me Will, all I want to know is what the hell this guy's doing. Is he staying, is he leaving?"

"I think he's going to leave." I mentioned.

"Yeah he probably ran out of money." Marc mumbled under his breath. Tommy laughed.

"Should we chase him on foot?"

"I think that's the best option we have right now, what about you Marc?"

"I don't want us running him over, that'd be nice though."

"So what are we doing?"

"Let's go, if were gonna catch him we have to go now."

"Yeah look, the other guys going inside."

"Now ours chance."

"So go!"

All of our doors opened at the same time and we started walking to the bar. Ryan didn't take notice to us yet so we kept moving. Maybe if Marc wasn't such a show off we could have walked the entire way but he had to open his big mouth yelling and cursing that we were going to kill him.

"You'd better start running asshole, you're dead!" He sounded like a specific actor.

"God damn it." I thought.

He took the closest corner he could find running and screaming random names to give him a hand. A friend of his was running with him. I'm pretty sure neither of them knew who we were chasing so they both took off. We weren't too far behind him, but when you're running for your life you can do almost anything.

"Man this crack head runs fast!"

The sidewalk we were running on was not leveled at all. Grass was growing through the cracks and we all almost tripped several times, but we kept catching each other and ourselves. Ryan tried to cut us off by running across the street and around somebody's back yard, but we didn't give up.

The sounds of our footsteps grew louder when they hit the road. "Come on you little snake, keep running, keep fucking running!"

Some many people were standing outside watching us in the chase, pointing and yelling for others to come and watch. Nobody was concerned for any of our sake, they just wanted to watch something other than TV, and it was a joke to them. It was like having no witnesses at all.

Even if we turned a blind eye for a second, it wasn't hard to keep up with them. All the gates were still open and we could see them struggling to hop the fences. Every fence got us that much closer because we could climb them faster. I couldn't run any faster than them because if I were the one to catch Ryan, I didn't know how I was going to keep them both down until they caught up. The last yard had no fence, but a big back yard connecting to the corner of the road. We turned left and saw the orange coat just make it around another corner store. We were getting closer to the canal which would have eventually cut them off and only have two ways to turn. Something was in store for me.

I reached the corner just a few seconds earlier than the others and I could see Ryan lifting his arm pointing the flare gun right at me. "Shit!" A flare blast isn't anywhere close to the sound of a real gun, but I think the pain is either equal or greater. The flare went off course almost in circles. It just caught the left side of my chest burning away my shoulder too. The pain woke me right up, the only thing I could focus on was getting the fire out, but it was in my skin tearing away my shirt.

I tried so hard not to scream in pain, but I couldn't help it, I grunted and moaned slapping the burns away. I could feel it spreading a bit and the rest of it was burning on the road. I kept looking at how much smoke was coming off of me. In front I watched Marc beat the crap out of Ryan, smashing his flare gun, kicking him in the face brutally.

Everything was getting blurry and my shirt was torn off me from behind. I was being dragged away by Willie, "Are you alright? Come on, kid, you're alright. Come on!"

"I need some help man, I need some help." I screamed spitting all over myself. My feet would not move while sliding off the road. The last thing I saw was Marc running back with blood on his hands. I wasn't completely knocked out. I remember hearing some voices but the pain was louder. Everything was dark but my eyes were not closed. It stung like a million bees, pins and needles.

Dark burnt blood covered the top left half of my body. It numbed my arm and body somehow.

"Come on buddy, you have to get up, come on you can do it!"

"Eva." She was the only person I could think about. "I have to see her later."

"He's up!"

"Fuck, this hurts."

I only passed out for a couple of seconds. I could still see the corner store being dragged away. My legs got feeling again and I tried getting up, both their hands reached and wrapped me around each other.

"Can you walk?"

"Yeah, I think so."

"Oh come on you guys, the fucking thing shot him in the arm. He can walk."

"You have to try Alex, come on."

Easier said than done. I walked on my own. It was a struggle, but I did it.

Insulted by Marc's harsh words. Willie took off his sweater and insisted I put it on to cover the wound. They helped me run a bit until we were far from the scene.

"Cover that up."

"Try and not look obvious will you?" Marc just did not understand that I could not help it. His belief was that everyone was a solider, and shouldn't feel pain. I could still feel the burns gaining heat. The small winds felt like great pain. I knew this was going to scar me.

"Fuck you." I mumbled. The car was still in front of that bar where there was a crowd of people, and they could have been friends of Ryan. Our goal was to walk as if nothing happened and look unafraid of anyone, ready to fight again. Before we got there I was told probably ten times not to hold the wound and keep my head up, "Be strong kid." Was what he repeated to me over and over again.

I walked and walked feeling every bump on the road. In the heat of the moment I couldn't feel as much as I should have, but I knew it was going to kill later on that day.

There was a family of friends all sitting on their front porch just watching me walk with my eyes dazed and mouth hanging open. I probably looked like some junkie.

"Did you kill him?" I asked, I sounded as if I were freezing.

"What?"

"Did you kill him?"

"You're nuts man, no."

"There's blood all over your hands."

"Guy sniffed too much shit, his nose busted open like a fucking zit."

"I can't believe he fucking shot me."

They stuffed me into the back of the car and I laid down bleeding all over myself. I ripped some of the burnt pieces of my shirt out of my cuts. There was one piece that was still attached to my shirt and it was the most painful thing I have ever felt getting it out of there. Like melted cheese, it stretched off my chest.

"Alex we cannot take you to a hospital, but we can take you somewhere where you can get patched up." Tommy told me with a concerned look in his face.

Great, it wouldn't be that duct tape doctor would it?"

"No, it's my friend's mom actually."

"All I really need is some cream stuff to rub on it, clean it all off and get some sort of wrap thing, right?"

"Hell if I know, but you might have met him, he's a hacker like you."

Carmine Burton, or just 'Bee' as some people called him. Why we weren't friends since birth is a question I wish I could have answered. He and I became brothers instantly. Their house was uniquely built and the yard was different as well. The driveway cut to the back and to the front right on one of the busiest roads in town. It was right near a beautiful park too. This family had their stuff in order and were all very hard workers, nobody believed in living a life of crime, drugs or anything illegal, but they all supported there surrounding friends who did.

The house felt very safe too, there were two entrances just to get to the main door. The house was held with very heavy doors and phone activated alarm system. The men in the family were both Carmines. One with electronics, the other with fixing and building very reliable things.

We called ahead to make sure they were home so we weren't just dropping in with some bleeding burnt kid, thus not making the same mistake when we dropped off Sanko.

When we arrived I watched Marc check his bloody boots and he just sighed to himself he must have been stomping on Ryan, or was upset about getting them dirty.

By now I could feel even the lightest tap on my shoulder and chest. We were waiting for somebody to answer the door. When the door finally opened it was Carmine Jr., with some of the messiest hair I had ever seen. "Hey Eric, how's it going buddy?"

"It's Marc."

"Sorry man, come on in guys. My mom's just inside watching some TV." The way he stressed both letters in that word was hilarious. I even muttered a giggle.

They seemed pretty normal for a situation like this. He was eating a hot dog when he answered the door and was a little off from the rest of us, he must have just woken up. He was overly nice and not totally clueing in to our problem. His Mom already had the table cleared for me to lie down, "You must be him, come on lay down and I'll get you all fixed up." She said.

"I think I just need to sit down, it's only the front part of my body."

"Oh okay. Well then, sit down and take your shirt off."

"I really appreciate this, by the way. Thank you."

"It's no big deal," My shirt was off and she started cleaning the cuts and burns. "This might sting a little."

It stung so badly. It felt even worse, the sensation of rubbing alcohol.

"Come on, stop being a baby." She was the perfect resemblance of the nicest nurse.

The constant sound of Willie opening and closing his phone was driving me nuts. He kept walking back and forth with the same two-step radius looking all over the house taking somewhat deep breaths.

"Hey Willie, call Kenny Pollock. Tell him what happened." I said.

"That's a good idea."

He went outside to make the call, then the mother looked up at me and said, "Damn phone was getting on my nerves too." She said jokingly, and I laughed a bit. It was time to meet a friend, so I gave my introduction. I looked her in the eyes went to shake her hand.

"Alex."

"Kelly." She shook my one finger as a whole hand and smiled.

"Don't you want to know what happened to me?"

"Maybe another time." She smiled. She really knew how to make feel comfortable.

"Thanks again."

"You can stay here the night if you want, I bet you're tired."

"I am."

"We have a spare bedroom upstairs if you need a place to stay for a couple of days?" She suggested to me. She was looking at my burns, and knew why I was there. Not only could I not go to a hospital, I could not go home or to Eva's. It was not like to me to hide, especially at somebodies house I had just met. But this all came with the territory, and I did not really have a choice.

I took everything out of my pockets and put them on the table. "I don't have much money to give you."

"That's okay, Alex. I know you'll pay me one day."

"Thank you, Kelly."

"Will you stop? You're a sweetheart, but just go get some rest. Carmine will take you to the guestroom."

CHAPTER IX

Nothing to Lose

(Monday Morning, 9:00am, April 6th)

Three weeks later, is a deadly amount of time for many reasons. I don't know why, but I ended up staying at Carmine's house for about two days not getting in touch with anyone besides Tommy and the others. They were the only ones who knew what I just went through and why I hadn't gone to see Eva or set foot into my own house. I was just easier to hide from everybody and the world.

These cuts and burns weren't going to be easy to explain, especially to Eva. But on the third day I finally called my sister to tell her I've been sleeping at my buddy's house, but my mom was home for once and she was yelling and screaming at Meghan for her to give her the phone. She kicked me out of the house and had even told Eva I was an idiot when she called looking for me. My mom was going off about how I haven't called and I missed school and I was not allowed to come back home. With the set of new circumstances, I could have cared less. I didn't feel like I had nowhere to go and I didn't even yell back at her, I quickly accepted it and moved on and in with Carmine's family.

It turned out we knew a bit about each other already, and could have possibly met at some time during our separate lives. They really liked me. They thought I was a good kid with a lot of potential. They treated me better than my own mother and father. Rules were a new thing for me because that my mom was never home, which gave us all the freedom we wanted within those walls. Carmine's dad didn't talk much. I always considered his few words of wisdom were worth listening too.

"You're a smart kid. I just think you never had a chance."

This was the starting line for me to write and publish a book. It was only rough notes and ideas but I got the idea down in my head. I had one little black note book that if anybody read, they would not understand the quick statements and ideas thrown together all out of order and unorganized. I was the only that could understand this story because it was original. It was my biography and my personal feelings upon almost all the world's problems. I wanted to twist my story though, to make it more of a novel then a biography. I figured I had some creativity to write since I had a lot of bad memories to count on. It's unfortunate to think that in today's world its people's bad memories that sell.

One night I stayed up until the sun was coming up and saw that Eva would just be getting up for school. My notebook was almost full already and I had this great idea for a story. My character was getting to my head. A go-happy, funny guy just throwing his problems aside with a 'shit happens' attitude.

So I picked up the phone and called her. I was totally forgetting that she had no idea where I had been, and that the last words from my mother to her were very negative. She answered sounding as if she were still asleep. Her groggy voice still sounded sweet.

"Eva, are you awake?" The second she heard my voice she snapped up and was wide awake now.

"Alex!" She paused. "Where are you?" She sounded like she was going to cry almost.

"I'm at my friend's house, I'm so sorry I haven't called you."

"I even tried calling your cell phone, I've been so worried. I was finally able to sleep last night."

"My cell phone?"

I checked my pockets and realized that it was missing.

"I must have lost it."

"Come over after school, I want to see you."

"Yeah, you're going to be proud of me, I think I'm going to start writing a book."

"That's so cute, Alex."

So I was in the clear with her, but maybe since she was just waking up, all of her thoughts didn't kick in right away. Later on that day I went to her house and we got into this argument about why I got kicked out, and why I haven't called her in a couple of days.

She could tell I was not telling her the complete truth. When I sat down I'm guessing I pulled the top of my shirt down a bit and showed some of the bandage. It wasn't my first priority to hide it. All I needed at the time was for Eva to stop demanding that I tell her everything. She was convinced I was some sort of drug dealer, the truth had stretched so far that apparently I was even doing lots of cocaine.

"What the hell is on your chest?" Her tone went down, while my heart skipped a beat.

"What are you talking about?"

She had to physically tear down the top of my shirt to see what had happened to me. Her mouth was open, her eyes watered, she was speechless and shaking. She covered her mouth and stepped back a little bit. I didn't know what to say either.

"How did that happen to you? Is this why you have been so distant with me?" She asked. I could not think of anything. The burns were in such a weird spot that I could not say it was some sort of accident on my part. I just came out and told her the whole story, even Shawn. Half the time she would not listen. She just kept cutting me off yelling 'Why, how and when'. She felt obligated to leave me because I wasn't the same person anymore, when I still was. I would have thrown it all away for her and I tried to tell her that more than enough times, but she would not have it.

In the morning we were fine. I kept my regret that I wish I never told her, but I didn't want to lie to her.

"Alex I want you to leave."

"Eva! Listen to yourself, please just hear me out."

"Oh I think I understand perfectly, you're hanging around idiots and you're going to get yourself killed!"

"Fuck that and fuck them! I want you!"

"And I want my Alex back you're tainted now with all this shit! I don't even know who you are! I can't even look at you anymore!"

"We aren't some fucking soap opera Eva! Were different, and I know you know that."

"You're the one that's different now. I can't be worrying about you like this Alex, this isn't what I want."

"Stop being so dramatic! Please?" I kept yelling.

I knew this isn't what she wanted. She kept crying then she'd get mad and then suddenly start crying again. The fight lasted almost three hours. My throat felt ripped and I was so thirsty struggling to keep my tone as high.

"You think this is what I want, to lose the only person that means anything to me?" I begged.

"Just shut up." Rolling her eyes.

"No, listen! I will piss this life away, in a heartbeat! I would do anything for you!"

"Then why did you do it in the first place?" Her cry turned into that cocky attitude.

"I, I don't know."

What was I supposed to say to this? Everyone around us swore us to be together forever. I never expected anything to come between us. I thought she was my life and money wasn't even in the middle.

"My dad's going to be home soon, I don't want you here anymore!" She was screaming like I've never heard before, it was unbelievable! She tried leaving the house to storm off but I kept grabbing her trying to keep her with me at her home. "Let me go!"

"Eva! Eva!" She was clawing at my face and punching me repeatedly, she was a stubborn one.

"I fucking hate you!" She slammed her hand and on the burns and kept saying she hated me, but I didn't let her go. She was my world, if she left me I didn't know what I would do.

"I know you do, I know you do. Please just listen for a second." I cried trying to hold her.

"No! No! Let me go!"

"What the fuck is your problem? Calm down!"

"Leave!" She bawled.

She finally got outside when I yelled for her to come back. I chased her to the road with her back turned to me. I tried to surround her to look at her face, but she was circling with me just telling me to leave and to get out of her face. "I love you Eva, don't do this to me!" It almost sounded like she was hyperventilating. Her face was red and soaked in tears and eye makeup running down her cheeks.

"Don't you ever say that again! Get the hell away from me!" Cars were passing and watching us fight. I did not care and didn't even look at anyone driving. We were alone in this world and nobody could have gotten in the way, they didn't even matter.

"So what, are you going to break up with me? Is that it?"

"We're done Alex! Go home!"

"No! Listen to me!" I just watched her walk away right and out of my life. I stopped dead in my tracks. It was all over.

"Eva!" My scream sounded bloodthirsty. I was frozen, stiff and numb as it echoed on. I was angry and wanted to keep going, but something told me to just give it up, walk away.

She kept her eyes on the bright road. Her arms crossed and I could tell she started crying again, she wasn't walking straight. With my legs locked onto the sidewalk, I rubbed my face holding back the tears. I didn't want to feel weak so I started thinking about getting home, I was on the opposite side of town without my phone, I didn't even get used to it yet and I had already lost it.

My wallet on the other hand had two hundred dollars in it for some reason, I went to look for some loose change but there were ten mint crisp twenty dollar bills. My guess was that Willie put it in there when I was sleeping the other night to pay Kelly for allowing me to sleep there. I quickly got to the nearest corner store to call the first person on my mind: Eva. I only hung it up and kept my hand on the payphone.

"I can't believe this is really happening." I thought to myself. I started slamming the phone up and down, yelling at it fearlessly, and began to cry again. I finally picked it back up calmly thinking of a number to dial. There was an old drawing on the phone next to thousands of others but this one caught my eye. It was a gas mask that reminded me of Andrew, my best friend. So I thought I'd give him a call.

We got together and back to the heart of our town. All I could talk about was the fight thinking of some way I could get her back. The two of us were sitting around a table both fidgeting with something while Carmine's parents were at work.

"Give it a month, and you'll be fine." He kept saying.

"I don't want Eva to be the one that got away man."

"Maybe down the road when you two are a little more mature, you'll both think things through better."

I could barely hold on a second, let alone years from now. Nonetheless he was right. In time I grew to accept it a little more, but it still hurt.

"Do you really think your high school sweetheart was your soul mate?"

"Yeah I do, I got lucky and fucked it all up."

"It doesn't matter!" "If she's your soul mate you'll get her back."

"Andrew, that is not how life works. Yes, the possibility of us getting back together is still there. But no fate, or destiny, or soul mate bullshit is going to do it for me."

"Then go do something about it! What the hell did you call me for then?"

Our easygoing talk turned into a lecture from Andrew. I was confused though. Right then and there it seemed that's all I've been since this entire thing started. I was biting my fingernails thinking about this and the room was quiet. I was getting an idea, a way to show everyone I wasn't some scared loser. I had the potential and the opportunity to help me get started. What did I have that these guys didn't? What made me so special that I had the right to be expecting some gratitude? They've been doing this for years. Why should I have been scared?

I make my own choices. It was my decision to pull that trigger, my decision to chase down 'flare-gun Ryan'.

"Andrew, I think I got it." An opportunity we should have taken for granted.

"What?"

I had nothing to lose anymore, and it was one of the happiest days of my life. I never cared about myself, it was always my friends and their opinions, my family and Eva. My life started over. In this very moment I felt incredible. I wanted and thrived on this new life of dramatic crime, it would be my story. It has always been my opinion that in life you should always have a good story to tell. Of course I missed what I lost, but it wasn't like they were dead, I would still eventually talk to them again and they would be close by. I wasn't transforming into somebody else. I was just going with the flow and watched where my feet were taking me. I was reborn and redeeming myself to my regrets.

"I say we grab this business by the balls." I said.

"What are you talking about?"

"There's a lot of money held between these guys and they like me. Let's work for them and make our own names for ourselves."

Quiet kid or no quiet kid, I could tell that Andrew was very interested in this idea. Eva was still on my mind, but easily I pushed aside and did not allow it to get in the way. If we truly were soul mates then I should have let her go. She could see that I was living off on my own and I wasn't desperate about the whole break up.

The plan kept getting better and better and I wanted to let a few people in. Chelsea for her looks and ambition, Andrew and his dark minded ways, Sanko for the supplies deals and money, Tommy, Kenny and Carmine. Since I was kicked out of my mother's house, I mentioned that I should go and get my own apartment. I could now be an individual and do things at my own risk.

I thought maybe for all the favors I had done I could get a loan on the place. They certainly had more than money to throw around.

I knew I wanted to live somewhere in town, where the same rumors would float around, giving everyone my story.

I was getting ahead of myself. Daydreaming about nearly the impossible, but now it wasn't. I had a chance and I wanted to take it. I used this for an excuse to rid my mind of anything unsettled, a distraction. Love is blind.

"I don't want to go against the others, I want to work for them and make them proud of us."

"That doesn't make sense Alex."

"How doesn't it?"

"You just said you wanted to grab this business by the balls."

"Sometimes I think you just argue to hear the sound of your own voice."

"I hardly say anything."

"More the reason." I laughed obnoxiously.

He didn't say anything as he titled his head at me, and tapped finger on the table. The good mood I was in just got me screwing around with Andrew.

"Sorry man, I'm just busting your balls." I smiled.

"You were saying?" He asked.

"We'd be like the side project to these guys, our own little group."

"I've met Costa, probably twice. I don't think your idea is going to work."

I knew I might have been wrong and the whole thing could back fire in my face, but I still wanted to at least try.

"But it's worth a shot."

"True." He agreed.

The table we were sitting at was very close to two long vertical windows. We could both see the blue and faded gray color of outside. It was the quietest part of any day, no matter what day it was. Everything was chilly but the house was warm. I thought this was the time of day that had people getting ready for their plans that evening. So using Carmine's house phone I called my cell to see where it might be.

It turned out that Willie had it in his car the day I was shot. He was driving when I called him. He came to pick me up and hear this idea I had. It quickly grew into something bigger. I was very irritated with Costa's constant talking about it as if it were his own idea. Everybody connected with him knew about it and he seemed excited about it. His drinking habit wasn't much help either. Almost every night he was so drunk he would say the most outrageous things.

We didn't do much but talk about this for the remaining three weeks. We had also discussed that idea of a loan for my apartment. They had agreed to give it to me but did not get around to it for a while. At the end of the third week we had just made this five-course meal. We were sitting in Costa's living room picking at our teeth and lounging around talking about how full we were. Then out came Costa's drunken outburst,

"You know what I think?" Holding his bottle at shoulder height, staggering around.

"I think that we should all get matching tattoos or something, you know?

"That's ridiculous." Tommy said.

Chelsea was sitting next to me, she wanted me to get my own apartment more than I did. She always asking about it and wanted to help me move in and buy some things for me. She started to dig through her giant purse throwing around makeup, key chains, about four different bottles of perfume. I could have sworn I saw a matching MP3 player with her cell phone.

"What about Alex's apartment?" She asked out loud waiting for anyone to answer.

"Have you found a place Alex?" Tommy asked.

"Oh there's a great place up near the bridge, it's got a balcony looking over the canal."

"Found it!" Chelsea shouted, pulling out a ripped piece of newspaper.

She had gone out of her way to circle apartments I might like and passed the room. It was a lifesaver not having to do that myself. "This place right here is near my house, get this one."

"How much is it a month?"

"It's not that expensive, so don't worry about that kiddo. You keep doing what you're doing and you'll make lots of money."

"Yeah plus if you got a part time job or something?" Chelsea suggested.

I was almost speechless with Tommy. I couldn't believe he was doing this for me. He treated me like I was his little brother and looked out for me in any way he could.

"Thanks Tommy, I owe you a lot for this."

"I'm going to get you into this apartment by tomorrow, but I am not paying your rent." He was stricter with me than anyone else. He knew I had to be toughened up and learn things without them being given to me.

"I wouldn't want it any other way, Tommy."

He looked back at the newspaper, counting up the first and last month's cost of the apartment.

"Well then let's go to the bank, friend."

I flew up out of my seat to the car and was handed fifteen hundred dollars cash, and was told not to spend it on anything until he called me with a meeting place with the landlord. Within hours that same night he had already gotten his hands on the contract. All I had to do was sign. The next day was painfully slow. I could hear Carmine's clock ticking and even a cigarette lasted what felt like half an hour. Every time my phone rang I thought it was going to be Tommy. Even when the house phone rang. Finally the one time I didn't expect it to be, it was.

"A couple of us are going out for dinner, you want to come?"

"What about my apartment?" I had to ask right away, I could not bare the wait anymore.

"Yeah, were going to take you their afterwards."

"Sure, come pick me up."

I was ecstatic. My very own place all to myself. I was just hoping that Eva would find out and maybe come and see it. I thought this might have impressed her or grabbed her attention, but it only drove her farther away each time I did something like this. Dinner tonight was the first time any one of us had heard of 'Freedemption'. That's what my side project had become.

Tommy, Costa and I were eating around a table far in the back, discussing *Freedemption* and what exactly it was.

"It should be the name of your book." Tommy said.

"What the hell is a *Freedemption*?" Costa sneered to me.

"It's freedom, with a sense of redemption, to redeem yourself by any means necessary. I don't know it's just something I made up about my moral responsibility. It's sort of a catchy title."

"You think you're going to save the world, is that it?" He asked.

"You are. I know you are kid." Tommy said under his breath to me. I knew he had faith in me.

"I'm not writing to redeem myself, and true freedom will never exist. But it would be nice to send a message."

"So this, *Freedemption* is everything a 'good' person is supposed to do in their life?"

"That's not what I said, Costa."

We weren't communicating very well, what I always believed in was truth. Being truthful to yourself and the ones you love. It drove me insane how many times I watched people suffer from rumors, drama and how tough people thought they had to be. I figured if what I was fighting for it, this *Freedemption* could have a little bit of truth in it too.

It was a way of life. Not a basic revolution or even a name for ourselves. It was a hidden agenda in the back of our heads reminding us that were better than most people. We seemed to have the good morals in this business we've all chosen. Nothing in life makes sense. So why not follow something we made up? It seemed right to feel free, truthful and to redeem yourself to how you saw fit. We all needed redemption in some way, and that's what we fought for. We needed to figure that out. Besides it sure was better than money and trying to fit in and be cool, but the money would still be coming in.

Along with freedom itself, our plan did not exist and it could never happen. Truth was no matter what you say or how you say it, somebody in your crew is going to stab you in the back and you will never see it coming and you may never find out. I should have strongly recommended to anybody that if they ever felt that vibe or that bad gut feeling about someone, get rid of him or her instantly. People are very good liars.

What I thought made us so special from everybody else, was that we were put together by rage and frustration from our own separate pasts that we could somehow all relate to. It did not occur to me at all that I was meddling in own my self-loathing, unaware that my mentality was not whole.

"You have to go through hell in life, to be happy." I'll never remember who told me this or if I just made it up in my own head, but it means that you'll realize the things you have in life when their almost out of reach. That's why we hated a lot of the people that were just given greatness and success without ever having to go through half of what we did. Another thing we wanted was to show people that life is what we make it and people should not be so selfish.

I leaned back in my seat after finishing my meal and looked around the room and watched everybody else have conversations about their daily lives. Maybe we were the idiots, but at least we had something to live and breathe for, a reason to wake up every morning.

CHAPTER X

---◦◦◦✠◦◦◦---

Redemption in a Cage

(Tuesday, 10:33am, April 7th - Six Months left)

My apartment was amazing. The pictures in the newspaper did not come close to how looked in person. Everything was brand new, the floors, the fireplace, the odd shelves and hidden cupboards. The whole place had a cinnamon color to it. It was all brown with a little bit of red and orange. It suited winter perfectly.

The space in each room and how it all joined together was big and unique. I was already picturing where my stuff would go. My bedroom had a cubbyhole that you had to step up to and it was its own little private space. It was a two-apartment brick house located near the east side, regrettably.

My bed was not moved in yet. Hardly anything was but a few boxes of cereal and blankets that my sister brought me the night I moved in. She was so proud, but questioned how I got my own place so fast. She was just jealous because she was still living back at home.

"You can stop by anytime Meghan, and thanks again for bringing me some stuff."

"Where are you going to sleep tonight?"

"Here, right on the floor."

"Okay."

"Thanks again, Meg."

"Do you want me to bring you some more stuff tomorrow?"

"Yes, I think I can get my hands on a truck or two to grab most of my stuff."

"Like your bed?"

"Yeah, like my bed."

Since I was born I never had my own king size bed until this year. So you could imagine just how much I loved it compared to my twin or single. It also had some sentimental value. It was the only bed Eva and I could sleep in and she picked it out for me. Tommy bought me some beer to have when everybody left. I sat in front of the fireplace wrapped up in the only thick blanket I had and just sipped on my beer thinking about the next day. I never thought being bored could be fun. Thinking aimlessly about what the apartment would look like. For a couple of hours the emptiness had me pondering a lot of other things.

When I woke up the next morning, I felt great. I could still smell the unused walls and carpet. The house was spotless and it was all mine. I looked outside my big bay window into the street watching the new lifestyle of the side of town I lived on, my house matched it. The only difference was, I at least took care of everything on my property. The inside was nice, but the outside was somewhat of a dump. The windows looked weak, some of the white paint was chipped off, and my radiators were those big brown bars that stick out in the most inconvenient of places.

I took another look around with a bowl of cereal. I looked again at the second bedroom, and it made me think that nobody lived in the upstairs apartment yet. I was all alone close to the side of town that I hated. I took note of the people who lived next door. They owned an Italian bakery and looked very elderly. My side window was matched with theirs and I could see them all working peacefully. I tried to tell myself that I was on the broader of both sides, and the corner of the road set the marker.

I was unwelcome, but this was something I wanted at the time. I was looking forward to being scared, powerful, and courageous and to struggle all for the story I was writing. I vowed to not leave this place until my novel was done.

There were no pens, pencils or paper to even write some rough notes. I was so eager and impatient to get moved in that I could not find the time to pack some things the night of. I made a call. I needed everything from toilet paper to my dressers, food, a television, a shower curtain, pots and pans, silverware, dishes, even a can opener. The only things I had already owned were bedroom materials aside from my computer. These were things I had to slowly but surely gain my entire life. Buying things like this really adds up, a household with everyday pictures, plants and little things bought throughout the years must have cost thousands upon thousands of dollars.

Life is expensive and until the money system breaks, over more than half of regular people today are going to suffer and struggle for the everyday necessities. That alone is very senseless and idiotic, this was another reason why I wanted to do what I did. With technology advancing every day, our world is only going to get lazier, and less motivated to do something for themselves or the ones they love, it's just going to get worse.

My mind wondered about these things. I've always come up with the greatest ideas in the shower of all places, one thing reminds of me something and it grows from there. Again, if only I could speak my mind. After getting all the necessary valuables in place, tidy and organized I walked back into my front living room. I watched Kenny get up and pass me, going right for the fridge. I watched him open it up and grab all this unopened food then he started cooking it. He made himself God knows what and left me all the dishes and a big mess to clean up. The plate wasn't even rinsed properly and I could see chunks and crumbs of food all over my countertops.

"I just finished furnishing this place, and you make a mess for me to clean?"

"I'll go and clean it when I'm done."

"I find that fucking hard to believe." I said under my breath.

There were a group of us that worked on the house almost all day just moving me in. We opened brand new boxes, we set up desks and entertainment stands, but Kenny just sat around on his phone not lifting a finger to help us. Sure enough he never cleaned his mess, leaving stains and unwrapped food all over my countertops. Other than the mess, the place looked legit and it had a homey feeling to it. It had a mix of my favorite band posters and artwork of fruit and flowers. It had my name written all over it. Obsessive-compulsive disorder meets a heavy metal freak's potential.

"We deserve a break kid. Let's go get some booze."

"What should we go get big guy?" Kenny yelled

"We're gonna get fucked up tonight."

"I have no plans tonight! Let's do it!"

"Yeah, and you're paying for not helping us today."

I wanted to throw a party. I had never thrown one just in my name with no strings attached or with my mother breathing down my neck with a million rules. I decided to throw my first house party. It was kind of a ticket to show this side of town that I was connected now. All across this side had its ten-year-old, beat up minivans and pickup trucks, while my parties had its gorgeous sport cars and jewelry seen from a mile away. People were leaving and coming back in every second of the night, half of them left their shoes on and tracked the leftover winter through house still extending their hands for a greeting. I didn't mind, after all, I was getting handed drinks all night with arms being thrown over my shoulder for some reason of gratitude. Everyone had stopped by to show their respects and everyone else that went to my local high school introduced me to people I've never met.

In the last two weeks I had met over twenty-five new people and I loved every second of it. I was getting the drunken and sober love of over half our town just tonight. The drunken ones were doing a lot of weird things that I never seen before. Tommy kept trying to start fights with everyone outside of the crew, arguing that they were weak and stupid. No matter how many times you shook hands with somebody, they would probably forget in a matter of seconds and do it again.

House parties are not like the movies make them out to be, everybody just does their own thing and has conversations about the last party they were at or they sit and play drinking games. The house was filled with smoke and nobody was dancing, nobody was almost having sex on my floor. It was a loud relaxation point driven outside from the drama.

I mostly just observed everything trying not to get too drunk. I was standing next to Willie having a beer with him.

"I just realized, do half the people here have a reason to celebrate?" I asked.

"No, that's just what alcohol does to people."

"They're going nuts."

I watched as people were screaming, hugging, stuttering their words of so called wisdom and falling over laughing, all because they had a bottle of booze to drink to themselves all night. The truth that comes out of people when they drink is a riot.

There was this girl I went to elementary school that almost pushed me against the wall and her breathe reeked of vodka. She was very attractive, a brunette too, her name was Summer.

"Summer, are you okay?"

"Alex, my god! How have you been?" Her voice was going higher than lower, slurring the simple words.

"I've been alright, I haven't seen you in a while."

"Yeah, ever since you dated that *Kylie* girl." Basically spitting on her very image

"Eva." Correcting her.

"Whatever Alex, did you know that," She said putting her fingers up my chest. "That I've always had a crush on you." I just laughed looking at Willie switching my beer to my other hand.

"You're drunk."

"I'm not drunk!" Her vodka soaked lips told me otherwise.

She was a beautiful girl that I used to have a crush on myself. It was long before Eva and I thought it never would have happened. Now I just wanted her to get off of me. My goal was Eva and not to have some pointless drunken sex.

"You're no fun." She said strong and disappointing.

She started walking away and I looked over at Willie, "What the hell was that?" I lifted my eyebrow, embarrassed yet very comfortable, and laughing inside with a huge visible smile.

"You might want to check out your woman." He pointed over to Summer as she was hanging out the window and it looked like she was puking. My bathroom was filled with people doing the same, or probably doing something that didn't require a bathroom in the first place.

My house was getting destroyed, that brand new carpet was getting ruined from people's shoes, ashtrays and spilling their glasses.

"I think it's time for people to leave, Will."

"I think you're right."

We rounded up the guys as they helped me end the party, walking everybody out.

"Okay guys, party's over, it's time to go." At first we tried to be nice, but nobody had the intelligence to listen to what we were saying. They could hear us, but they were not listening well. Teenagers cannot drink, period.

"Were leaving, don't worry Tommy." He licked his lips rolling his eyes and tapped his foot.

"Now!"

We had to all physically push people out while they screamed about how much they were having.

"Killer party, Alex! We gotta do it again!"

"This is the party house!"

"Yeah!"

The door was shut and the place was quiet. The rest of us helped clean my house and it was spotless once again. We must have filled over four garbage bags with paper cups, and cigarette packages. I was left alone with news of tomorrow's plan for some fun.

"I feel like I just got used for my apartment."

"Everybody wants to go to a party Alex." Tommy said.

"I was getting way too much respect from people I didn't even know."

"They were kissing your ass."

"It would be more respectful if they just kept their mouths shut."

Instead of lying to my face, I found it more reasonable to just talk to your friends that you came to see.

"You're growing up kid, and people see that. It's not like everybody used you." Said Tommy as he stressed the word 'everybody'.

"Does that include my new friends?"

"I wouldn't doubt it."

"Tonight was insane, I'm wondering why the cops weren't called."

"You're on the side of town where cops don't exist."

"I'm pretty sure that my next door neighbors are almost eighty years old."

"There Chinese, man! They don't give a shit."

"I think they're Korean."

"Korean, Chinese, Japanese, who cares?"

Conversations evolve from point A to B very quickly. I never understood racism, the only thing separating humans today are skin tones and that's it. If God exists, he must think we're all stupid arguing over this matter.

"We all have our differences."

"Sorry man, I get it from Costa."

"That doesn't surprise me."

"Yeah! Costa's a real fucking character, eh?" The truth that came out of Tommy drunk was unexpected. He was almost passing out lying there swigging around his bottle going on and on about much he wasn't a big fan of Costa.

"He doesn't give a shit about anyone but himself. He's not anything. He's gonna end up going down."

"You two are like best friends."

"Far from it, we used to be though. Back then, during the good old days."

"What happened?"

"Forget about it." He wasn't drunk enough. "What about that girlfriend of yours?"

"Eva?"

"Yeah, that one, what happened? Why'd you two break up?"

"Forget about it."

"You're funny."

Shortly thereafter, Tommy picked up his bottle and headed out the door. He put his hand on my shoulder facing the door, and taking another sip. "You'll be alright, kid." The fact that I was drinking my problems away only made things worse. The longer I wasn't thinking about her just reminded me of pain when I did. Sometimes I had completely forgotten we had broken up, I had lived on but her face was still smiling at me. When reality blackened everything, I wanted to break down right then and there. She was so upset and disappointed with me. Tommy had finally started up his car outside and left on his way back home. I sat in the same seat wondering if I should call Eva or not, constantly opening and closing my phone, losing my mind. All the lights in my house were on, I had to turn them off. It bothered me how bright it was.

I went over to the light switch and it was next to the little hallway leading to my bedroom door, it was wide open.

I could see my bed from where I was standing. For a second, it looked like the same bedroom as the one I had at my mother's.

"Eva." I muttered. The room screamed her name. All the memories and moments came rushing into my head feeling like a migraine. I closed my eyes and slammed into the wall, sliding down still facing the empty bedroom.

"Why is this happening? How could this happen?" I thought to myself. It felt like a dream when I was screaming in pain, how much I missed and needed her. I kept slamming my hand down as if I were being stabbed. I couldn't believe how much this still hurt me, and I didn't even understand sadness until this moment. I was alone because of my own choices. I was the only person who had this faint sense of death before dying.

My legs were sliding back and forth on the floor while my hand covered my face, in less than a couple of minutes they were drenched in tears. "No, no." This was the worst feeling in the world to lose something of this value. It was the only thing that could make me act like this. I was trying to let out a sound but I could barely breathe. After everything we had said to each other, it turned out to be a lie. Everything we had done was for nothing. I was hoping that she was just as upset, and not forgetting about me completely, and so quickly.

"Eva, look what you're doing to me." I was doing it to myself. I knew I should have at least tried to call her. But I was stubborn, I felt like such a hypocrite and did not want to admit it. I sobbed for what felt like an eternity and pulled on my skin to ease the pain. Every time I pictured her voice fading away and realizing that she was actually gone and wanted nothing to do with me anymore broke my heart. I would have done anything to erase this agony, it was too much to handle I thought. The ghost inside of me grabbed ahold of myself, my conscience whispered to me that I still had the potential to win her back.

So I let out the last of my tears, "Sometimes it's good to cry." I thought.

I sniffed and was finally able to breathe out of my nose, heavily I did. I pulled myself together. There seemed to be a million broken pieces all over my floor, but I would just kick them away.

"Nobody is going to feel sorry for me but me, and crying is not going to bring her back."

This was the moment I didn't let her interfere anymore. She wasn't real or in my existence. I brushed her away with my broken pieces and redeemed my conscious. I stood taller than I ever have, chest out, ready to throw the world off my shoulders.

Freedemption had to make a difference, and at that very second, I realized what it meant. It's everything good in a person, to pick yourself up to make your own difference. We are human nature and we're all more than smart enough to not care about the things we actually do. The important things don't matter anymore to society. The few left in the dark are the ones we should be fighting for. Freedemption had a vision greater than a simple goal. It was a story of good integrity with intendance, instincts to look past money, war and ignorance. It's the last style of world peace caused by its own anarchy, a fight to stop fighting.

"We're going to go down as criminals, but hopefully, the world is a bit of a better place." It needed a symbol, a book cover recognized by both the law and the streets. It needed a motive and a first target of success.

I walked around barely lifting my feet, thinking over and over again about the symbol. I snapped my fingers and ran to the side door leading to my basement. I had only seen it once and it was in the middle of a renovation but the tenants before me never finished it. I could see an endless pile of wood, puddles of water, and a broken window boarded up what looked like half of a picnic bench.

"It's a like zombie movie down here." I started to dig through all the tools looking for some spray paint, when I finally found a black can of rust coat. "This'll do." I said to myself.

I had numerous blank brick walls ready to be painted on. I thought since it was my idea for Freedemption to begin with. The symbol needed reflect me somehow. I tried a lot of different pointless designs, and none of them caught my attention. I couldn't think of any artwork to portray me, and then I thought of my own name.

"Maybe I should keep it simple." After all, it would become the cover of my novel.

I started to spray a straight vertical line making a capital letter A on a slight slant, the right side of the letter was diagonal, then a straight curve stretched farther then the vertical with an X crossing through the longer side. I was anarchy reimbursed and beefed up. I wasn't a punk. I wasn't just going to sit around and talk about what I believed while everyone else across the world did my dirty work, and took the hypocritical blame for it.

I did not move. I had a fantasy about this wall covered in Freedemption, this was it.

I could see myself standing in front of this new aged masterpiece. Anybody could draw it, and hopefully some would follow it, they would follow my words and my morals.

Every day so far had its own story. Earlier I was in the best mood walking around my empty house, and now I was in the darkest basement proud of something I was creating. I started to think this was my purpose and I didn't need an ordinary job, I could have been a writer. I had to start to somewhere, and first thing on my mind was to get this design all over town.

CHAPTER XI

Having Some Original Fun

(Wednesday Afternoon, 1:45pm, April 8th)

Tommy had these ideas of original fun, at the same time he called his own style of work. I had stopped thinking of the night before. This was because of the attitude Tommy had when he was with me, it made me feel different. I felt like anybody in a conversation with him would feel intimated. My own friends before I started to write Freedemption started to look at me different. They left my friendship thinking I was changing and that I wasn't true to myself anymore. Which was ironic considering I was writing a book about it.

I was eager to keep working to build up a reputation, and a belief about freedom while not having anybody to care about anymore.

My laugh with Tommy became obnoxious and loud, filled with insanity and patience for the next job we had. We weren't employees for a job, we were more or less mercenaries. We had been giving ourselves a mission for anything like greed and self-esteem against everybody following a pointless ambition.

I was getting sloppy and forgetting about my own goal and purpose. At the time it was all about my team of recklessness and taking my advice. I was throwing out my main friends from school and didn't even bother giving them a second look. My phone number had been given out at school. Just when I thought my cell phone was mainly for the crew, I was getting a million phone calls all at the same hour after school.

"You're throwing a lot away just to be cool."

"I'm never coming to that house, I don't like the people who go there."

"You're not going to see me until you smarten up."

Most of the calls were from girls a bit younger than I. I was friends with almost everybody at my school because I was the class clown and the girl's favorite sweetheart. I used to be the shoulder to cry on, the person everybody could talk to and I was the one to the girls looked up to. Chelsea once told me, "You're the guy that girls love, Alex." Well in the back of my head I wanted to be more than that. I wanted to find at least one girl aside from 'her' that found me attractive. I was always shy and could not talk to girl the way other guys did.

With Tommy, I felt no matter what I said or did I would not be judged. I had finally stopped thinking twice about my actions and just let myself go with whatever the world was throwing at me. My purpose in life was not just to take up space. I was not going to be another soulless, annoyed person, feeding off of a daily routine job, begging for an answer, any answer.

"Will you sit down?"

"I'm thinking."

"About what? You've been walking in a circle for half an hour."

"A few things." I said biting my nails.

"Not about that girl are you?"

"No, that's the last thing on my mind." I had kept my word about brushing 'her' off.

"Then what? Will you relax?"

I didn't say anything back for a second, I could think a lot better when I was moving around or doing something productive. Everything had been happening so fast I didn't bother to think about how I was going to feel ten months from now. I felt high and unaware of my own actions these past few weeks. Everything past today was blank. I did not know where I was going to end up and I kept wondering how this was something I was looking forward to.

What if I didn't? Maybe I was just another fool thinking about being the next guy who could have changed the world. I heard Costa laughing at me in the back of my mind. I could make a difference about my own belief. Should I have been selfish? Should I have been more concerned about finishing Freedemption? Every direction I felt I could have taken had a real bad outcome. I was stuck. Dwelling on the past was the worst, I had to remember that this was all for a greater opportunity.

"I'm thinking about myself." I finally said.

"What's the problem?"

"This fucking town."

This was where Tommy usually came in to comfort me, his points of interest and words of wisdom.

"You just gotta remember that it could be so much worse."

"So then, it is bad?" I asked.

"That's not what I meant."

"What did you mean?"

"I mean, no matter where you go you're still going to deal with stupid shit."

"So what makes us so different?"

"We've already had this conversation before, Alex."

"What could be worse then?"

"Were in a small town with nothing to do. We just get high, or drink out one of our hundreds of bars."

"That's pretty bad Tommy."

"Yeah well, just remember we're not in New York, or Boston, or Jersey."

"So it could be worse, with more gun fire and robbery?"

"Kid, you're not listening."

"Then enlighten me."

"Forget it. You'll figure it out on your own."

Just having this conversation alone had made us different. I was starting to understand the picture a little more. I was repeating myself over and over again, coming to the same answers just after I had figured it out. It was my personal problems that were stressing me out. Tommy had gotten up to go to the bathroom but on his way he said, "Just be you." I was so paranoid from being this side of town, getting caught by the police, 'her', my friends, the judgment, it felt like my head was going to explode. I grabbed a sheet of paper followed by a pen and started writing down all my problems one by one.

It was a short list compiled by all my recent doubts, sorted by the possible and impossible.

The impossible list was the judgment and the side of town of I lived on. I could not change these two things so why bother with them? Slowly I had already started to calm down a little bit.

The possible list was my idea of taking baby steps towards fixing the problems, like you-know-who, the police, and moving with this life style for my own enjoyment and story to tell. My new team was loyal to each other. However, some my friends I had put trust in for so many years were already turning their backs on me, and for nothing. The main problem turned out to be Freedemption, it just kept coming back to that. Everything else could have been fixed solely because of it. If the message got out on what it was about, people wouldn't have their finger to point at us, or at anyone for that matter.

Maybe then 'she' and my lifelong friends would understand. I had a long way to go, but time was the best part considering time heals everything. I was getting my foot in the door, a decent start to something that might change everything.

"What do you want to do today?" Tommy asked.

"Let's get out the house for a while."

"You're looking to do something productive?"

"Come check this out first."

I took Tommy downstairs and he said the same thing about my basement. "God it stinks down here."

I had revealed to him my symbol, "Pretty cool eh?" I asked.

"It kind of looks like a sideways seven." He looked uninterested.

"It's the first and last letters of my name."

"What's your point?"

"Oh never mind, you'll figure it out." I said with a smile.

He lifted his finger and started bouncing it up and down towards me. "You're clever, very clever."

"You're going to be seeing this all over town soon."

"Well I'm glad to see you got your spirits back up. You ready to go?"

"Where are we going?"

"To do something, productive."

As I was walking back up the stairs I could see a black burnt spot on the wall connected to the stairs, it reminded me of my own burns by the flare gun. I stretched the collar of my shirt, looking down at my chest to see it almost fully healed. It had been a few weeks since I had seen any action and that got my spirits up even higher. I had only hoped that Tommy had something in store for us later that evening.

"The burns on my chest are almost gone."

"Oh! That reminds me!"

We stopped half way up the stairs while Tommy bit his tongue.

"Marc's been missing since that whole ordeal, so I'd keep an eye out."

"You think he was kidnapped?"

"I doubt it."

"Yeah. He looks like he could hold his own against a couple of guys."

"Exactly, I just wouldn't trust him."

Tommy could not really put his finger on it, but it wasn't our priority. When we got outside I didn't need a sweater or even a light jacket, it was such a nice day out I could have walked around in just my T-shirt.

"What a beautiful day to get some work done, eh boy?" Putting on his sunglasses, yelling and raising both arms for the entire town to hear him.

"What kind of work?" I asked.

"Do you want to drive, Alex?"

"I've only ever driven a car once before."

"I'll teach you, come on, it'll be fun." He opened up the door and tossed me the keys.

The first car I was ever going to drive was going to be this nice. I was in town so I started thinking if my friends saw me driving this. I may have considered not driving for a split second, but was eager to get behind the wheel.

"Alright!" I was so excited.

I ran around to the driver's seat of the car when Tommy had thrown me the keys. I quickly started up the car and wait for some sort of instruction.

"It's not how I pictured it, Tommy."

"Are you scared?"

"Yeah, a little bit."

"Don't worry, I'll be your guide."

"I know a little bit about driving, I'm not too illiterate."

"Then give her some gas." The engine started to go but the car remained still.

"This isn't an automatic, put it into drive."

"Oh, right."

We were on a straight road with a ton of left and right turns. I wanted to just keep it straight for a while. I was going so fast down our little roads that every time I hit the brakes both our heads would be thrown forward then back.

"Lightly let the break down, Alex!"

"Stop pressing the break so fucking hard!"

"Sorry man."

I had come to a stop sign. Tommy's face was filled with sarcastic disgust. I forgot completely about turning signals so it made us both jump a bit when I started to turn.

"Lightly press the gas, lightly!"

"Okay."

"Then turn the wheel until the car is facing the way you want."

"Then start going faster?" I asked.

I was doing exactly what he said. Then when the steering wheel had gone all the way to the right, I had let it go to slide back into place, I started going faster too soon. I could hear the tires screech from behind me. The car threw itself more over to the right and I had to steer back into place.

"You couldn't even turn, at a complete stop?"

"You sound ashamed of me Tommy." I added laughing.

"I'll have to teach you another time, I'm driving."

"Come on, let me try one more time?"

He just looked at me with a blank stare and sighed to himself.

"Alright, but you have to listen to me."

"Let's go by the high school."

"You want your friends to see you driving this don't you?"

"I won't lie, it's a nice car." Admitting the truth.

He put his head on the seat mumbling at the roof, "Just listen to me and take it slow."

"Just tell me where to go, and I'll get us there in one piece."

"I'll have to give you the directions one by one, I don't even know what the place is called."

"Maybe you should drive then."

"Thank you." He said relieved.

Him driving the car suited the situation better, he really knew what he was doing as I watched him peel off the road. I had no idea where we were going. I just looked out the window and had this strange song stuck in my head. I remember I could not stop thinking about this one part. I could not get past the first chorus, it would not get out of my head. It was a song I must have heard on the radio because I still do not know what that song was either. I could hear the singer, but I was not able to understand what he was saying, just the faint beat and rhythm of the song just being repeated in my head.

Drifting off and daydreaming about this song got me unfocused as to where we were. We were both in car staring at what looked like a car auto shop. It was a dump. The barbwire fence with the ripped grocery bags made it that much more appealing. Everything was rusted and disgusting. The hot sun beat of its black tar roof. It seemed dead everywhere you looked.

"What are we doing here?" Tommy didn't answer.

"Are we even town anymore?"

I looked behind me just to see a sandy, rocky, dusty driveway leading up to this hellhole. For a second I thought maybe Tommy was going to kill me. "We work tonight." He simply said.

"What, here?" He kept his eyes on the run down building.

"There's a lot of money in that place."

I couldn't even read the beat up and burnt crooked sign hanging off the wall, and he believed there was money in there?

"If there was any money in there, it was already stolen." I said.

"That's the beauty of it! It's not money, there's some brand new titanium stuff."

"This place looks over a hundred years old."

"It's still operational though." It seemed to strike his curiosity amongst mine.

"This place is actually up and running?"

"Hard to believe, isn't it?" He must have been joking.

"What the hell are we going to do with titanium?"

"I don't really know, but Costa said he can sell it."

"Titanium?" I asked very rudely.

"Apparently, yes."

I shook my head a little bit thinking about this. The titanium was in thin-stacked lines, bundled by twenty-five piles. We wanted to get our hands on at least eight of these piles. Whatever the material was exactly, somebody wanted it and would be paying for the effort along with it.

"How much money is in this?"

"A lot."

Figuring out the size of the packages, we would need another vehicle, a bigger one.

"We're going to need a truck." I suggested.

"Maybe two."

"Can you get your hands on them?"

"Of course we can." I knew he was going to say that.

"Two trucks might be too much of a risk Tommy."

"There is no risk involved if we come back later."

"Are you sure?" I didn't like this one bit.

"Of course I'm sure, I know the guy who owns this place."

"And you want to rob him?"

"Well no, Marc knows him."

"Marc knows him, that's just great Tommy." Taunting him.

"Are you scared? Marcs the one that wanted to rob this place months ago." He did a good job convincing me.

The way he pointed and explained everything assured me that there was no risk in doing this. He made me feel stupid comparing my worries to his confidence.

I should have spoken up though. "This place has no security, how hard could it be?" He said. I just wanted to tell him that I had a funny feeling about it, but I thought maybe I was just being paranoid. We drove off as we agreed on tonight's new plan. Sure it seemed simple. We could easily get caught stealing two truckloads of heavy equipment. It felt easier to do more dangerous things because they mostly took up less time. The only way it wouldn't take much time was if we had more guys to load the trucks. That would also create more noise and taken space.

I would have hoped that Marc really did mention it months ago and completely forgotten about it since. The fact that he was missing and everything was probably the reason for my concern and stomachache. Something was not right and not settling too well with me. We pulled out from the old building heading in a random direction.

"Where are we going to get the trucks?"

"I think Steve drives one."

"Have I met Steve?"

"Probably at that dinner we all went to a few weeks back."

"He is the really tall guy?"

"Yeah he's got short black hair, he's a laid back guy."

"I remember him."

"Good, because you're asking him."

"What? I met the guy once!"

"Just be casual, act like he owes it to you."

I turned and just looked at him funny, without a nudge of understanding.

"Remind him that you met him and that we need it."

"I just can't see why you don't ask him."

"You have to get involved in every little way you can." It's true, it really adds up.

"How would this benefit me asking him."

"Stay there a while, have a drink or two with him."

"What about you? What are you doing to do?"

"I'm going to get the other truck."

We were heading towards Steve's house as we spoke. He lived just outside of town in a one-story bachelor pad.

It was brick house with a garage filled with bike parts, skateboards, spray paint, and he was working on his car. He was the guy I'm not sure if I spoke to all, or even just once. He lived by himself and the music blaring out of his house was just my taste.

I could tell when I got out of the car he recognized me right away. I put down something and started towards me, I was listening to the song, lightly head banging singing the words in my head.

"Steve, right?" I asked.

"Yeah man."

"Hey I'm Alex, I met you a couple weeks back."

"Yeah, yeah I remember you."

"Good tune, I like this kind of shit too."

"Thanks man." I needed to get straight to the point.

"Hey listen, I need a favor."

"Well come on in."

He was very welcoming and nice. He was nothing like the others and didn't seem too involved with much. I had seen more than him in my first week in this business, he was more a friend to everyone that made his living with a normal job and steady income.

He didn't look any older than twenty and he was doing very well for himself. The house looked like it was just a built. The garden had just been planted, and I could see some of the plastic tarp that hung off the windows still attached. The oak trims were brand new and barely sanded down. The foundation around the house was still a little rough and patchy.

"Are you renting this place?" I asked.

"No, just bought the place."

"I like it."

"Thanks, I appreciate that."

At the time it probably seemed like I was sucking up to him to get easier access to his truck, but I wasn't. I liked the feel he had to the house. I knew right away he was on his own and ran an honest living.

"I'm serious. It's got a very, nice feeling to it."

"Do you live alone?" I asked.

"Yeah."

His house still had a ton of unopened boxes, a lot of them were half spilt all over the floors just waiting to be picked up. I noticed that most of the things that were unpacked were sports related, his trophies, medals and awards. He loved to smoke his pot too, but not cigarettes. I could see pipes and bongs all over his table neatly organized for his next hit.

"Do you wanna toke?" He asked pointing at his bong.

"Oh no thanks, I wouldn't mind a drink though." Referring to Tommy's idea.

"There should be something in fridge, go take your pick."

I was always told that if ever got my own place, not to let anybody in unless you could trust that person. I was curious to know if Steve knew my name before I gave myself the introduction. His house design was a lot like Eva's. The front door leaded into the living room and a hallway to the left with the bedrooms and bathroom. The dining room and kitchen was straight ahead and a bit to the right behind the living room wall. Even the fridge was in the same spot.

He had his fair share of different alcohol. I picked up what was left of his whiskey and brought it back out to the living room.

"You want a drink with me?"

"Sure. I think I have some glasses right under here." Sitting at his coffee table, he reached under into a little cupboard and pulled out two glasses.

"Sorry the place is such a mess."

"Don't be, you just moved in."

"It's been like this for a week." Pouring us each a drink.

"Thanks."

"So what's this favor?"

"I need your truck for the night." I felt like I had to get straight to the point. Nobody likes somebody who beats around the bush all day.

"That's it?" He asked with no distraction.

"Yeah." I thought it was a big deal borrowing somebody's vehicle for something illegal.

"You know what we're using it for, don't you?" He stood up with an empty glass, brushing some crumbs off the table.

"I don't want to know," he said. "but I can imagine."

"You're sure then?"

"I'm positive, the keys are right over there."

"I don't drive, I mean, I don't have a license."

He thought for a second, he looked out to see if Tommy was still in the driveway.

"Call your buddy. I'll take you over to him."

I flipped open my phone to make the call, I could sense some hostility between the two of them. Something must have happened a long time ago. I thought about it while the phone rang.

"You're going to be noticed kid." He said, out of nowhere.

The phone was ringing, but I quickly looked over at Steve. He meant that in a general. Everybody was giving me this speech. For the months to come, I wondered what else was going to happen to me.

CHAPTER XII

Rawest War

(Later that night)

The road seemed extra bumpy, and time stood still. The night was quiet and we were on our way to the target. I was in the back seat with my back set straight and every muscle tense. Every few minutes I looked at my hands to see them shaking, but I wasn't nervous or scared. I think my body was trying to tell me something.

We had an estimate for how much money we could possibly be making. It ranged between eight to ten thousand dollars, all in packages that had equal weight. I had no knowledge of what exactly we were stealing, I knew I had to be lifting very heavy boxes, and load them fast. I could smell the mint flavor gum from my mouth mixed with the cool air from the barely open window. It reminded me of my middle school when I had first met Eva.

"Alex." Her voice said.

I looked right over to the other side of the car. I swear to this day that I saw Eva sitting right next to me staring out the window. She had her black coat with thin faded gray strips down it. She looked over at me and grabbed my hand. She looked bored resting her head on her other hand. She just gave a quick careless smile while rubbing my fingers, as if we were still together. The hair on my arm stood up I was so shocked and amazed. Somehow I knew it wasn't real. I looked back out my own window with my eyes closed not accepting this illusion.

"Eva." I said back, facing the window wishing she really were there.

I looked back to see that she was gone, it was fake. How did I imagine something so out of proportion? It was unusual and unexpected, was I losing my mind? Her voice was perfect, I could smell her perfume. I even heard her coat ruffle against her arms when she turned. It was too real, she was right in front of me for that spilt second, and the touch of her hand felt, familiar.

"Alex." It just kept playing in my head.

Normally it would depress me and make me cry or get sad, but not this time. I felt like I knew I was drifting away from her, like I didn't need to worry about our problems and just focus on myself for a while. It drove me mad, and made me angry that my own mind was playing tricks on me. I couldn't stand it, or believe it. I had only seen things like this in the movies but I always considered things like that *could* happen, but if and when it does, it will blow your mind.

Have you ever felt your heartbeat? The sound and feeling made you concerned about just how much anxiety is pouring through your veins? I was thinking about getting there, and how it would feel when we pulled up to the broken down car shop.

"Tommy." I mumbled.

"Did you say something?" He asked.

"Tommy." I raised my voice.

"What's up?"

"Do you know where the stuff is?"

"It should be in the back."

"I hope this is as easy as it sounds."

"You're paranoid, I promise."

He couldn't see the future, how could he have promised? He was so sure that we wouldn't get into any risk or danger. I brushed my fingers through my hair, taking a deep breath. I felt as if I was holding an assault rifle and I was loading it ready to go into a battlefield. I zoned out for a second and placed myself into the last thing next to reality. Imagining myself in a third person view if anything went wrong.

I was sweating in this trance, picturing a field I could escape in. I could see Kenny yelling telling me to hurry only a few feet in front of me, and then it ended. The truck had hit a rock that threw me off my imagination. We were pulling up the dirt driveway to the shop, while Tommy turned off his headlights.

I took one more deep breath and opened my door running around the right side of the building. The other truck was pulling around the back as I saw the lights. I waved my arms signaling them that we were here and ready. Tommy's truck pulled up from the left side by side with the other one.

Kenny and Tiny got out and walked towards the circle we all met in. The four of us met in a circle near a back door. We could not see each other. Not even a streetlight from a distance to give us a shine of light.

"Tiny is that you?" I asked.

"Hey it's the little guy."

"I thought Rant was coming?" said Tommy.

"That idiot couldn't lift a bag of fuckin' milk."

With Tiny being there, he would watch over all of us, we must have all felt secure. His stories about getting stabbed and showing the scars to prove it made him monstrous. He was one tough guy supporting the little stones we walked all over. The mud was pressing between our footsteps, squishing between all the grooves. The business in operation I guess had some business considering all the footprints making the dirt wet and muddy.

"I forgot you had a truck, Kenny."

Our flashlights were all facing the building searching for the red and white packages, Tommy had thought they would be on heavy-duty shelves, but I had seen them through a window stacked neatly.

"So this is what we're stealing?" I asked shining my flashlight. All the flashlights pointed to the second floor's window.

"That has to be an attic or something." Tiny said.

"How do you figure?" Tommy questioned his statement.

"I've been in here a million times, not once have I seen a flight of stairs."

I cut in. "I wouldn't doubt it if it was hidden."

"It probably is."

"What the hell are we doing out here then?"

"We should hurry." I suggested.

The building cracked and rattled with every footstep inside. Some of the wood was rotting and it smelt like a damp sock. "For an auto shop, I don't see a lot of cars."

"Bad time of year?" Tommy said.

"I would never bring my car here."

"You don't even drive Alex."

"I'm just saying."

Tommy's head was underneath a short white string connected to the roof. None of us had noticed for a minute while we looked for a way to the second floor. We were digging and scraping for a light, bumping into little tables and tools, it was a tight fit. You could tell who everyone was by the sound of their footsteps. Tiny's were heavy and slower while Tommy's slid across the floor squeaking. Mine were quiet and restless. I was observing the roof checking for any color difference or something would give away the hatch.

"Tommy you're standing right underneath it." I pointed.

"Oh my god, I am." His teeth shined with a smile.

He pulled down a set of stairs that reclined as you pulled it. We all went straight up the stairs to check it out. The first thing in sight was the red and white packages, and we all went straight to work. We all kept laughing shining the light on them, it took two of us at a time to lift these boxes because they were so heavy down the awkward and unsafe stairs. After a few of the laughs died off, we didn't speak much.

We just went through the same routine. Lift, one step at a time, load it in the truck neatly stacked, repeat. It took almost half an hour to load the first truck.

"We're halfway there boys." Tiny yelled from the top floor.

My arms were sore. The rush kept me going. 'Halfway there' I thought. Every box was getting heavier and heavier. One almost slipped right out of my hands at the top of the stairs.

"Watch it man, you don't want to kill yourself." How comforting.

"I got it."

Struggling with the box, Tommy called out to me, "Hey I got an idea for that book of yours."

"Yeah? What's that?"

"Freedemption is where responsibility comes first." He said it as his own quote. He voice struggled as he lifted another box.

"I don't get it."

"I'll explain later." The idea sounded too simple to be explained.

I was at the bottom going straight for the back door. That's when I heard somebody else waiting outside. He was alone and trying to hide in a crack near the door. His figure looked familiar. I didn't notice it might have been a threat until I got closer. His face was dark and hidden in the shadows. His blue jeans and brown boots gave him away. He was starring right at me and we were both standing still. The vibe was scary, whoever it was seemed high off something.

It was one of those things you didn't want to look at it, but you knew you could not look away. You were frozen in this state and stare. I was getting to know the exact colors as my eyes adjusted to the scene.

"Who is that?" I asked shaking. But he sat against the wall not moving. I knew somebody was standing there.

"Tommy! Somebody else is fucking down here!" In an instant the body moved and took off out the back door, he slapped the waving door open and I could see Marc's face for a split second.

"It's fucking Marc!" Tommy yelled already at the bottom of the stairs, chasing him.

"Come on kid!"

"Why the fuck is he running?" I heard.

I dropped the package and took off running, I heard Tommy yell to Tiny to finish the job and that we would call him. The field was empty but we did not stop looking.

"Get in the truck!" He yelled. Our lights had shined on another vehicle trying to escape. Their headlights were not on so we had to stay close.

"Are you sure that was Marc?"

"I'm positive Tommy!"

"Then we really have to catch this guy."

He slammed his hands numerous times on the steering wheel cursing and frustrated.

"I thought you said there was no risk!"

"I'm sorry kid, we'll talk about this later." Always with the procrastination, everything came later and we never seemed to get there.

We had to watch where he was going. He was clearly with another person driving somewhere. The chase would never end if we kept on him, so we made it seem like he lost us. We stayed close, just barely in his sights, hidden from the darkness. My phone started ringing from a number I didn't know. I thought it might have been Marc himself telling us to back off.

"Hello?"

"Were all loaded up, where are you?"

It was Tiny. His truck had been filled with all these highly illegal packages while ours was still full as well in pursuit to stopping Marc from whatever it was he wanted to do.

"Put Tommy on the phone."

"It's Tiny." I handed the phone over.

"Buddy, I've almost got him, he's pulling up to a corner house, or maybe this apartment building."

"Where are you?"

"Not too far, I'm still in town, across from that,"

"Across from what?"

"Shit." Tommy said looking out the window.

We weren't discovered, but the apartment building was having a party on the top floor. All our enemies were all bunched up in a small place and we just watched. Marc had this smile on his face like he had just accomplished something. He was a snake that slithered away scared.

"Tiny, I'm at Marc's place."

He was the owner of the building. He could do whatever he wanted. Almost the entire building was being rented out to his friends, good profit living a life to party. Marc was a good muscle before he had betrayed us. How did it happen? I didn't want to believe the rumors, but something else was calling to him that was more than what we could offer.

I hated this pointless war. It was raw, uncensored and undesired, but it was this town's way of life. All the deadbeats and addicts bunched together thinking they were some kind of force to be reckoned with.

"What do we do?"

"What can we do Alex? We have to go in there."

"But we got the stuff, can't we just go?"

"I can't get rid of it for another couple of days."

"Are you? You're kidding right?"

There was silence. His eyes were focused on Marc shaking hands with the some of the dirtiest people I had ever seen. You'd think that with the money they had they would have bought some decent clothes or shampoo. The deeper you went down into this side of town, the worse it got. Stupidity rained over everyone and everything was about selling drugs and fighting. Self-esteem did not exist, half of them were liars anyway.

We drove around the corner to meet with the others. We were alone on this one, four against many. We had to take action because Marc had all the answers as to where the packages were and without a doubt he would attempt to steal them. The four of us were ready. We parked the trucks over a mile away and walked for the target. Everybody was inside and the music was shaking the entire building.

"Are you coming in kid?" Tommy casually asked walking in with the others.

We were asking to have our heads kicked in. Think about how dangerous our situation was, we were barely armed with any weapons and we were clearly out numbered. I had to make sure we had alternative.

"I'm going to look around back. I want to make sure we get out of here safe."

"Hurry up." He went up the stairs, and I went out back.

The fence didn't even cover the entire property. It was like Shawn's old fence but worse. The playground was a giant broken bottle scattered all over the slides and swings and the sandbox was more a death trap. I ran into a cobweb between the crooked gates. I pulled it off my face spitting looking up at a loft apartment where the party was. Marc was hanging off the balcony talking to some girl.

"It's not on the top floor." I thought.

I ran back to tell the others but they were already a few floors up. The stairs led all the way to the top and that's where they were headed. They could have been trapped a few floors above with no way out. As tall as the building was, there was not a single elevator. The place had nearly thirty floors.

"Tommy!" I tried to whisper and yell at the same time. I started to run up them faster and faster not having a care about the echoing footsteps. I skipped three or four steps at a time looking down at brown squares and upswept steps. The music must have blocked out any noise we were making, so why struggle to be quiet?

"Tommy! Tommy!"

"He's on the balcony." I said.

He didn't answer back he just concentrated on what door he was going kick down. He was running to every door listening to the inside from where the party was. We found it almost halfway up the building and we covered the sides, two by two.

"Nobody could have grabbed a pipe or something?"

"I grabbed my tire iron at least." Kenny laughed.

"Fuck it, just rush in and grab the fucker."

"He's by the balcony."

"We heard yah the first time."

"It's all yours kid." He gave me a chance to kick the door open in one shot. I grabbed both sides of the frame and winded up for strong kick. It broke open, but not enough. Near the handle it busted in a triangular pattern, pieces of the thick wood stuck out like knives. One more boot would bust it right open.

My second kick was faster without holding onto the frame and the others rushed me to get in first. Instantly they started shouting, "Turn off that music!" or "We're looking for somebody!" repeatedly.

They pushed through while a bunch of guys the same size as us just sat on the couch scared. I always thought they'd stand up to us, but they were scared and couldn't walk the walk. Speechless and unready to do anything themselves, they were judging and unsure what exactly was going on. One guy got in our way but all Tiny had to do was push him over and he fell into a tall shelf covered in graffiti. A girl was leaning into the shelf and the guy fell into her. She was still holding a cup of alcohol spilling it all over herself. Her pupils were huge and she seemed to be the only girl there that had any energy.

She started kicking and screaming and grabbed hold of Kenny, "Get your fucking hands off me!"

I went to help him out but my phone was vibrating in my pocket and it distracted me. He threw her to the wall while she tried to bite him. Tommy was already on the balcony with Tiny punching and taking turns beating Marc.

"You're coming with me!"

"Kid! You go with Pollock and get outta here!"

I finally got to my cell phone as I was pushing my way out of the room. I was heading back outside keeping my head down. It was my mom. I didn't want to pick it up. The last time I had talked to her was when I lived at Carmine's house with Kelly. She probably didn't have anything nice to say so I didn't want to hear it. We all walked out of that house untouched and we shook ourselves off running down the stairs screaming in joy and happiness that we didn't just get killed by a bunch of drunken psychos.

"I bet they were all on coke! We got 'em all paranoid!" Skipping almost an entire flight of stairs Kenny yelled. We were laughing, all four us. We got out first and I'm still not sure what Tiny or Tommy had done to him. We saw them dragging him while he was barely conscious still giving them a wiggling fight. Kenny started the truck and we were gone.

"This is going to turn out ugly."

"What do you mean?" I asked.

"Everybody saw our faces. A lot of stories are going to start."

"What do you think they're going to do with Marc?"

"I have no idea. Tiny is fucking crazy and he'll probably beat him out of town."

The gunshots to Shawn's kneecap those weeks ago came flooding back into my memory. That damn white flash in between every couple of seconds gave me such a headache. We weren't the good guys either. We were just as bad and nobody in this greedy war deserves to be in such pain. But again, in today's age it's either kill or be killed. This time we weren't wasting time interfering with other people's business. We let them sit there all day and talk behind our backs while they threw their life away for drugs and alcohol. Nothing had made sense up to this point.

"Get in, get out." I heard repeating and echoing away from that moment. I couldn't be doing this every day. I needed to clear my head somehow.

CHAPTER XIII

———∞o◦)◦(◦o∞———

Of All Mercenaries

(10:30am, June 1st - 3 Months left)

My mother had been calling me almost every day since that night. I was so busy dealing transactions with Tommy's packages and wondering about Marc that I hadn't gotten around to see her.

Her spirits convinced me not to see her. However, I thought since she is mother I should pay my respects. The entire time I was there she had gone off about how she wanted me to back home. Then she would turn around and yell at me for my mistakes.

"You're a fucking freak you know that?" She was putting me down endlessly making me feel as if she was the victim to her sick game. The fact that I never wore dress shirts and stonewashed jeans with spiked hair and a great report card made her furious. I was always her punching bag compared to my perfect sister. Just thinking about it now gets me as angry as her, I never wanted to play her games. I remember fighting with Eva and not yelling back certain things because I knew it sounded like something my mother would have come up with.

I never understood how she could treat me like this. She was smart and could fool anybody and still was able to make me feel bad about her own actions. She's my mother and I love her, but I hated her as a person. Our fights were about her and nothing else. I couldn't feel sympathy for her anymore. She had no sorrow, no mercy, she just wanted the attention and it drove her nuts that I didn't deliver. She was fierce and powerful. She also had her own sources of information around town, I wondered if she knew anything and was just waiting to use it against me.

"I'm smarter than you Mom! You just hate the fact that I have the balls to move on."

"I kicked you out, son!"

"You just invited me to move back. I don't even know why I talk to you anymore. You're nuts!"

"Because I gave you birth, I am your mother!"

"And I'm your fucking son! Look at what you're doing to me! To us!"

"I have given you everything you've ever wanted!"

"All I wanted was to come home from school and not be scared every time I saw your truck in the driveway."

"I've done nothing to you."

She must have been a compulsive liar. She truly believed everything that came out of her own mouth. I never wanted to fight with her, but somebody can only push you for so long before you bite back. In this case it had been almost eighteen years and I finally snapped.

"You are not my son, I wish you never born." It's kind of sick when that doesn't affect you. She had said that to me at least twice a year, and for nothing. I had finally had enough and walked out the front door.

"I love you Mom, but god damn it I fucking hate you too."

"Get out of here!" I could hear her screaming furiously from inside the house.

I wasn't on her puppet strings anymore. I slammed that door as hard as I could and kicked her garden lights up the driveway. I had called for a ride back into my side of town.

It was a brand new and bright month, all of my problems were washed away and I was rising up in our world. The people that should have been scared were terrified. The people we respected showed us the same values back. Everything was too good to be true, but money puts a dirty smile on people's faces.

A unique war had started in our town, but we did not know our own enemies, or what exactly we were doing to fight back. The town kept raving over how insane a few of us were, like Costa and his brother Rant. I was in the dark, along with Chelsea, Andrew and Sanko, hidden from all the outsiders trying to get a scoop on our story. A lot of heat was coming down on us, it made it that much harder to be unseen. Everything was moving so fast, the drugs, the money, and the stories that suggested we take all of it before somebody else got their hands on it. It was a contest to see who the toughest guy in town was, or who would do more crazy stunts or tell the funniest jokes.

I remember watching a news channel stating reports of 'gang activity' coming from our small town. We did not get paid doing things like the party raid. Sanko was pulling in more than enough profit to go around. He was a typical drug dealer, and was not gang related. We kept it simple but only selling marijuana and it was perfect. The other half of cash we received was from stealing electronics and things we could sell.

I was always happy. I always had money, new clothes and I was able to buy some things for my friends and family. Everybody around me was proud of me and I was never home to put my feet up to think otherwise. I was always moving, giving advice and running through game plans. I hadn't sat down in over a month to play a video game or to just sit back and have a drink with a friend. The only person I could talk to now was Tommy.

Nobody had understood my book's meaning, of *Freedemption*. After a while that's what I wanted it to be. I could have been judged by a lot of people who found the idea ridiculous and to me that was embarrassing. I loved the idea I had come up with. I didn't want any posers or people that would criticize the idea.

People just started to recognize me as a movement. A book of self-rehabilitation. I was *Freedemption*.

I started to always carry a can of spray paint with me late at night and I would look for an untagged building and spray the symbol I had made in the basement. I only spray painted the buildings that I had a memory in or some sort of accomplishment. I never went to any place that might have been a possible regret. I kept them on a level like where my first job was, my best friend's old abandoned house, the place where "her" and I had our first kiss, the frustrating lifting bridge. A lot of people's faces were still new to me. The last thing I wanted was to look like a punk painting their property. I had my own place to understand the values and could not disrespect somebody with a can of black paint. It sounded too childish to me.

I was leaving Sanko's house out the back one day, he was located almost right next to the train tracks and one of the busiest roads that cut off into an island. A moat of deadly water spilled and sucked through the undertow of the only two bridges connecting to the island. You could hear the angry water as you went up the small hill behind Sanko's and my eyes struck a big bright white wall with one signature, a black heart.

"Chelsea." I whispered cheerfully. We had put it there a long time ago, when we first became friends.

This had been of those memories I could spray the symbol on, I pulled out my can of paint and I went right for the wall. As easy as the graffiti sounded to make, it was not a two second job. I had to keep both letters connected and equal in thickness. Next to this white building was a bumpy path leading to the road. I could see it to the left of me. With all the cars driving by on the opposite side I would not be able to hear any cars coming. As I was putting the paint away a cop cruiser pulled up right next to me. "Shit."

He was parked there and didn't take any notice to me as he typed away on his computer. I thought he couldn't see or thought I was on my way to do my own business. So I quickly switched the can for a smoke and went to light it. I had just made it past the officer, he called out to me. "Hey you."

You could tell from his voice that he was just waiting to put me in cuffs or write me up for a ticket. He sounded delighted and he tapped the outside of his door like a drum set.

I walked to him without any hesitation. Only my chest was shaking and felt like I was pregnant with a pro boxer punching me from the inside. I wondered if he was going ask me if I knew anything about my recent events. He seemed like one of those cops that just beat around the bush, chewing their gum with a bad tone, smiles and radio calls about your stupid response.

"What's up?" I asked.

I still lit my cigarette. For once I didn't acknowledge that this was somebody with a lot of power to put me away.

"Are you, Alex Smith?" He asked, looking at his computer screen.

"Yes I am, sir."

"Born, November 18th?"

"Yeah."

He continued to type while I waited outside of his car enjoying each inhale. I just wanted to get it over with. He didn't even wink a lash of interest at me. The radio reports in his car were all indicated by numbers. The girl speaking them out sounded like she must have had the most boring job in the world. Yet the impatience and professional organization between both the officer and I kept any possible consequences off of my mind.

"Sir, is this important? I kind of have to be somewhere."

"Do you know why I pulled you over?" He was a casual guy putting me to the test.

I could have simply lied. I could have just said no and had a chance to walk away, but my head was curious about this police officer. My delayed response made my answer obvious, so I told him the truth.

"This spray paint?" I turned to my side revealing the wall with a fresh black symbol waiting to get charged for defacing private property.

"Maybe, what if I just drove off and let you go?"

"I don't understand what you're asking me."

"What's it mean?"

"What does what mean, sir?"

"Your symbol?"

Anybody could tell you that he already knew what it had meant. He was pushing my buttons and almost taunting me to just come out and say it. I didn't want my eyes to get off track. Every second I was thinking about something else, I even tried to think of anything else, but the moment was so unknown.

"It's my signature, it's my initials."

He got out of his car and stood almost a foot taller than me. He pushed me aside and observed the wall. I thought it was the end for me but my fear was replaced by a handshake. He had put his hand out, "Hi Alex, the name's Roy."

"Officer Roy." Of all mercenaries, I thought.

"Nice to meet you, sir" I said.

I had pieced together by now that he met with a few of us before, but should I have asked? A lot of cops are never normally somebody you can trust. It's their job to fool you into telling them something. At the same time I knew some of the connections that Costa and Tommy had. I was neither surprised nor falling into a trick.

"This isn't a trick." How convenient.

"You're a cop, what am I supposed to think?"

"I'm not asking for a bribe either." He laughed.

A bribe? Who was this guy? Our conversation had been getting too deep too quickly.

"How did you know I was here?" I asked.

"You have a good thing going for you. Take my card."

"What the hell? How did you know I was here?"

He kept everything simple and on the level. He knew all the questions that would be pouring through my head. He looked me like he had met me before, or as if he had been watching me in the act of my crimes. He grabbed my shoulder and I didn't move. I kept my eye contact as he moved in closer.

"I won't sugar coat this for you Alex."

I grunted while my eyes tightened, "What?"

"I like you and Tommy, but some of your *other* friends."

"You mean Costa."

That was the point he was trying to get across. Immediately his arms were taken off and he patted my head.

"You're smart. You call me anytime if you have any problems." This wasn't your everyday conversation. I just looked at him strangely, he gave that a second.

"You don't have to trust me, but you can." He finished.

"Yeah that sounds like something a cop would say."

He looked fed up on not being able to convince me, he struck up faster than before and was dead serious.

"I know you kid, I've watched you grow up, and I know you're better than this."

"What the hell are you talking about?"

"Your mother, she's made your life rough and I know it's hard."

My life was all about going from one thing to another. One day it's about business and making money, the next is about my mother. It never ended.

"You were one of the cops that arrested my mom?"

"Everybody at the station knows who your mother is."

"And you think I'm following in her footsteps?"

"If you keep on hanging around this Costa character, yeah I do."

Too many times had I been through this with her, the way I always saw it was that you have to go through hell to make yourself happy. That fact alone is what reminded me that I was alive and that I should value my own values. Every family has its ups and downs, mine just had more downs.

For as long as I can remember I had always seen dramatic things ripping my family apart, the police coming after school to pick my sister and I up, past drug problem, the physical, verbal, mental fights we've all had with her.

"You really don't like him." I said.

"He's a fake and doesn't see what *we* do." The same vision and belief that goes through our minds every day, and the very same thing that I did not think existed yet.

"What is it that we see?"

Some people call it 'being down to earth' or 'realistic'.

"Anything more than what we wear." He said, and for a cop, he was one weird guy.

"You have my number, I'll be around if you need anybody to talk to."

"Do you want mine?"

"I'm a cop. I already have your number."

"How assuring." I threw him some attitude.

I had just developed a friendship with an officer. I knew right away I had to talk to Tommy and the others to see if what he says is true.

His dislike for Costa had my head in knots. I knew what I believed in was the right thing to do. What if Costa had more up his sleeve than anybody else had known? When Roy had driven off I just stood there, waiting for an impulse to take me to an answer. An answer that made sense, an answer that would change some of this.

It wasn't easy being in this position with people pulling me in every direction now and trying to convince me otherwise. I looked back at the spray paint and threw away the can.

"This *revolution* is stupid."

I knew now what I had been thinking about people in general had been no mistake. I was right and did not need to prove it with some type of resistance, it wouldn't go anywhere but I felt proud for the belief itself. My story would be told and I had dreamt that I could help one person on the face of this earth. Something was happening to me and I kept thinking in my head that it all be over soon. It would just another phase in my life that would slowly fade. I thought at this moment that I could just walk away, but my phone started ringing.

"Tommy." I said bluntly.

"Hey buddy boy, you want to go for a drive?"

"Yeah, where are we going?"

"We're gonna go pick something up."

"Party treats?" I asked.

"Good guess, where the hell are you?"

"Ritz Sanko's, near the tracks."

"Be there in five."

I had already forgotten about taking off. I was already focused on telling Tommy the news about this cop. I figured I was just stressed out, I'd mention it to Tommy later that day that I needed to relax for a day, clear my head and just see some old friends. It seemed harmless but it would catch up to me no matter how far I ran. A cold breeze lifted up my thin sweater and the clouds went grey by the time I was picked up. It seemed like winter had started over. Tommy had lifted me from the dark feeling and I brought the cop to his attention. An everyday conversation built with people in every department. Roy was telling the truth, he wasn't a crooked cop, his target was Costa and he told us all that from the beginning. It seemed like a personal vendetta.

"So I shouldn't worry about this guy then?" I asked.

"Not at all."

"Does Costa know that he's got a cop up his ass?"

"I wouldn't doubt it, but I wouldn't bring it up to him either."

"This is pretty serious."

"You're the one that shot that guy, kid."

"That feels like a bad bribe Tommy."

He started to laugh, he knew I was joking and that my good mood sounded just as bad as my complaints. The number of people involved and how big everything was turning out to be reminded me of a good mafia movie. I was doing something with my time other than watching my school football team run back and forth. It was never about being tough, I just wanted to be happy. I wanted to wake up every morning with something new, and no matter what direction I would take I would have that little bit of stress to keep me alive.

So I followed my instinct and stayed in the car, because after you obtain everything you want, what would be left?

I was the writer and the third wheel. I had done my part to fit in so I wasn't going to quit.

We went to go pick up something in exchange for all the money we had made from selling those packages. It wasn't a typical deal. We had to pick up Willie and Tiny for this one. Costa had met them over the internet, of all places. Without a doubt he used a fake name, Dave Michaels. He said he used to live in this town and he knew almost everything there was to know. Without the proper questions, we didn't know where he was coming from in the first place.

All we knew at the time was to wait on Albany road for another car to meet us. We were waiting next to a small park next to a crowd of Victorian houses. A nice place where nothing could go wrong. I switched places with Tiny and sat in the back with Willie. The road was long and quiet, It stretched almost as long as the town itself, one of the longest roads in town. Before every deal you would be worried of anything and everything. You could easily be busted by the cops, get ripped off or sold out. When you do it enough times it barely fazes you and you forget the minor details.

Two cars were coming our way and we all shut up as it grabbed our eyes. When they slowed down Tommy started counting his hundred dollar bills ready for the exchange. He waved down the first car he pulled up to Tommy's car. He threw two big bags of pills over to us and Tommy threw the cash right through the windows.

"How do I know this stuff's good?"

"How do I know I got all the money?" Tommy grunted with a smile, his head nod had trust written all over it.

They had never met but acted very professional. The second car passed and the driver had his eyes locked on me, he smiled nodded his head at me. It got me wondering if there was another little guy like me wherever these guys had come from. Another story being told just like my own, an artistic life written down on paper.

"Hey kid!"

"What's up?"

"Have you ever tried ecstasy?"

"I drink, Tommy. That's all."

"Come on, live a little."

The car started to move up and Willie smacked my shoulder sitting next to me.

"Come on, you'll love it." He bugged again.

"What the hell does it do to you?" He looked at me frozen for a second.

"You'll love it."

CHAPTER XIV

—∘∘∘≫✖≪∘∘∘—

A Delayed Phase

(3:30pm, June 2nd - 3 Months left)

I   was taken to a bar that looked like a dump on the outside, it was right next to this giant bridge in town. I've passed it all the time and I was curious why they were taking me there. We had over two thousands pills locked away in the car, untouched and unknown.

"You want a drink?" Tiny asked.

"I don't have any ID."

"You aren't going to need it, do you want a drink or not?"

"Of course."

The inside had a brown square bar surrounding the bartender. It was plastered with a weird tarp and hardly anybody was in the place. The tables were separated far from the bar, next to the free games of pool. The bartender was a girl that looked like she knew what she was doing, as if she made a career drinking what she was serving. She would dance to the music and was obviously filled with life, or booze. She kept calling me 'sweetie' or 'honey' and was very generous with the drinks.

"Nice to meet you, I'm Alex."

"I know all about you honey, I used to be friends with your mother." Again with my mother.

"Seems everybody has."

She laughed at almost everything I had to say. I'm still not sure if it was because she wanted to be nice or she seriously loved my sense of dull humor. I asked for a pen and paper so I could take some notes down for the book. I was given a handful of pens and giant pad of paper.

"I heard you're a writer."

"A few pages."

"You want another drink?"

"Sure." I smirked.

"Not much for conversation, are you?"

"Usually, but I think I'm stressed out, that's all."

"You think?"

"I just," I brushed my hands through my hair. "I don't know where to even begin."

"That's life."

A bartender is somebody good to talk to. I think they carry some good advice, if they're willing to give it to you.

Just think of all the people that come in to solve or start their problems. She's probably seen a lot of action and drama, with tears and fears. Bartenders knew people, drunk and sober, and the truth would eventually come out. We talked as long as five filled pages and she could see that I was determined. Every couple of seconds gave me the opportunity to write some more while she served the other few customers. Her and Tiny were the closest of us all. They knew almost everything about each other. The conversation was filled with laughter and I got to see a side of Tiny that a few people have. I noticed his tattoos and they all had truth to his stories, whatever half of them were. I could tell that he hadn't always lived out here, he was an outsider. I asked him a few things when the topics were brought up, and eventually he got up and kissed the top of my head.

"You're gonna be my son." He got the load off my mind.

"I think you're the only guy I would let kiss my head, Tiny" I laughed holding my free drink.

"Is this all for your book?"

He had a buzz on and I could smell the beer, his arm was wrapped around the chair as the other was going through the five sheets.

"Just some notes, more or less."

"My son is a fuckin' genius! You're going to be famous, kid!" I could hear Sandy laugh from a distance. I put my head down in a funny embarrassment. I smiled and lifted my head to another direction. Half the conversation he had with people they ended up pointing back at me for being his son, the slurred words kept my head up.

"Alex, my boy! Come shoot a game of pool with me!" He yelled. I was going to keep writing, but I had done my part for the day I thought, so I agreed.

"Alright. One game."

"Are you any good?"

"I used to be, but I haven't played in a while." He was starting to set up the game as I walked up to the table.

"Am I going to be playing against professionals or something?"

"I'm no professional, but Sammy, wow."

"Sammy? Who's that?"

"My brother, now he's a professional. He could beat everyone in this bar with a blindfold on."

Almost all day we just had free drinks and games of pool. At first I couldn't sink a single ball, but after about eight games I was starting to beat Tiny. We played almost twenty games with nothing but good quality beer. My sense of humor grew more and more used to the surroundings of the people I had met only a few times. We were truly all becoming friends outside of working. It seemed as if I had been living my dream, it was the same dream that a lot of people followed. I felt untouched and my hands were washed from all the blood.

"What kind of music do you like?" Tiny asked me.

"Oh here we go." Willie yelled from the bar. "The kid loves everything, I'm surprised he hasn't started already."

"I like a lot of different things, heavy metal, all types of rock, a little bit of the softer acoustic side."

"Like an acoustic guitar?"

"Yeah, half the time I wanna put my head through a wall listening to my heavy shit."

"Then why do you listen to it?"

"Because most of the time it stands for something, there is a lot of emotion put into the stuff I listen too."

"That's it?"

"Let me put it this way, have you ever been in a mosh pit?"

"No, I'm not big on your music."

"Well you're missing out man, it's almost better than sex." I don't know if it was the alcohol, but I felt very comfortable and naturally in place. My bones loosed up and I was focused on something else.

Tiny yelled over at Costa, "He really loves his music eh?" In the distance I heard quietly. "Told yah."

"It's not just that, more than half the world listens to this rap, hip-hop shit when there's no talent."

"So? It sells."

"Exactly, they're rich enjoying the same thing every day, money, and lots of it."

"Everybody likes money."

"Yeah well, a lot of us need it." I took another shot while our conversation continued, it was last game before we went back over to Costa's.

"Good point."

"I win."

"What?"

"I win."

Tiny looked at the table and saw that I just barely beaten him. For the first time, he looked back at me while I shrugged my eye brows.

"Talking helps me concentrate."

"Well, it took you long enough." Turning and laughing with everyone else.

We walked back to the bar and sat down in the tall chairs and ordered another drink. I looked out the window and saw the sun just starting to go down. The shine off of the canal's water glowed a wicked color, the orange reflections off the wall reminded me it was the end of the day, but only to wake up some more.

"This is my favorite time of the day." I said out loud.

"Is it?" Sandy asked refilling my glass.

"Yeah, it's the time of day where everybody's getting off work, or getting ready. It's just perfectly quiet at this time."

It was too hard to hold a conversation with her. She was always distracted by the others and never gave me the clue when she wasn't listening anymore. Her eye contact was strong and she always meant what she said. She was just a sweetheart.

The front door was pushed open with some force, my back was facing it so I had no idea who it was but when I turned it was a great surprise to see Chelsea, Sanko and Andrew with a couple of others all waiting at the door with happiness written all over them.

"Hey!" I yelled just as happy.

"Let's go man, we got one hell of a night ahead of us." Sanko said.

"What's going on tonight?"

"We got a big bag of drugs, a lot of booze and a lot of people coming!"

I was in a good mood so it did not convince me not to do drugs, I felt incredible and just went with the entire feeling. I had some self-esteem problems and always felt judged, the nice feeling of how the day went made everything go much smoother. We were far from invincible. We had an understanding about communication, and that was never about being as tough as the next guy. We were all friends that had something in common. I saw this now and didn't want it to bother me.

Despite my greatest efforts, something always did bother me, the feelings where I could feel the painful beats of my heart. I felt like glass everybody could see through. I was crazy like a little kid past his sugar limit. I felt good like I had been before all of this happened, the old jokes in front my classrooms and schools, my best friends to guide me through hell.

By now, hell didn't seem so bad, because in the back of my head I knew something was wrong.

Something also seemed right. It could have been the cool feeling of walking out of a bar, underage and with obvious intentions of a known crowd. I looked over and saw a woman looking right at me from a distance, she looked disgusted with concern. She seemed to have something going for her life, a nice car, new clothes, a good job. She must have worked hard for a long time to get hold of some of things she deserved.

I could see her looking right at me while I stared back almost in the middle of the road. This is when I had the idea for the beginning of my novel. The judgment from all eyes wondering what I had been doing, a story based on my own biography. I thought my imagination would have covered the rest, seeing as how this woman was looking at me, and only me. I lifted my hand and tried to wave at her, but she drove off in the same speed as the rest of the traffic as it continued. I pondered for a moment, wondering what she was thinking.

I quickly got back into my party mood. I was ready to try some new things that were against my own morals. I saw fit in what I was doing, and knew better than to become a junkie or addict. In the small parking lot stretching across from the bar, three cars were pulled up with everybody talking to everybody. The others had the cars started up and were ready to go, I was going with Tommy in shotgun. I saw two new faces outside standing out of what was obviously one of their own vehicles. One was covered in tattoos and seemed quiet. The other was filled with life having a cigarette heading for the bar, laughing and smacking the others shoulder. They must have both in their thirties, and you could easily see that they've both done a lot of time in prison.

"Who's that?" I asked. Tommy looked back and came back crunching the leather in his seat.

"That's Mancuso, and I don't know the other guy."

"Which one is Mancuso?"

"The black and blonde hair guy."

"The one on the left?"

"Yeah, I never see too much of him."

It turned out that he had been in and out of jail several times, for several different things. He was the last thing from a killer, but I was told he had done some time for some big operations. He was good on keeping his mouth shut, very loyal and he cared about his loved ones. This bar was familiar to their faces, and ours. Thinking about Costa's father, I realized that these two were in connection with him. A man I have yet to identify.

"He can't really read though." Tommy mentioned, looking to himself.

"What like books?" I paused. No answer.

Tommy was too busy pulling out of the parking lot heading towards this party. That's all anybody had on their minds. Once we were on the free road, our cars kept passing each other screaming about how excited we were. I even saw Sanko pulling out his bottle in the back seat of another car chugging back some vicious vodka. His sour face was priceless from my distance. I started to wonder about Chelsea's condition. I was more than sure she hadn't done any chemicals before. This would be something to see.

This was all for my story to tell, it was going to be fun but I did not think I would learn anything from it. This was a delayed phase of mine that everyone had already been through, drugs and whole nine yards. It seemed like I was with professionals. I looked back over to their window and saw cocaine being busted up onto a CD case. It was passed around in the car out in the open while they just sniffed it away, including Chelsea.

"What the hell is she doing?"

What was I seeing? I could not believe it. She was smaller than me and I had thought she looked up to me, had this been her first time? I was amazed but it was a little upsetting. I had hoped she didn't just do it to fit in with this crowd. Cocaine is such a dangerous world that I never wanted to live in.

"I've got some news for you." Tommy said.

"Another one of Tommy's wonderful speeches, I assume?" I put my arm against the window holding my head up, looking at the driver.

"Do you want to hear it or not?"

"Of course I do, go on." We laughed.

He forgot what he was saying for a moment, he was going to start laughing again but his mouth closed and he got to the point, with laughter behind him.

"There is going to be a lot of people at this party man."

"Isn't that bad news for Costa?"

"Why would think that?"

"It's at his house, no?"

"No, he's hosting it." Correcting me.

"Still."

"It isn't illegal to party, Alex."

"No but, I know, but," I rolled my eyes trying to explain. "a lot of people cannot be quiet."

"You worry too much about other people, man."

"Like I haven't heard that before."

"If you can save your own ass, we can too."

"I don't get it."

"If it gets too loud, which it won't, it'll be every man for himself."

That sounded great, you know the risk of getting busted with a bunch of drugs and our plan was *every man for himself.* Parties got everybody wild, nobody could focus. Especially by the time they got high. Costa wasn't exactly the host of this. He was the one paying for everybody, and a sample test for his new product I guess. We were pulling up this very simple two-story house. All along the entire road they all looked the same. Every roof was in sync with each other, it seemed like this part of town was shut out from the rest of us.

There was a typical five-foot fence that everybody kept calling the co-op, surrounded it. The driveway could barely fit two cars let alone a truck under its low garage, the thing didn't even have walls. The door at the end of the landing opened up and I saw a woman open it faster than we had pulled in. Cars were pulling in everywhere. At least fifty of us had arrived at the same time, against the sidewalks, on the grass, on her yard.

Tommy had known the woman and they greeted each other with great respect. Willie and Tiny had done the same. I waited by the door for Chelsea and the others to catch up. I looked over at Kenny already pouring shots down his throat with a group of people before they even made it to the driveway.

"Well he's done for." I said to myself pointing at him.

"He's going to be puking." Chelsea said.

"Hey stop for a second." I snapped my finger and she came back in my direction.

Her eyes wandered and vibrated her cute little nose while she they widened made my questions harder. Everybody has headed in and the others were coming up to the door, so I had to keep it brief and quiet.

"What the hell were you doing in that car?"

"What?"

"The coke, what the hell are you thinking?"

She just gave me this look that said, "None of your business." If only eyebrows could talk.

She continued to walk inside and I followed her in. The house already seemed trashed with toys and kids were still running around everywhere. It felt a little out of place to be smoking, drinking and sniffing something with all these little kids. They had to have been only five or six, too young to see what we were doing. I was the only one that noticed this, everyone was getting to know each other all lighting up. I didn't have any physical reaction, I just sat at the end of a small table observing everyone. This one guy, had teeth blacker than oil, his hair looked like it was ripped out, and he just sat at the opposite end of the table and he kept screaming.

"Are you asking me something? Or are you telling me something?" Whatever that means.

Stressing his anger, I don't know how many times he stomped down his feet. He was a wreck and didn't look more than twenty five, a young disaster. The dining room and kitchen were both very small and joined together surrounded by a crowd of people being a little more reasonable than this guy.

"Hey kid, let me tell you something." I refused to turn my head, he was that pathetic to me, but I blinked in his direction.

"Yeah, what's that?" I asked.

"You seem all dressed up, huh?"

"Excuse me?"

"Your clothes, they're nice."

I looked around and everyone had nicer clothes than me, my blink turned into sarcasm disgust. I didn't respond.

"Hey! I'm telling you something."

"Enjoy your whiskey, sir."

Again he stomped his feet and I couldn't do anything but cough a laugh. It was forced out, there was nothing I could have done.

"Hey!"

"What!" I yelled.

"Are you asking me something? Or are you telling me something?"

"Jesus Christ."

"Hey!"

"What the hell do you want me to say? You're not making any fucking sense!" I slammed my hands down on the table. He got up from his chair and stumbled his way over to me, I only wished his breath smelled like whiskey, but it smelled like garbage.

"Are you asking me something, or are you telling me something?" I swear he must have heard this from a movie or something.

"I don't know what to tell you."

"Look at these!" Grabbing my arms.

"What the-? Get off me, man!"

"You've got nothing on these!" Showing me his biceps and then lifting my t-shirt to spit on my arms.

"What the fuck is wrong with you?!" I screamed.

I quickly got up knocking over the chair ignoring everybody else, but they quickly got in the middle of the fight ripping us apart. The woman who answered the door was real tough, just the look in her eyes told me to sit back down, but I couldn't. I was too stubborn to let this addict looking guy get the last word in. She was more focused on the drunken guy more than me, she even yelled, "He's a good kid, you wait until my brother gets here!"

"I don't even know you man!" I yelled again and again, then finally I spit right in his face and the fight became worse. He came at me with everything he had. Everyone was tearing us apart, I was mad. I was struggling to get out of the arm lock and just beat the ever-living crap out of this guy. Tiny and Mancuso got in the door at the same time and saw what was happening and slammed it shut. I could see them coming in my direction and I started to calm down as fast as I could. The Mancuso guy looked at me right from behind the crowd.

"Don't worry, he's outta here kiddo." This wasn't something he hadn't already seen a million times.

Kenny was the holding me back. He had my arms locked in pretty tight but I looked back and simply said. "Alright, come on, let me go man." In the background of all this I could hear the drunk screaming and kicking as he got dragged out of the house. Kenny let me go and I walked over to Mancuso who was leaning against the counter of the small kitchen. He stood out from everybody else, he was older and well known by the looks of it.

"You want a drink?" He asked.

"Oh my god, yes I do." I said a little out of shape and breath.

"Here." He passed a fresh unopened bottle of scotch.

"No shot glass?" I asked.

"Straight from the bottle, boy! Come on!"

I took one of the biggest shots I possibly could, and I didn't even make that same sour face Sanko had made earlier. I had an adrenaline rush from that stupid guy and finally clapped my hands together, ready to get them messy. The night went on like this, and I just kept drinking and drinking and drinking, making jokes and hanging out with the originals, as I called them, Sanko, Chelsea and Andrew. We sat around the table playing cards and enjoying the entertainment the entire house brought. I was even smoking like a chimney.

The kids were forced several times to go upstairs when Costa arrived. He was the key to the party, what took him so long to get there didn't really grab my attention just yet. This was one the few times I hadn't seen him so mad, he was almost the life of the party. As soon as he and Tommy returned with the ecstasy everyone was almost in a line up ready to get some samples. A lot of people were paying under the agreement that if you did these you could not leave and we were forced to stay in this house. It was a small handful of people that didn't want to do it. Their booze was enough for them. Mancuso and Andrew were some of them. Lines of cocaine and ecstasy were being passed around the table. People were rubbing the leftovers in their teeth, already wanting more.

Sanko leaned back waiting for the buzz, the coke got to everyone almost instantly. The music had to be on and it had to be on loud. Everyone loved whatever it was they were feeling, all the girls kept screaming for nothing. Yelling at the top of their lungs just to say how much fun they were having, there I was, alone in my own little world contemplating what my next move was going to be.

Finally the tray was passed to me. It was the on top of an old text book from school, filled with multi colored lines. Pink, green, white, and all of them mixed in stains all over the tables and countertops.

"Fuck it." I grabbed the rolled up bill and sniffed the biggest green one I could find.

It burned the entire way up and all the way down, the taste was awful. "The drips." They kept saying I had to wait for, eventually I started sniffing more and the high came in really fast and all at once. I started drinking as the music was being turned up. I looked around and I started to value everything.

"Go and look at your eyes man!" Mancuso yelled laughing, knowing this was my first time.

I literally ran to the bathroom filled with energy, eyes wide open and grinding my teeth. My mouth was open and I looked like an animal, or a monster. I shocked myself looking into this reflection. I was hideous, sniffing all the drips down my throat. I was getting used to the bad taste, after a while I learned to like it.

I wanted more.

CHAPTER XV

—∞∘❄∘∞—

A Rotten Overdose

(4:15am, June 3rd - 3 Months left)

Time was flying past me and nobody wanted it to end. I felt great but I had a little bit of a headache from all the whiskey earlier. All these girls dancing kept me observant almost all night. Cocaine and Ecstasy together mixed all your emotions, but to some other people it drove them wild. Events were happening almost every couple of seconds, fights, a crazy girl screaming and dancing on a table, paranoid freaks chewing what was left of their fingernails.

"Do you have any gum? Do you have any gum?"

Straws, cigarettes, gum and tooth picks were all key ingredients. Unless you were talking to somebody you hardly knew about everything possible. I heard so many people talking about solving the world's problems or about how much they love the person they were talking to. Two guys I had never met before were standing by a window that was covered up by a dirty blanket, going on and on about what would be a good idea to help someone's situation. A lot of things were promised to each other, and Kenny was the worst.

"Come here!"

"What's up buddy?" I asked.

He gave me this serious look like he had just fallen in love with me and he gave me, just like many others had, a giant hug. He squeezed trying to pick me up and he would not let me go, I laughed and patted his back. I looked at the dancing girls and questioned them with my eyes about Kenny. They laughed too as they came closer. Their shirts looked like they were ready to fall off. They were beautiful girls with so much potential, but I didn't care, I was amazed by their beauty and did not have time to consider their professional life.

They had these outfits that looked like they just got out of a dancing club. They looked as if they were in their mid-twenties with voices like high school cheerleaders.

"Who are you?"

"I'm Alex." Struggling with a smile kept on, while Kenny squeezed me a little harder.

"What are you doing here?" She asked in such a cute tone.

"I wish I could tell you."

"How old are you?"

"I'm seventeen, what about you guys?"

They looked at each other and smiled, "Were eighteen." The one said. The one I had my eye on was a brunette, while the other was a blonde. The blonde seemed more girly while the brown haired girl seemed her age. When the blonde said how old she was, she didn't convince me. There was an age difference in these girls.

"You do not look eighteen."

I could feel my teeth grinding again, I stopped right away and pulled myself off of Kenny, I put him at arm's length.

"Kenny, I appreciate it."

"How old do you think I am?" Asked the flirt.

It wasn't a surprise to me that Kenny already knew these girls, Melissa with the brown hair, and Nadine with the blonde. They weren't too fond of him though, they brushed him aside. Without any knowledge that Kenny had been turned down, he went off to go do his own thing.

"So, how old do you think I am?" Nadine asked again.

I had no idea, my instinct told me that she had been lying and that she was younger, but this girl looked older for her age.

"I don't know, seventeen?"

I looked over at Melissa and she was still smiling as she mouthed the words, "Fifteen."

"You're fucking fifteen?!" I yelled. Normally I wouldn't have done such an obnoxious move, but I was amazed. Besides, Tommy had given me a huge lecture a few days back about how to talk to girls. He believes that if you 'call it out how it is' they would be the ones to chase you.

"Just be an asshole." He said, and oddly it works.

Nadine's face had turned bright red, but was not at all embarrassed by her own lie. It brought her closer to me. I could not believe this stunning of a girl was younger than me. Anybody would have been fooled by this face and body. I was amazed. This beauty, as high I was, did not get me attracted to her in any other way, these girls were not my type. I knew that they were every other guy's type. The fact that the drugs kept my thoughts on Eva just bothered me to move forward or play ball.

"I turn sixteen in a month though." She said, like it really mattered.

I went to take my first step out of this situation, I felt pathetic talking to this girl. She was nice, but she did not have to try, she had fake smile with shiny hair. I paused looking over at Melissa. She seemed different, she was just enjoying her age while she could. For a second I could not say anything, this was a girl you were meant to be nice to.

Her jaw lines lifted up as I saw her smirk a little, hiding herself. She had these natural highlights to herself and the last thing from a fake smile, it was real.

"It was nice to have met you." I shook her soft hands. I was never sure if it was the given circumstance of the night, or if I really felt something for another girl aside from my typical loss.

I had never seen something like this before, people half naked, sweating, smoking and moaning. The burned carpet was covered in the plastic wrapping from several cigarette packages, burn holes and spilt beer. The entire room smelled like sweat and smoke. The air was a light moving gray, and I could see all the individual rings forming from the exhales. I noticed stupid small things like this all night from mostly the ecstasy. I walked through all this in slow motion and I saw Costa, Sanko and Tommy with a few of the others sitting around a glass table covered in plastic cups, bottles and ashtrays. All of our eyes were half down, everyone had been mixing different types of drugs and alcohol, and it was for this reason that most of us spent time looking at things we normally wouldn't.

I sat on the ruined couch next to Costa, feeling oblivious to get his attention.

"Costa, Costa, hey Costa!" I patted his arm.

Impossible to get his attention, Tommy had looked over for a brief second giving me the index finger asking to wait. They were all laughing as I sat on the end corner of the couch waiting for an answer.

"All we have to do is hit them where it hurts!" On these drugs, you could not imagine how stressful it is to get your point across, that's if you can even finish your sentence. Talking was by far the most important thing happening around this table. I would have loved to have seen somebody on these pills standing still without trying. Everyone was blinking too much, always playing with their hair or wiping the sweat off their faces. The three of them were so caught up in a conversation about all those goons that hung out at Marc's apartment building, or something along those lines.

"No, no we have to hit them where it hurts." Tommy stressed.

"What? Like kicking them in the balls?" Idiotic Sanko, trying to fit in.

Even I knew that Sanko had no idea what they meant, drunk, high or sober. Tommy looked over at me, then Costa with his hand out and shoulder shrugged, shaking his head.

"No, Ritz, not like getting kicked in the balls, not like kicked in the fucking balls at all."

He had a blank stare at nothing. I might have mumbled something back but the music covered it. I sat on that couch for hours on end, just talking and running to the bathroom countless times to wash my hands and use the toilet, I could not stop drinking. A beer here, a shot there, it seemed like an endless supply of problems that you never realized the debt, until you wake up. I still wanted more, but one thing had stopped me.

The music was still loud, people were still doing exactly what they had been doing for hours on end, and I could see the sun coming up. It was that same blue feeling outside from when I was picked up that one morning. My body was damp with the room, I needed fresh air. I headed for the depressing door out into something that seemed new and Tommy followed. I opened the door and the breeze hit me like I had just been released from jail. It felt so good up my arms and through my shirt, the sun coming up and it really bothered me. I always liked my sleeping schedule.

"Beautiful! It's a beautiful morning." Tommy said with a girl wrapped in his arms, her back to his chest as he leaned on the small railing. It was concrete steps with a small square landing back to the door, and we stayed. I started to feel weak and angry. I was coming down from the drugs and seeing the day in front of me, while Tommy was still enjoying himself with his beer and women. I thought, "How the hell could you always been active, and always so fucking happy?"

He started screaming, "Yeah! This is perfect, wake up town!" Laughing at his own jokes.

"Tommy, I've never seen you like this." I said.

"Neither have I, friend, neither have I." He chugged the entire beer afterwards.

"I need a refill, you coming in kid?"

Before I could even answer he was already running up closer to my face, "Hey, you, you coming in?"

"I'll be in a second."

We all stunk like the ashtrays all over the floor and tables, my twenty-four deodorant smelled like a lit cigarette, all our hair was in strings hanging over our faces, bunched up or just messy. My night was almost over and somehow I wanted more drugs so I could get away from the headache. With the energy I had left I decided to walk home without anybody else knowing. The sidewalk hurt my feet, every once and awhile I would slip or hit my foot off the misplaced concrete. All the walking made the aches worse, at some point I wanted to just stop and die, plus I think I was still drunk.

But in a strange way, I wanted to keep walking, and standing still seemed completely off course. I tried to think of numerous things that would distract me from the self-torment, I knew I did this to myself and that's what it kept coming back to. I knew in the end I would feel better, but I also knew I overdid it for my first time. I suffered during every step acting like a zombie.

"Everything is in a circle." I said.

I knew my walk had to have been another twenty minutes or so, and I slipped to my side walking on the morning grass. My shoes were soaked from it, and the bottom of my pant legs were too. The awkward feeling walking with wet feet made me so mad. I slid my hand up my face and through my hair, I was dirty and did not want to walk into my house alone, nobody to have a conversation with.

Tonight was twisted, I might have been the only one, but the way I saw it was that we all had such a fun time. I could not remember when some of the others left, or even the good jokes that were told, I only remembered the night and feeling in general. I wanted more, I needed more, I thought. What a pointless ambition to have for myself. I hated the feeling and everything that it came with. A headache would have been acceptable, but this was more of a fear. I felt like I hated myself and death could have been an easy way out.

As every step felt like a rusty needle digging into my knees and feet, I finally reached home. It had to have been almost 6:30 in the morning because the sun had made its original color, I had four steps to reach my front door, lifting my knees on each one killed me. My door was locked, and my key ring was attached to my belt line, I wondered, "How the hell am I going to do this?"

I used every key, upside down, turned around, and with my luck it just had to be the last one. After the main door I repeated myself with my apartment's door. When I had finally gotten in, my phone was ringing. I ran to the phone, I forgot it was cordless and stayed by the base. All I could hear was static and I seemed frozen in time, my headache got a million times worse in a split second, it felt like it was being cut in half.

"Eva?" I asked.

Somehow she had still been on my mind, I was lost and hurt. "I'm sorry, but I don't know where I am." A wave of heat came through my entire body, everything had hit me at once. A cold chill went through my entire body and I started to instantly seat.

"Are you there?" There was no answer, and I started to think nobody was even on the other line. I checked the battery and turned the phone off and on, back and forth I could keep together the phone idea, but everything else was blurry. I was standing on the brink of an overdose. My eyes started to feel heavy, I looked down at my dirty shirt and thought back to the laughs and senseless answers, I started to deny it ever happened.

"I'm better than this aren't I?" I thought, or said. I called back the first number that came to my head, it wasn't any phone number, just a series of randomness put on the phone. I think I may have only dialed three numbers.

"Hello?" I stumbled to catch myself, but as I fell I watched the phone stay in midair. I was in a slow motion trance, watching the phone stick to the air. This was actually happening, I was half illustrating a belief on something from Hollywood. That's all I could think about, as I fell to the ground watching this floating phone I kept thinking that this was incredible. I hated it, but at the same time I thought it was kind of cool. Somewhere in the doubt I knew everything would be okay, it was just in the present darkness I knew I could not do anything to get over this awful feeling. I was becoming numb.

Finally, I had hit the floor and rock bottom, I could not move a muscle but blink very slowly. I stared at the nothingness of my walls. A million things were coming to mind, my mom, her, my sister, my friends, my life, my regrets. I could not stay on the level with myself, my arms were falling asleep. I started to think about a day and age when I did not care about anything or even myself, in this dream the sun was bright and I was happy. The book I was writing seemed stupid and I hated myself. This new version of me was a rip off of another poser.

But somehow I knew better than all this, I knew I was better than to sell myself out for a handful of drugs. Finally my eyes felt sewn shut, and I passed out. The second I fell asleep the pain was gone but I was going on a mental trip around my world. My memories were not so remembered, but the general feeling was around me, I seemed to have been living in a nightmare. It went back years ago, things I thought I could never remember.

There was a situation almost four years ago when I was thirteen years old. I was treated in a dark hospital for carbon monoxide poisoning. The night before was just a normal night, my mother had made dinner for all of us, even with desert. I'll never forget the little things about this night. My step dad at the time was a respected officer with a lot of respect. He never yelled at us, he was the entire reason I wrote my story. He was stocky and bald, he was so innocent and had no reason to die. All of us seemed fine that night, my sister and I, my mom, David, and my two dogs. He had called the gas company three weeks prior to come and check out a gas leak. By their mistake and incompetence, they left no report while we inhaled poison into our systems that entire time.

David at the time was painting in the basement next to the furnace and my room. I guess I lived through the ordeal because he had sent me out to get a bag of potato chips and dip. The amount of fresh air I got into my system was enough to keep me alive throughout the next morning. I woke up in the middle of the night sicker than anything I had ever felt before. I walked over to a pile of my dirty laundry and collapsed on top of it. I thought I had food poisoning. I woke up the next afternoon in my own blood, vomit and piss. This had to have been the worst pain I had ever been in. Somehow I got up, dizzy, dirty and undead. Apparently I did die, but the fact that carbon monoxide lifts up and was rising past me kept me alive and I had collapsed on the floor which also saved my life. My room was in the basement right next to the furnace and where David had been painting. I made it to the stairs and anybody who has experienced this pain will tell you that it is a silent death, you feel as if you could lift your legs but in reality you aren't moving much at all.

I banged my feet up every wood step to the bathroom straight across from basement door, once I made it I started to puke out pain and blood. It was yellow with chunks of dark red blood, and I could not stop puking.

"Oh my god." I had still thought it was food poisoning, my head was in such pain and my stomach felt like somebody was grabbing all my organs and bones and twisting them with their hands covered in barbwire. I was still standing while I cried with my hand against the wall, I kept my balance as my other hand was tightened on my shirt and putting pressure on my chest. I tried to turn around but even looking around with my eyes hurt, there was a pain behind them.

The window in the living room gave away the time of day. It was just after noon and I had never slept in that late. We had just moved to this town so my mom had to drive me all the way to school in another town, she hadn't even come to wake me up. "Are we all sick?" I thought.

"What the hell is happening?" I was so high I made some disordered steps to the couch, I could not move once I was lying down. I wrapped myself in a blanket and turned on the television to some cartoon. In the dream though, I looked up and saw the new me, I was older and had a bit more sense of style. I felt the age I was in during the dream, in that reality, it wasn't a dream, I was reliving the twisted moment. I had the same sense of humor, the gothic side of hair and the rings. The new me seemed like a mystery. I was just standing there, quiet with a presence I was focused on. I had a very nice wristwatch on that was bright and I had a different hair style, with more color in my clothing and barely any acne on my face.

"Is that me?" The younger, wrongfully me asked.

This dream was like time travel, I felt alive in the young body of myself. The new me seemed sad, there were no words, but we both knew what we were saying. It seemed like I was trying to tell myself something. I quickly snapped out of the illusion facing with what I thought was real. Ironic how in my own dream I was convinced to be somebody else looking back at the modern image of myself and thought I was high.

The dream had gone on. I heard a loud thump coming from upstairs, and my mom was crying. I could hear her falling over and over again. I heard her pick up the phone and dial somebody, there was no answer and she fell again. Only the sound was closer to the top of the stairs. I tried to lift my head, but I was almost dead, I could not speak.

"Mom, Mom!" I tried to say.

Her tears were the sounds of something that just been taken away. Barely calling the police, she managed to pull through.

"Hello? Hello, my husband, he's dead." Those were the first words I heard her say.

"178 Elgin Street, please just hurry I don't know what's going on." Hanging up.

She fell all the way down the stairs, she had bruises all over her body, and her eyes landed on my sick face.

"Alex, honey, David is dead." I had already known this, but it shocked me again. "What?" I could finally speak, hardly.

I did not cry yet, I felt somehow I should be strong for my mother.

"Where's Meghan?" She asked.

"No." I prayed I did not lose her too.

I blacked out, and in a split second there were cops all over the house with this strange beeping noise following them. The house phone was constantly ringing and the beeping was keeping me awake. An officer was holding both my arms looking me straight in the eyes yelling at me to get out of the house. When I came out from the black out I was somehow sitting up, mouth dry and wide open, eyes dazed and bloodshot. I was seconds away from death, and when I looked over at the floor I saw mud prints everywhere, they had been here for some time.

"Where's my sister?" I asked.

"Come on, kid, were going to get you out of here." Kid?
"Why?"

"You need some fresh air, you'll be okay. Come on, you'll be okay."

"Okay."

I started to get up and then the officer lifted me and carried me with one arm, I think it may have been Roy.

"You're going to be okay, Alex. Come on, you can do it. One step at time, that's it."

I couldn't reply, I just moaned a little bit feeling the horrible pain and aches through my entire body.

"Once you get out here you'll be okay, just take it easy." We took the back door out so we had to pass the washroom I had just puked in. I looked over at it and saw my blood and vomit all over the place and little spits of blood from my feet banging off the stairs. The back door opened into a sun room, only it was the middle of winter so I could feel the cool air hit me. It felt exactly like it did walking home before this nightmare. Only, this air wasn't enough, I had to be outside. Two police officers were at the bottom of the small staircase that led out from the sun room, one was a woman, I think. When the sun and fresh air hit me I took the biggest inhale and then vomited all over the place, all I can remember is that I wanted this to be over.

The air I inhaled must have been too intense for my body to handle, it hurt. I started to choke taking several deep breaths as fast as I could. My heart was jump started I could feel it pumping blood through my cold veins. I got a boost of adrenaline and started to ask about my sister. Before they could answer I looked around to see her strapped to a gurney being carefully carried out. I looked to see if she was alive and she was still breathing.

"Oh thank god, Meghan, Meghan!" A cop held me back and would not let me get close to her, she was in a coma. She had seen David's dead body and had a heart attack.

"Is she going to be okay? Is she going to be okay?"

"Answer me!"

I skipped ahead to the hospital, the bright white light was fading away and I don't remember even getting there. I was in an emergency room lying next to my mom. I could not talk, something was strapped to my face. I tried to look around but my peripheral views did not exist, everything that was visible repeated the pattern to the things I could not see. Like a glitch from a computer screen or video game. I remember two railings on each side of my bed, but the texture of them were not there either. I was hanging on one of them, an invisible railing.

"Are you thirsty?" A man's voice asked.

"What?"

"Are you thirsty?"

"Yeah, where's that thing?"

"Excuse me?"

"That thing, it was on my face."

"We had to take it off, do you want something to drink sir?"

"Yes."

This person was a blur, he looked like the outline of some detective from a comic book.

"What do you want?"

"Ginger ale."

I was handed a two liter bottle of ginger ale with a shot glass of a paper cup. I thought, "What the hell am I going to do with this?" so I just took the bottle and started to slam it back, only thing was my arms were still weak, so I had to repeatedly put it back up with both hands and take small sips. The man was still standing there waiting for me to finish and I finally got through the entire bottle. I was still thirsty.

"I'm here to ask you some questions." He said, but everything had skipped ahead again, I was still in the same room facing my mom.

"What's going to happen?"

"I don't know son."

We were soaked with tears, we didn't know what to think, we were just as angry for some reason as well. I squeezed her hand and I kept trying to figure out what happened, but I ended up falling asleep, hooked up to all these machines. Asleep I started to become myself again, I felt my body stretch apart as I got taller, my headache came back, and so had I.

I thought I woke up in my own bed, it was just as comfortable. My blanket seemed thinner, and I could hear people talking all around me.

"Andrew? Tommy?" Nobody was around, where was I? It didn't make sense, but in a way I wasn't fully awake, I wanted to sleep in. They sounded like mothers, a crowd of women writing on something, professional and official. The echoes drove in and out of my head.

"He's waking up." One said.

"Hello?"

"Alex, you're in the hospital, how are you feeling?"

My eyes opened wide and I seemed well rested. The weird dream had ended and I saw my eyes open as they focused into the light. I was looking directly into a nurse's eyes. Her face was too close for comfort. I just looked at her for a second, my mouth wide open and it did not smell too pretty.

"Excuse me, sir?"

"Yeah?"

"You're in the hospital, are you okay?"

"Yeah, I think."

"Do you know how you got here?"

"Do you?" I asked.

"Yes, but I'm asking you sir."

I tried to think hard, but the last thing I remembered was the floating phone and living in that odd fantasy.

"I have no idea."

"You're sister found you, you were having an overdose."

"Meghan? She found me?"

"If that's her name, than yes, she did. She is downstairs."

She must have thought I was insane, like I was getting into a bad crowd. I could not believe it was my sister that had found me. I hoped I was still dreaming, I prayed that it was not her or my mother that found me.

"Short little brown haired girl?" She asked. My sister was blonde, and just as tall as me, so the only answer I came up with was Chelsea.

"Yeah that's her, is she still here?" I lied.

"Yes, she's in the waiting room, would you like to see her?"

"Yeah."

Without a response she left with a smile on her face. I tried to find something that I could see myself in to fix my hair up so I didn't look like such a loser, but I had to improvise with just my hands. Seconds later, Chelsea walked through the door, she couldn't see me at the end of the short but long room, she checked the other patients blocked area then found me.

"You're a real piece of work you know that?" She punched my arm.

"Hey man," with a smile. "How did you find me?"

"Well, you went up and left this morning so we went out looking for you."

"You and Tommy?"

"Yeah, we found you passed out on your floor."

"I know, and I had the weirdest dream."

"How are you feeling?"

"Good actually, but I have to ask you something."

"Go for it."

"I wasn't like, twitching, or anything was I?"

She laughed for a second and put her head back down, "No, you were out cold."

"Thank god, I would have hated to have you see me like that."

"You over did it last night." Stressing like I had done something stupid.

"I don't even remember to be honest."

"Well, you tried to kiss me."

"What? No I did not."

"Yeah, yeah you did." Assuring me.

"No I didn't."

"You did."

"I'm sorry Chelsea."

"You're not the only one, at least you understood after I told you."

"What do you mean?"

"Willie, wow." Rolling her eyes.

Willie could not keep his hands off Chelsea. He did not get the clue to stay off of her. He tried everything in the book, smooth talking, mean talking, just trying to be nice, pulling her towards the bedroom, dancing, his objective was strictly Chelsea.

"Everyone was really fucked up last night."

"You're telling me."

"You must have blacked out, I have never seen you so hyper."

For a second I remembered seeing myself laughing at the living room table explaining a story, everyone was laughing with me.

"Chelsea, did I make an ass out of myself?"

"Not really, you were more the life of the party, but at times you were a little too much."

"I'll keep that in mind next time."

"So, do you know when you can get the hell out of here?"

"I'm fine, I should just walk out."

"Alright, meet me outside."

"Who's all here with you?"

"Kenny drove me here. He probably still thinks he had a chance." She giggled.

"That's it?"

"Yeah, but call Tommy, he wants to talk to you."

"What does he want to talk to me about?"

"Apparently he's all worried about Costa, he doesn't trust him anymore."

"I have that feeling too, but we'll talk later, where's my stuff?"

"It's all in that closet right over there."

"Hey Chelsea!" I called out to her as she was walking out the door.

"What?" She stopped.

"Thanks for coming." I meant it.

"You would've done the same for me." She smiled and then shut the door.

I put my clothes back on, they still smelt like smoke and seemed stuck onto my dry skin, my hair was a mess and I stunk. I could not wait to shower when I got home. Then that got me thinking, I really hated being alone, eventually they would drop me off with no mission of something to do, other than to make a phone call. The morning after a great night was depressing, it reminded me of ending a great relationship. Ten years of greatness is not worth the first three hours of agony and pain you feel in your heart.

I was a people-person, a leader, social, not a follower. Only thing is that I can't understand myself, I never could. This wasn't something new because I always just went with the flow, reacted to the new people and events that came with my life. The things I think about during the weirdest times are my best thoughts. I looked back on the drugs, sniffs, drips and the headache. I knew this wasn't going to be my life, I experienced more in life already than most elders, and I refused to go down in life as an addict. I was proud of myself now, I knew I was different "I'm better than this." I really did wake up.

CHAPTER XVI

Riddled Vendetta

(June 5th - 3 Months left)

Two long days passed as I constantly thought back and forth for a good game plan. I went for long walks just listening to my music trying to figure out something. I was trying to figure out something to figure out. I did not know where to start, let alone how to handle it. Sometimes I thought I had it, I wondered if I should just get a job, go back to school, pay my rent the normal way. I was concerned about my reputation if I even had one and if people were going to jump me. Everybody talks in this town so I wouldn't be surprised if everybody had known what I was up to, or if they even cared.

I was off the earth when I had those headphones on, sometimes I had to walk over people's houses and back. I kept my head down, mouthing the lyrics from the music, but I walked with pride. I'd watch hundreds of cars go by and I'd get looked at by almost every single person in every vehicle. I always said hello to the people walking by me. A lot of emotions came out of me, one second I'd be in a good mood, then I'd get mad or upset just going off into my own head. The things that have happened to me and things that I'd seen gave me an opening to some creativity. I was always told I had an imagination when I was toddler and my real father told me I was going to be a writer.

I thought that maybe I should go see him, he was only a couple of towns over, it had been so long since I last saw him. He was a lot like me when he was my age, he used to be in a band, smoke, and drink and lived a dream. I had heard he got his act together and really picked up the lost pieces. He was wealthy and with a good woman, he should have something good to say.

It could have been a mistake. Should I just have admitted it to my mother and sister? As I walked past the place where I was shot, I wondered again if they were going to be around to do something similar. People around here were stupid that way, but again my mind wandered off. The music was playing in my ears, but I didn't hear it. I used the loudest of music to mute everybody else out, and it worked. I could really think and approach everything with some time in-between and take baby steps. One problem at a time, I just loved to listen to my music.

"Hey, you're that kid!" I looked up watching this guy waving his arms at me.

"Yeah, you!"

"Do I know you?" I asked taking my headphones out.

"You don't remember me?"

He looked a little familiar, but he just one of those faces you could not put a name to.

"I can't say that I do."

"You're Alex right?" He seemed a little shifty, not like he was hiding anything, but, something wrong was just there.

"Well, what's your name?" He asked again.

"You're right, it's Alex."

He quickly patted his legs and started rub his shirt like he was itchy. He was high!

"Hey listen, I'm friends with your Uncle Nico, you want to help me out with something?"

"Uncle?"

"What you don't know your own Uncle?" He had a dark laugh that told me he was desperate.

"What do you need help with?" I asked.

He leaned in closer to me but I kept him at arm's length.

"Can you spot me like, fifty bucks?"

"What the fuck, no!"

"Come on, calm down, you don't have to yell, you know?"

"I don't even know you!"

"Yeah you do, your uncle, come on man. Help me out."

"Forget it!"

I was standing in the exact same spot where we had parked the car the day I was shot, and across from me was that same damn bar. Nobody was outside to hear me yell at this guy.

"Oh come on man, please?"

"Are you out of your mind, buddy? I said no."

I started to walk away but he was following me. I could hear him getting mad, not say anything for a second then he came out with another stupid offer.

"Come on, I'll give you my wallet and everything to hold onto." With no response from me he grew angrier.

"Just give me the fucking money! You don't know what I can do to you!" Yeah, threaten me. That will make the money appear in his hands. He was getting desperate.

"Please man, I got a little kid to feed."

Even if he did have a child, I still wouldn't have given him the money. That kid could have probably taken care of himself better than his or her own father. With the money given to him regardless, I and anybody sane would know exactly what he was really going to do with it. The thing about the threats he made was that here's somebody that is asking a kid half his age for dope money. That fact alone said he didn't have any power at all. He was just talking a big game with no walk. No more talking to this guy, I thought and I just kept walking. I made it seem like I was listening to my music, but it was on pause. I heard him run over to the bar and it sounded like he was going to have an angry cry. He was moaning over nothing, which to him seemed like everything. Perfect timing to give myself a pat on the back, that could have been me craving a needle filled with trash.

"Yeah run and cry you fucking loser!" He yelled at me, making it seem like he had the upper hand in front of his friend. I turned around stopped dead in motion, and looked at him. My face was filled with disgust. I started to get mad.

"What the hell did you just say to me?" I was fed up.

"You heard me!"

"No, I don't think I did."

I started to walk over to the bar in hopes he would meet me half way, but he stayed by the only protection he had, a steel door. Even his friend could care less about this scruffy and scared loser. The cigarette he had lit was worth more than their so-called friendship. He returned inside and the other guy followed. So casual.

"What am I, a ghost?" I thought.

I walked to the door and the bastard had locked it. In a dictionary, he would classify a coward. I wanted to find out his name. I knew that face, but the way I remembered him was not so grimy, or dirty. I think he might have been one of my mom's old friends or something I met, when I was younger. I turned around and walked away. I turned the farthest away from where I was shot. I must have walked all over town, I saw a lot of my friends walking, driving or biking all waving at me. Summer time must have been close for them, the smiles showed the will for freedom, away from the teacher's rules and to just enjoy the time apart.

I dropped out this year, I had no vacation saved up. A lot of plans were made while mine stayed the same. Old friends would be working to save up for something nice, others would just party. I myself was going to be doing the same thing I had been doing since it began. I missed the feeling of long waited events. Time flew by so fast that I had just realized that I could be wearing shorts. The sun glared off the beautiful full green leaves, the wind gently brushed them to the sound of happiness. Teenagers the same age as me living in a younger state of mind, and these were my friends. I did not feel cold, I did not feel hot, I felt nothing. Just the music playing into my ears, no sweat, no shakes, everything just remained a picture for me to observe.

This type of weather was not created for people to be locked indoors, being an addict, shutting themselves out from a life that is not so hard. Life is what we make it, complaining about it only makes it worse, we're here now so we might as well make the best of it. Stories and tales make the world run a lot smoother, legends and beliefs are what cause conflict. As the world turns we get older submitting to a thing we call time. I always saw beyond the picture, the very nature of how we were created and what we've created is a mystery, and we waste a talent of communication to complain or become something that will eventually be forgotten. Something I cannot stress enough is to just live today like it really is your last, do whatever makes you the happiest.

Doing harsh drugs can be an experience, it most likely can become a problem, and this isn't a hobby to be proud of. It's a waste of time and money. This guy had thrown his life away for his next hit, maybe he did have the thought of paying me back, but I know when the hit was over he would care about the next one.

"He can wait." This is a thought in most people's heads, reality flies by before you realize how much you've missed.

It's a sad sight to see so many people in such a state, but it's what made us stand out. That's all we cared about, a few of us anyways. I noticed some of the others were all about the social perks you get, I saw a lot of fakes. It's the fake people that cause a problem in this sort of world, when it comes down to any deadline or unsuspected situation, they are the failures, and they are the various reasons aside from anything positive. No secrets were kept and they had no true goal. Everything kept in the open for everyone to see.

I figured the best course of action would be to get back in touch with my best friends. Andrew was the first, he and I were exactly the same at heart. Before a lot of this happened we used to make videos and upload them to the Internet, or just sit around and play video games. I missed those days, but we were smarter than to just go back to that life, it would never be the same. Plus, we were enjoying it at the same time. That's the part that always confused me.

I got tired of the music, I might as well have just gone on with my day. Question was, where to start? I started to head over to Andrew's house, before I even crossed the road I could feel my phone vibrating in my pocket. I had seen the number before, but there was no face to it. I wondered if I should pick it up, since I had known the number a little bit, I picked it up.

"Hello?"

"Alex, I didn't know who to call, you have to come quick!"

"Who is this?"

It sounded like somebody my age, could have been Andrew himself, or Sanko, I wasn't sure. It sounded as if they uncovered a dead body or something.

"Just get over, everything's up in flames!"

"Who is this?" I demanded.

"Carmine, it's Carmine!"

"Carmine! Where are you?"

Carmine, the good kid. I hadn't heard from him or his parents since I had moved out from his house. I really truly hoped it wasn't his house that was on fire. They had worked so hard for every little thing in their home. Even the dust that collected on everything had value to them.

"Costa's house! We're all here. He's piss drunk and doesn't even know what's going on!"

"I'll be right there!"

I snapped the phone shut and started running. My pants kept falling down and nearly off, the belt was not tight enough and one of my arms was used to hold them up while I ran. People were watching me run in such a panic over to Costa's. I tried to tighten my pants at the same time running down a street filled with sunshine, while a darker person running to an even darker fire or fate. I prayed that it was his fault for burning down the house and that it wasn't some personal vendetta. Running out of breath wasn't an option. I could have run for the rest of my life. I was comparing my speed to the cars that drove by, I wasn't too far behind.

I found reason to keep running, those deep breaths felt so reviving. The music was gone but I could still hear it, the perfect tune to my situation. As I ran I heard the sirens from Costa's house get louder and louder. A cop was driving behind me with his sirens lit as well. I looked behind me as I slowed down, it was Roy waving his hands at me. I thought he would pick me up but he kept driving on, though his wave only signaled me to hurry. I nodded indicating that I would follow. Everybody was gathered around this giant fire, I could see the black smoke lifting into the sky.

When I got there everybody was surrounding the building throwing any source of water they could find on the burning wreck, buckets of water, Costa's garden hose, probably even spit. I wondered what had caused the fire. It had barely made it to the second floor, and it looked as if the entire building would collapse in no time. A crowd of people were surrounding us just watching, not lifting a finger to help. Costa was nowhere to be found, neither was Carmine. I could only see Tommy and Willie doing whatever they could to put the fire out.

They stood out from everybody else risking their lives getting as close as they were. The flames were growing as if oil was burning underneath. I could feel like the heat and I was standing at least twenty feet away. Nobody was talking and if they were it was a whisper, everyone just watched as somebody's home burn down to the ground. The sirens I heard were only police cars trying to block off the area. The fire trucks had not arrived yet. I'm guessing that's why Costa was nowhere to be seen. Out of the corner or my eye I saw his brother Rant in tears about all of his possessions.

"All my stuff, all of our things!" He cried.

I ran over to him as fast as I could, even still I did not like him.

"Hey! Where's your brother?"

"I don't know," He sobbed. "I don't know." I let him be alone.

The trucks were starting to pull in, everything and everybody was scattered all around the property, I had no idea where to start. It never ended, something new was happening all the time, whether it is good or bad. It would only be a matter of time before something like this would happen to me again, it seemed like history was repeating itself in a small town. The police started to move the crowd back, including me.

"This is my friend's house, he might still be in there!"

"Part of my job is to keep you safe, now please step back."

It sounded like somebody behind me was telling him what to say, play by play from a book. I could easily tell that he did not have a care in the world, his voice was damp and sarcastic. I was shocked, I was mad and I wanted to push this cop out of the way, but there was way too much authority to stop me. All the windows were shattering, everything inside was breaking and cracking, we could all hear it. I couldn't get past the invisible line blocking me, it was best for me to call Carmine back.

"Carmine? Is that you?" He picked up the phone in seconds.

"Yeah it's me."

"Where are you?"

"We had to leave, Costa started puking and the cops were everywhere man."

"How did you guys get out?"

"Easy, we walked right out of there."

"Where did you go?"

"We're over at my place, he's out of it man."

"How did the fire start?"

"You got me there, I have no idea."

"Shit." I could not think of anything myself. "Alright, I'm coming over."

"Alright, the doors unlocked."

The firefighters were doing a good job at putting out the fire, by the time it was out, everything had been destroyed. Costa had lost everything.

CHAPTER XVII

---∞◦❈◦∞---

Repressed Fate

(June 8th - 3 Months left)

Three long silent days passed us since the fire happened. Everything was about Costa, every ten seconds I heard another story about him. I was getting sick and tired of it. Apparently he used to be some sort of psycho and always loved his cocaine, he made a lot of money from it. He didn't have to sell it anymore, or be a muscle to anybody. He made a name for himself over the years, things were all starting to tie together. The way I understood it, was that some people hated him, feared him or loved him. I knew a lot of girls that wanted him bad, maybe for the money, maybe for the attitude, or his past. The first couple of days I met him, he seemed sober and legit, but now all he did was drink himself to sleep and if he wasn't sleeping he was high on coke. The town with no name had all its stories, and you could not pick or choose which ones to believe.

We found ourselves sitting in my living room, myself, Tommy and Carmine. We seemed bored because of how quiet the three of us were. Something was different, our friendships grew stronger the less we cared about the fire. Costa was turning into our enemy, and it trapped us. We believed because of the fire that we should feel that bit of sorrow for him, but even he didn't care. The day of the fire I saw him with Carmine laughing like he had wanted this to happen.

"Carmine, run this by me again, how did that fire start?" Tommy asked.

"I've told you both a million times, I don't know."

"Insurance fraud?" I wondered.

"He doesn't need the money."

"That's true."

"It must have been an accident."

By then, none of us had cared anymore. We were being separated with no idea where Costa was. We all pictured that he was out having the time of his life without a care in the world. I was sitting on my couch with my knee bouncing constantly. It seemed that destiny, karma and fate had become distorted. I never believed in destiny, but I always had faith in an ultimate fate. All I wanted to know was what was mine, and if anybody like Costa was going to steal it. Karma came into the picture because I wondered if that's what configures your fate, I had to find him.

I heard a knock on my door, before answering it I asked from the couch. "Who is it?" I sounded angry.

"It's Willie!"

"Come in."

He came through the door and took his shoes off in some sort of excitement, or like he was in a hurry.

"What's up guys?" We all had simple responses.

"Listen to this," he took his wallet out and threw it on the table and made himself comfortable right next to me.

"Costa's already has a new place down on Main Street, he can move in tomorrow."

"It's been three days since the fire, who can move that fast?" Tommy asked and looked demanding.

"Probably his dad," "anyways, he wants to throw a party."

I could not even bare the word party, it never stopped. It's fun to party sometimes, especially when you've done something to pat yourself on the back for. Parties over and over again get boring very fast, it's always the same people, same drama, same stories, and same regrets. It made me sick thinking about whiskey and cocaine, and I just started to get mad. I sat up a little bit and stretched my back and got everyone's attention.

"You guys aren't going to go are you?" I said as I started to vent.

"Might as well." Tommy shrugged.

"Fuck that." Sitting back in my lazy state.

"What's the matter with you?"

"I'm just stressed out man, so many things have gone wrong."

"Like what?" Willie giving me an attitude.

"That's a pretty stupid question, just forget it."

"No, I want to hear it, after what we've done for you."

I was very thankful for the apartment and the money but the memories were not worth it. I was too weak hearted to be doing this all the time.

"Ever since that damn party, remember?"

"Which one?"

"It was months ago, Sanko almost died."

"I remember, go on." He was not making this easy, he was getting cocky with me trying to get on my last nerve.

"I got you out of there in one piece remember that?" He yelled.

"Well maybe you shouldn't have! Ever since that night I've stolen a car, I fucking shot somebody! I've been shot and I lost the love of my life!"

"Welcome to life Alex! Join the fucking club!"

"This is not life!" I cut him off and yelled over top of his voice. "Kids should not be holding guns to each other's heads!"

I could have sworn that if a couple of more seconds had gone by, Willie and I would have gotten into a fight, but Tommy started to yell over the both of us.

"That's enough! Alex we're out of here, go and clear you're fucking head!"

Carmine just walked and stayed as quiet as me, he was calm while I was pumped to start hitting someone, soon they left, and I was all alone in the house. I thought about their laughs, all of them. I needed to get out of the house. I felt like I could not function properly. Something was blocking me from finding an answer, I could not be myself anymore because I had no idea who that person was. Everything was staged and presented in front of me, right down to what to say and how to say it. I knew how to be everybody else and I knew how to think, but the words and actions of me would not come out.

"I need to watch a movie or something." There wasn't a chance in hell I could sit through an entire movie, calm and stable.

I was a different person, Costa was not the only person that changed. These months had flown by as I went from somebody that never got out, to somebody that can stay in. Most of my friends used to write things into my journals and agendas, all the girls used to write things like 'stay golden' or 'you rock, don't ever change'. I missed that, because now I wasn't anybody with a trait other than how to come up with a few easy bucks. Things could have been worse, a lot worse, and I knew this, but it's the fact that our problems are raised with us and everybody in the world gets stressed out at some point.

I felt like I had nothing, Costa lost a lot of things in the fire, but he did not lose himself. Something had to be done to stop this. I had to stand up and fight for something that I truly believed in now. I had written half of a good novel and people said I was a decent writer, maybe that was my calling. I decided to get down my hateful feelings on paper.

Once I started I did not stop. Anything that came to mind I wrote down. A couple of weeks had gone by of me shutting everybody out. I boxed myself in the house in hopes that I would become a writer. All my feelings thrown together became a life lesson.

"This is a ruthless story combining true events, the author's own biography, his friends, his family and they're all twisted into one story. It's a strong lesson in the end about not abandoning your moralities and to do what makes you happy as well as your surroundings, because sometimes the fifteen seconds of fame isn't worth it."

This is what my story was about. A true story mixed to let people see things my way, through my eyes and around my head. If I had this dream then I was sure somebody else would too. All I wanted out of life now was one person. Just one person to tell me that my book had changed their life and wanted to thank me for it. All I needed was an ending, a personal outlook giving a beautiful speech to shut everybody up who told me otherwise. I started a website from my home building on the books process, hundreds of e-mails were coming in daily from the eastern side of the world, mostly in Europe.

I was going four to five days at a time wearing a lot of the same clothing and not shaving. My hair was always thick and messy, and I would wear different colored socks. But July fourth was around the corner so I decided to treat myself. I pulled out what was left out of my bank account and headed for the canal. Every summer our town hosted an annual four-day carnival. It was divided all around town, it was beautiful. Once you crossed the main bridge from east to west, the town lit up with people's smiles, lights and laughter. This was the only time of year were cops did not mind you if you were out smoking a joint or having a beer in the middle of the street. This event was so big that people all over the region would come down and the town would be packed. Everywhere you looked there would be t-shirt stands, food stands, beer tents, rides, events, tall ships, boats, the smell of cooked food surrounded you. Bands were playing, every friend was reuniting and that was the best event of them all. Even in the cold winter people looked forward to this, because they knew that everyone bumps into everyone. I could not walk ten feet without somebody calling my name.

"Alex!" I saw Sanko and Andrew walking a large group of people. I wasn't even there five minutes before I had seen them.

"Hey!" I was so happy to see everyone again.

Old friends like Dustin, Annie, Mike, Sharon, Josh, Jamie, Bankes, Eddy, Brock, Kaileigh, Tyler, Ashley, Blackie, Shannon, Danielle, Telise, Melissa, Katrina, Sarah, Eric, Yeti, JJ, Kristin, Joy, Gelok, Sardella, Julian, Justan, Thomas, Taylor, Shawn, Richie, Chris, Chase, Adam, Keenan, Emily, Chad, Ryan, Sean, Andrea, Baird, Benji, Conor, Doug, Jake, Kyle, Keri, Vince, Biller, Elizabeth, Meagan, Kayla, Jocelyn, Erin, Eli and behind all of them, was Chelsea. Like an angel before the choir, it was good to see them again. I loved them all. We all greeted each other like a giant high school reunion, every year we had this. I was the funny one again. I set everything aside, my book, Costa, all of it. Again and again I saw these large groups of friends all calling out to each other. We all went on rides, ate delicious food, bought all kinds of accessories, watched the shows. For once, I could afford the beer for everybody, I bought a few rounds for the ones that were willing to drink, like Brock and Eli.

I had great respect for those two, they had a lot of muscle behind them and a lot of money but they worked hard for it. Brock had done his fair share of stupid things, he was thrown into jail for almost killing somebody, at this exact event one year prior. He really got his act together, as did Eli. Eli is nothing short than a damn genius. He is a bigger guy that loves to drink and fight, but he gets up every day for school and work. was an artist, she had different ways of approaching you, Connor was the amazing drummer and Justin, the only kid our age covered in tattoos. Each and every one of my good friends, that have been there through the thick and thin all had their own traits, ambitions, strengths and uniqueness to them. I felt very blessed to have so many wonderful friends in my life.

I started to realize now that it did not matter about being tough and hanging out with my new friends. I knew now that all of my friends were of equal value, I was no fool to society and believed heavily in myself that I would make the right choices.

I had done my regrets, but I've always told myself, "It's better to regret something you did do then something you didn't do."

I was whole again, and felt that old powerful feeling. I had every type of friend, and I didn't want to climb to the top anymore. My story was being told and I had lived what I could to the fullest. I ran into Tommy and the others in front of the old movie store. It was connected to a pizza shop with a famous back alley where a lot of bad things happened.

Tommy was with all the originals, but I saw some new faces. They all looked somewhat similar, like they were all brothers or something.

"Alex, I thought you died or something." Kenny yelled. That's what it took for Tommy to notice me.

"Oh my god, it is you!" He said.

I wondered what I had missed, I knew they were all still doing whatever they wanted. When I was at home writing, time flew. I was so lost in constantly sitting in front of that computer, I thought maybe a week had gone by, but Tommy reminded me how almost a month had gone by.

"What have you been up to man?"

"I've been writing."

"Your book?"

"Yeah."

"Are you serious?" Tommy was eating his cotton candy talking to me with his mouth full.

Kenny jumped into the conversation, "That baby is gonna make you millions, buddy."

"I wouldn't say millions." Although it was something I wanted to hear.

"Tommy, this kid can write!"

"That's all you've been doing?" He did not seem at all interested.

"Other than eating and pissing, yeah."

"Where the hell is your phone?"

I had forgotten about my phone, my guess was that it was dead just sitting under a stack of papers, either that or I had lost it.

"I kind of forgot I even had the thing."

I started to understand why Tommy seemed a little unhappy. After all he was paying for almost everything I had, and felt unappreciated. Without words we both just let it go and enjoyed the rest of the night. The sounds of the pirate ship blast away for the people entertainment was a sound you could only remember that very same night. Fireworks lit up the street and I had made peace with the ones I thought I had some sort of problem. I thought everything was too good to be true. Almost everyone had a bottle somewhat hidden from the authorities that did not care, like vodka in a water bottle or mixed drinks stashed in a flask. Andrew had a flask from World War II filled with whiskey, which he and I chugged back in a matter of seconds. As much fun as I was having, something still seemed off track. It was like trying to put a name to somebody's face that you can't remember.

Chelsea, my little angel and devil, the voice inside my head. Andrew, my best friend. We would both die taking a bullet for each other. Sanko, my frustration with a smile. My three best friends seemed a bit more distant with every day that went by.

I had to water them like plants. I could sense a lot of things were coming to an end, while a lot of other things were endless. It was a phase, all of it, getting shot, robbing somebody at gun point for a small bag for a bag of pointless narcotics, being betrayed, overdosing, pulling the trigger on somebody I was once terrified of. It was all a game, all a phase that would only remain in the back of my head. I would move on, they would move on, but this was fun and I hated change. I was teaching myself a lot of lessons without even realizing it. Phases came with new faces and situations, like moving to a new school with the same roads and signs.

"Come by tomorrow," He was not angry, but concerned about something.

"I need to talk to you."

"I'll be there first thing in the morning."

Tommy was a good guy, we connected and saw eye to eye to a lot of things now. We were on the same page, and we had the same questions about Costa, and I wondered if that's what he was talking about.

CHAPTER XVIII

—∘∘◦⬦◦∘∘—

Rock Bottom

(July 5th - 2 Months left)

It was an easy day, I was on my way to Tommy's house listening to my music again. It was hotter than hell, I could feel the sweat pour down my face. I always liked the colder weather better, if I was ever tense with stress in intense heat I felt pain. Literal pain, it felt like a million bugs would quickly crawl up my skin scratching their entire way up. It was always a problem I had since I was a little kid, outside wasn't nearly as bad if it happened indoors. I had no idea what it was and the itching only lasted a couple of seconds. I always paced myself and told myself not to scratch it. I was good at hiding it, the pain wasn't severe but I could notice it anytime, anywhere.

The sun beat down on me from the highest point in the sky, it was in the middle of the day and I felt cluttered with all the things I had in my pockets. My wallet, an MP3 player with headphone wires that would catch off my belt, with lighters and a cell phone. It was the weight from all things alone that was pulling my pants down, I could never just walk with my arms swinging back and forth, I was either choosing a different song, pulling my pants back up or texting Tommy that I was on my way. I took the back alleyways to his house or behind where I had met Roy. Seeing that symbol reminded me of how awkward he was, the dirty but clean cop. Where did he come in? I mean, he just made his introduction and I hardly seen him since. He was going to prove a trustworthy ally, I knew that, but when?

With no trees to block the sun I was walking faster than usual. I looked up the road to see how far the distance was and it refused to get any closer. I was in a good mood, but I was in a hurry, and the smell of sweat and fresh green grass was walking with me. It must have been the hottest day of the year, which followed for over a week. It seemed like its own little phase. I spent almost ten straight days at Tommy's house, and every time I thought about what we talked about, I could feel the heat in the background. If we weren't talking about Costa, we were talking about everyone else. The feelings I had about everything coming to an end were shared by Tommy and a few others. We never mentioned it to anybody else, who knows what would be said to who? Only the ones we had great trust for were the ones we talked to.

I had a good idea what Costa must have been thinking, but him constantly drinking and putting that garbage up his nose clouded his mind, he was just becoming a failure to a lot of eyes as he brushed it off and laughed. When he wasn't sipping on his bottle, he was on the phone. Somebody still thought highly of him, probably his father and others. A graceful tension was between us the few times we talked during these days, we sort of stayed out of his business as he returned the favor. Regardless of whether he was going to betray us or just fade away, something still seemed off. No matter how bad my problems could have been, I learned that they can always get much worse.

"I want to move out of this town, start fresh."

"A new beginning?" Tommy asked me.

If such a thing even existed, I thought. One night however, I was walking back home, dried up and used. All of my energy was gone, I had been walking all day and couldn't wait to take a shower. I was back walking by the symbol, I had never taken this way home before, only on the way to where I was going. A white van pulled up to me the same second my foot hit the road to cross. It was Chelsea with bad news. The way the van screeched down the road I could tell.

"Chelsea?"

"Alex, Willie's dead."

So simple to take in, but how could I react? So fast my problems turned into so many more, what was I supposed to think?

"What?" I asked, stunned but amazed in disappointment.

"Yeah, he's dead." She was trying so hard not to cry, but the tears just rolled down her face.

"He's dead?" I yelled but questioned again.

"He got into a car accident," With more news she added. "And Andrew's in the hospital."

"Oh my god, oh my god!"

"I know."

"No!"

We were both upset trying not to mention the comfort for each other, we had no words, no alibi.

"Come here," I said grabbing her shirt, I started to cry. I hugged her so tight on how tragic this was, I saw his life flash in broken pieces in my head. He had died a painful death, he burned and suffered for almost an hour. His death was the result of a drunk driver which had also died. Chelsea had to hear it from the news, she told me that it showed his face, smiling when he was bit younger. Why did bad things happen to good people? Seeing something like that

so unexpected leaves a million questions unanswered. Time
was flying by, I zoned out and just stared down at the road.

"When did this happen?"

"Last night." She said.

"Oh my god," What else could I say?

"How bad is Andrew? Is he okay?"

"He has major injuries and he can't wake up. They say
he's going to recover, but we don't know how long."

A death never hits you right away as shocking as it is, it
takes time. The first couple of hours left me speechless, and
I was asking myself why this happened, to all people. I had
even blamed myself. He was a nice person and I felt guilty
for fighting with him a few weeks earlier, he was just trying
to help. He was dead and I was glad to have at least one good
laugh before he died. The funeral was in three days, and the
news spread faster than ever. Everybody knew by the end of
the day, I called numerous people and over half of them said
the same thing I did but cried a lot worse. Kenny thought
I was lying at first, but when he heard my voice again, he
knew right away.

Willie used to be such an angry person, we used to pick
on each other when we were younger. His younger brother,
Dustin used to be my best friend. He was a genius that never
used his head as much as he should have. His family and I
were always close, we went years without talking but every
time we bumped into each other we were excited to see each
other and always found time to talk. Dustin and Willie never
got along, they were constantly fighting and sometimes
I got into the middle of it. The entire family was tough
by default, but Willie always pushed himself to become
stronger in both mind and body. This was so unexpected,
such a nightmare all built up in a matter of seconds. Who
knew where to begin if there even was a beginning, I was

asked by his mother to say a few words during the funeral. She had been taking it rather well but I could see that she was just being strong.

Everything was dull, the days went by quiet and rumors about his death were countless and stupid. Some people had told each other that he was murdered, or that he was the drunk one, or even got as low as to say he deserved every second of pain. It made me sick thinking of how he could not have an open casket. It made me even sicker that people were saying these brutal things about someone they were once nice to. It's all anybody could talk about. I had a dark feeling that one of those guys was Marc, and without a doubt all the little girls at school who just wanted to talk about it. I had never seen for myself, but I heard even Costa was upset, he did not cry but he was sad. I was told that he just took it in too quick to have a reaction and sat in his house alone that day.

We all kept our distance, and I wrote a speech that I was trying to make perfect. The funeral was in another town, Crystal River or something. Steve, the driver I had met months ago was the one driving us today. I was wearing an all-black suit that kept getting hair on it from the seats in the car. I was in the back with Tommy in the front holding a bottle of water with his head up. I could see that he was holding in so much, he just listened to the road go by. The funeral home was packed, people were in line to leave what they could on the casket. I held my own and did not wink a tear.

I felt I had to be strong, Tommy had felt the same way and we all spoke in whispers. Finally came the time for his remembrance. His mother was crying and so was his father, they both spoke at the same time trying to finish each other's sentences, this is when my eyes started to water. I had experienced losing somebody that close, and this time it was a friend and not family. It was funny how they both feel equal in a way. I put my head down with my hands locked behind my back, I blocked what they said, I just thought of all the good times we had. Everybody had said once or twice, "Now there is no way to bring him back." or that he still lived in our hearts.

I hated that, the only shape or form he could still be alive in anybody's heart was by thinking about him. You cannot hear him, you cannot see him. I would never again hear one of his jokes or his good ideas, and that's what broke me. I remembered all of his imperfections that made him perfect.

"A few of his friends would like to say something." The director said. It was painful to see that Andrew could not have been there that day.

Tommy went up first giving a powerful speech about their friendship and how much time they used to spend laughing. Then a girl that looked so familiar went up. It was Melissa, the one from the drug party. I could hear the microphone echo and her hands shaking has she held her speech, instantly I thought of her wearing those clothes she had on that night. She made everybody in the room cry just from her own tears, she could barely finish her sentence. Then, it was my turn.

"Hi, friends and family of William Daniel's, I have known William and his family for over a decade, and I know that he would not want to see us in such agony. His spirit was bright and he always kept his chin up, he could make a rainy day seem like angels descended down to shine the light we all wanted. He always made us laugh, he always made us think twice about something stupid." I froze, I could hear his voice in the back of my head. I sniffed a few times holding back every tear with as much strength that I had. The crowd could see this and felt the same pain.

"He will live on in the best of our memories, in hopes that he taught us all something. He taught me never to care what people think and to enjoy life yourself and whatever it is that makes you happy. He was a story of success and accomplishment, thank you." I could not finish it, my eyes shut themselves and I could feel my face turning red. I turned around holding the upper half of my face just about ready to break down. Somewhere along the lines of his death I felt a lot of guilt. Like what I could have helped prevent some of this? Everywhere I looked I saw pictures of him alive and happy. People were in such a trance watching the same twenty-picture pass by them in a slideshow. I had to leave.

The glass doors leading outside showed people smoking their cigarettes and trying to pick themselves up and get back together. Handshakes of sorrow and hugs of comfort surrounded the entire building. I slowly talked to everybody and told them how sorry I felt for them. I had paid all my respects possible and started to feel numb. I never wanted to think for or about myself again. How could I think for myself when I had no idea what I even wanted for myself? In the end I would figure it out, but I knew I should have stopped thinking about every little thing and just went with what was coming at me. Sometimes I doze so far off that I would daydream for hours, it was as if I was standing in whatever I was thinking about. All of this thinking helped me escape reality, which to me, was the closest thing to being free.

I had no time to think about Andrew's condition. All I knew was that he was hurt bad, a few broken bones and that he wasn't wearing a seatbelt which saved his life. If he had been wearing his belt they both would have burned to death in that wreck. I just wish they both had not worn them.

When I got home I started to rip through every newspaper I had. I had bunch saved up for my fireplace, which I never used. I was looking for more apartment ads outside of town. I had to get out of here. I called numerous people and landlords looking for a new place to live. Eventually they all asked me how I made my income, I told them all I worked in a shoe making warehouse under general laboring. A lot of them turned me down, even when I mentioned that I had already been living on my own. I was still wearing my suit with my shoes off and tie undone, I circled every apartment out of town. I would not be able to do this on my own, no matter how cheap the place was.

I had a lot of opportunities to make some money. One, ask Tommy if he wanted to come with me. Two, rob a bank, or three, get a real job. Logically I wasn't going to rob a bank and finding a job in computers wouldn't be hard if I found the right town. I called Tommy instead and he really liked the idea. It seemed like I had taken the easy way out.

"I think that's a great idea, kid."

"Would you want to move out of here by next month?" I asked.

"I doubt that," he said over the phone. "I want to stay a bit longer anyway."

Plus I had to see Andrew walk out of that hospital in one piece, so I did. It just made sense to keep it together a few more months in this town. I had never grown up here, I wasn't a local. I was an outsider. At some point before a lot of this happened, I felt like I fit in better than people that had been here their entire lives. Other times I knew I was looked down upon for having that bit of a different style and the way I talked. Maybe I wanted to move back home, but

I wanted to go somewhere new where the changes hadn't affected me.

"My head could be all messed up from this funeral."

"I was thinking the same thing." Tommy said.

"Alright, we'll give it some time."

"You okay, kid?"

It took me a second. "I don't know."

"You'll figure it out, we all go through it sometimes."

"I know."

Sometimes you have to go through hell in life to be happy and realize what you could be missing and not just get used to having everything handed to you. It goes in line with a quote, "You don't know what you've lost until it's gone." I'm sure we've all heard it. It's true though, time heals and kills all, change can be good and it can be bad. Life is what we make it, I've said countless times. I could not allow little things to get to me anymore I wanted to start enjoying life. I could see the people I loved being proud of me for some of my talents. My mom and Meghan, they must have missed me so much, I was the first person to ever get up and leave in a heartbeat and never come back begging for forgiveness. They watched me turn into this horrible monster, all for greed, money and for a story to tell.

This story was not worth it. I watched my favorite people all turn their backs on me. Not out of hatred or fear, but because I pushed them away, I pushed them too far. My sister yelled at me once, around the time I moved into this apartment.

"You are not the same person anymore, you're impossible to talk to, Alex!"

"I have not changed!" the fact that I was yelling at her at all should have been enough for me to notice.

"You used to be such a good person."

I shut her out believing it was small fight when I should have taken that in and swallowed my pride. I still was a good person, but I used to never care about what anybody thought of me. I knew that if I told myself this I could redeem myself. Instead of thinking it over and over again, I started to talk to myself. I walked between my living room and dining room arguing my own facts.

"If I know this, why can't I change this?"

Nobody in the world can help what they love or hate, but they can tell themselves otherwise and bury these thoughts until they come back. Strong willed people might be able to say otherwise, but somewhere in their head they know better.

"I'm still a nice person, I can still write."

"I know my regrets, we all live through them, and this is mine."

It was time for me to get this book off the ground and find a publisher who would take professional care of it. It was time for me to figure out some life goals before I ended up just another person struggling through life waiting for the next dime. It was time for me to become part of my family again, and put together all the lost pieces that I've missed these last couple of months. It has been the same thing over again, I was telling myself I loved every second of the power and social perks.

I came up with all these random facts about myself, both negative and positive. I was not having an epiphany, it was just reality. I started to feel more human instead of cartoon.

A new beginning does not exist. I called mine the next best thing. An awakening.

CHAPTER XIX

My Awakening

(Friday Morning, September 4th)

It was almost a month later and I got my first phone call from Andrew. He was in such better shape and they allowed him to make phone calls. Both of his arms were a little bit broken along with his knees and upper chest. A piece of his nose and his right ear were ripped off from sliding on the concrete. He was not wearing a seatbelt and flew right through the windshield when the car smashed into them. I asked him a million questions about what it was like, but he did not remember. He was drunk and unconscious. Now he was nearly healed up and ready to get out of the hospital and very excited.

Tommy had finally found the perfect place for the both of us. It was available for us in October first about an hour from this town. August flew by like nothing. The only main event was near the end of it. Costa had called us all like he used to months ago, and told us all to meet at his house. He had this over brilliant idea to steal us all a bunch of money, well a lot of things really. Apparently this guy who owed Costa and Tommy a lot of money just opened up his own pawnshop, which also had a lot of our lost possessions. With this new mood I was in, I almost refused. I figured Costa's talking was a waste of my time, but Tommy was fooled and brought me into it.

The back door was weak and this war was coming to an end. He was a thief that had been stealing from Tommy, Costa, Andrew, and Sanko, even the others like Marc and turned his back on Shawn for a bag of coke.

"This guy is a piece of shit, Alex. He deserves it." Tommy said.

Finally on the last day of August, he broke me. I agreed to do it because we could the extra cash at our new apartment. It seemed way too easy, the back door was weak enough to be kicked open with one good force. Everyone and I mean everyone was convinced that this plan was going to work, even I was. Costa seemed legit again, he was shaving every day, not drinking as much, and he was nicer to the whole lot of us. He even made me laugh a couple of times. Something about this seemed too good to be true, we were stealing gold, silver and electronics that could easily be sold and we would all get a cut of the profit. The fact that we were stealing from somebody that had reputation as low as dirt made me wonder how he could have opened his own shop.

The same trucks we used before were going to be coming with us and he had to get in fast. A lot of things were still on the shelves and were just waiting to be ripped down for them. There were TV's, DVD players, watches, rings, diamonds, guitars, mixers, rare trading cards, just the usual things. I did not want to do it, but I might as well. One last job then I would take it easy until moving day. My sense of everything coming to an end was getting stronger as the days went by. There was no game plan but to wait on a phone call to meet at Costa's house, he did not live too far from the target.

I pictured a person walking or driving down a street of your run down town. This person sees a group of teenagers meeting outside of a bar, a bar he or she has heard endless stories about. It was said to be coke central, drama heaven. Normally you'd think it these kids had nothing better to do, but the adults leave the bar had given them friendship and allowed them all to join them in their vehicles. Right away this person should know that something was not right. And one of these kids was me.

"Now that most knowledge is known, the beginning has become the end as the end was the beginning."

It was now early in September and I was in the worst state of my mind than I had ever been in. The stress was overwhelming. All I could think about, all any of us could think about was Willie. We all missed him so much, and it was hard to focus. Costa's house phone was ringing off the hook and everybody was sitting on the edge of their seats, because that night was supposed to be the end for everything. We were reviewing what exactly had to be done and made sure that we had everything planned right. Ritz Sanko, sitting next to me was one of them he passed me a cigarette. I couldn't recognize all the people there exactly. All the new faces crowding in the same small room Costa had called his new home. I kept my head down in anger, because I didn't trust a single one of them. This was a war amongst ourselves now, I had learned to hate half of them. I couldn't stop observing all of them, my eyes wondered the room as it filled with smoke and the ashtrays were filled with half put out cigarettes, everybody was fidgeting with something and there was tension in the air. I remember Kenny not acting like himself either, which wasn't like him at all, he had a lot on his mind He was quiet for the first time.

"Kid if you mess this up, we will all deny we had anything to do with you, and you'll be on your own." How reassuring, Costa.

I kept my mouth shut. "You're late." Costa mumbled under his breath to Chelsea as she walked into the room.

"I didn't get the missed call notification until after I left the hospital, relax." She replied taking her coat and bag off. The hospital provided no service to her cell phone.

"You knew tonight was important, it better not be because of you, Alex fucks this whole thing up."

"What the hell is that supposed to mean?" She asked. Wondering why I was the one to blame. The night was as young as me and I was already getting angry.

"Hey wait a second!" I finally yelled. "Why is this all on me? You're the one sending us to do your fuckin' dirty work! I don't know why you can't just do this yourself." I had to step in and say something, we had all been fighting for almost a month and Costa didn't like it too much when any of us spoke above him. He was spoiled, stubborn and unrealistic when it came to reasoning with him.

He and his big bugged eyed brother, Rant, gave me a real long dirty look, but finally his look became a smile and he started laughing. His face rearranging and molding into the demon he truly was.

"You're hilarious kid, just last year you were all hopped up and ready to do anything I said, then I say something a little harsh to this bitch you love so much and you try to make a stand?"

"Hey!" Sanko yelled, cutting him off before he could say anything more and create disaster in this small room.

"That's enough! Let's do what we came here to do, shut up and sit down!" He screamed.

"Aren't you always the peace keeper, eh Ritz?" He sarcastically mentioned without evening looking at him.

Nobody spoke for a second. Costa sat down and picked up a deck of cards, and his way to blow off some steam, he snapped them all over the floor. His attitude was intended for his own perfection, in his mind anything he did would never be judged or mocked. He was so full of himself. He had always been a little odd, but tonight, he couldn't sit still to save his own life.

"Okay I'm sorry. So Chelsea, why were you at the hospital?" He said without a care in the world.

"You forget that Andrew was in there? I went to go see him, but they told me his visiting hours were up and I had to leave," She started to dig threw her purse and pulled out something for him. "But I did find this in the gift shop for him."

She smiled and threw a book on the table and I grabbed it and looked at the title. It was a book about World War II, if anything could cheer him up it was anything concerning any war in history. He was a military fanatic, he was a solider and he would have loved to have gotten his hands on that book. I looked at Chelsea remembering how big of a heart she had. I could also see that she was hiding behind her fear. For the first time in her life, Chelsea was scared.

That feeling I had earlier didn't get any easier, my heart started pounding and I began to feel sick to my stomach, and nervous like the time Tommy and I stole that car. "Well, are you guys ready to go, or what?" Costa asked.

I just wanted to get it over with so I got up with Sanko, Chelsea and Kenny not saying a word and headed straight for the door, Kenny stopped us and gave me a sheet of paper that was folded up with fancy handwriting all over it, without Costa noticing. He shook my hand and said "Don't forget about old Kenny Pollock when that book of yours gets published, eh?"

I snuck the piece of paper in my coat pocket. "I won't, but I thought you were coming with us?"

"Oh, I'll be around watching you guys in case something happens. Don't worry Alex, I got your back."

"You always did, and it's good to know." By then Costa felt like he had to step in and push me and the others out the door and very bluntly said, "I'll call Carmine and let him know your leaving now." While slamming the door.

"What a fucking jerk that guy! God, I can't stand him." Chelsea snapped.

"I think he's just nervous about all this."

"Yeah well, maybe he should do it himself. He's has a lot of nerve yelling at me like that." She walked away muttering something else about him I couldn't hear.

Like always, I was the optimist and tried to defend him, and that made me wonder what would have happened if I had never met Costa, and how different things would be. We all had lots of money now, we all had the right people behind us, but also a whole new list of problems. Because with Costa as a broken leader everything was falling apart, it seemed like the only thing holding everything together was us, we were loyal and gave hope that no matter how bad things were, there were still people that cared. We kept this dying town alive. My phone began to ring. It was Andrew. "Hey you better not be doing that shit without me! I'm on my way!" He said. Chelsea ripped the phone out of my hand relieved to hear his voice. "I was just at the hospital! Where are you?"

"I'm on my way to the place, where are you guys?"

"Were heading the same way, can we meet you there?" She asked.

"Yeah but wait a second, did you just leave Costa's?"

"Yeah we did, we're just outside his place."

"Alright wait there! I'll be there in a few, put Alex back on."

Chelsea put her hand over the phone and turned to me, "He wants us to wait here, and he wants to talk to you." Sanko looked at Chelsea and almost started laughing, "Then give him the damn phone!"

Chelsea handed me the phone, and started arguing with Ritz in the background. "Yeah were gonna wait for you, aren't you supposed to be in a nice warm hospital bed anyways? We heard you were in and out of consciences."

"Fuck that shit, I ran right out of there, so they're probably looking for me, but shit I have to go. I'm on a payphone, and I'm still in my hospital pants and this fuckin' store clerk is looking right at me." Andrew arrogantly yelled, probably pointing right in his direction. Andrew was the kind of person that would fight anybody at any time.

I felt a little better knowing my best friend was on his way. "You sure you're up for this?"

"Damn straight I am, and I know you need my help anyways."

"Alright we'll meet you down the road from Costa's place, and after all this, we're all gonna talk."

"Alright, I'll see you there!" He slammed the phone down.

When he hung up, for some reason I kept the phone by my ear and I felt even weaker than before, I had realized that what we were doing was dangerous and one of us could seriously get hurt, or even die. I kept telling myself that after that night, we would all move on and forward from all of this. Enough was enough, and I was sick of being frustrated all the time.

Chelsea could see that something was wrong and asked me.

"What's the matter?" She looked concerned. Her eyes wandered into mine.

It had hit me then. It didn't matter anymore about the money, or the names we had made for ourselves, it all had to end sometime, and I knew it was going to be in the same night that I realized all of this, how ironic.

I shook it off like a bad gut feeling, and put the phone back in my pocket figuring I had one more chance.

"Nothing, but a lot has changed lately, hasn't it?" I had to ask to buy myself some confidence, but if I knew Chelsea, she was going to react the same way as me. She went quiet for a second then just simply told me, "Yeah, it has." Despite her social strength, she had a heart softer than mine.

We both looked at Sanko but he didn't care, his thing was always about money. He was distracted and eager to go, probably counting all the money in his head. The moment ended and the both of us stepped back into reality, ready for the worst. "I am going to rob this fucking place blind!" Sanko screamed in excitement.

Kenny's letter was still taunting me in my coat pocket as we walked down the street to meet Andrew. I wanted to read it. I quickly unfolded it and could not believe my eyes. It was a letter from one of the biggest publishing companies in Canada. They had heard about the book over the Internet and had to get their hands on it. They had offered me three great packages if I submitted to them a full copy of the manuscript. It was attached with phone numbers, e-mail addresses, fax numbers and location. The beginning of the letter was hand written by Susan Mercury. It was a note that clearly followed the rules but she had some personal reflections on what she read alone from my website.

"I can see that you are a talented student to society and you deserve the best."

I could see her face and hear her voice, like I had met this person before. Kenny must have had his parents do this,

his father was a lawyer and his mother traveled the world meeting all sorts of interesting people. I owed him a lot. I got a little caught up in the moment daydreaming in the darkest of nights. Andrew met up with us faster than ever still in wearing every piece of medical equipment. Bandages and cut off wires, he was covered in stitches and bruises. This would have been his first time doing this, he was more excited than nervous, he seemed to have lived for this. Something to reflect his love for the military, I was sure.

"Man, is it ever good to see you!" Sanko yelled, lifting his arm for some sort of high-five handshake thing. A few seconds later Carmine had met up with us and he was puffing on his cigarette constantly. He tried to act tougher, but we could all see that he was terrified. This was never his thing, he spent a lot of time in front of a computer. Around the corner from the shop we all met in a circle all looking into each other's eyes with what I felt, a bad feeling. The trucks were nowhere to be found, neither was Tommy.

"Where the hell is everyone?"

"We just got here, hold on." Carmine said. It didn't even seem like he had put the cigarette down from his lips.

"Andrew, are you sure you're okay?"

"I'm fine, what about you Chelsea?"

"Nervous, but how can hard can it be?"

"Exactly." I questioned.

Right there, I should have just called it off, but this was of those times I should have been speaking my mind. The others looked at me like I was going to do so, but instead I walked to the back door that looked almost brand new, but weak at the same time. I was too busy thinking about a reason that I did not come across a possibility. Something was trying to tell me that everything was about to go wrong. Our bodies were designed to run away, but that little bit of greed took over. Against what was right, I saw money and a new home away from this dump.

"Fuck this." I walked to the door with anger in my steps.

The door was weaker than I had thought, it only took a few good tugs to open the door. I had to put my foot up against the brick so I could get the door open. It was dark inside, without a flashlight or anything to give us the advantage we still went forward.

"Come on, the door's open."

The stones kicked up as we all looked over each other's shoulders. I checked my pockets for a lighter or something for any bit of light. My cell phone had proven useful one more time, I flipped it open and turned it over to at least see what was in front of me.

"Carmine, use your lighter." I whispered.

We were breaking the rules we had created, we should have just waited for everybody to arrive, and if they didn't we could just leave. The floor looked like it was covered in a dark dust. It smelt old, and we should have done some research about this place. There was no money to be made here. The shelves were covered in cobwebs and rotten wood. The place seemed haunted, and it had a very unwelcoming surrounding to it.

"I think we have the wrong building." Chelsea said.

"This is the right building." I said.

"You sound sure."

"There aren't a lot of back doors that come off so easy."

I heard something fall over a few feet in front of me, but the faded light could not reach what I was trying see. We all jumped and could feel that somebody else was in here. We started to get scared. The draft in the weak walls kept blowing out Carmine's lighter, we had no hope to see what was about to happen.

"I think we better leave."

"I'm calling Tommy." I said.

I turned the phone back into my face blinding the rest of us to see anything. They all gathered around me to see dialing Tommy's number. Quicker than ever we heard two footsteps run up to us and smack the phone out of my hand. I was punched in the cheek bone by somebody that was clearly twice my size and three people started pounding on all of us, even Chelsea.

"Guys, what the hell?!"

"Get them!"

"You dumb pieces of shit!"

I heard countless voices yelling. We were defenseless and my phone had been stomped, I fell to the ground and got jumped on with it.

"No, wait, please!" We were all screaming for help and trying our best to fight back, but it was useless. They had boxing techniques, and could run faster than us. Who the hell were they? What the hell was going on?

"Wait! Wait!" I cried.

I head Chelsea's voice cry in pain, and Andrew grunt from the scars being pushed in. These guys were real psychos. They used everything they could find and whatever they had brought with them, pipes, chains, knives. They were trying to kill us! They were going to beat us to death. Every time I tried to get up, a hard slam would hit me back to the ground. I busted my chin on the hard floor. I could feel blood pouring down my face and arms, and more blood being sprayed from the others. I was being grabbed by the collar of my ripped shirt and slammed up and down onto the floor. I had my hands wrapped around one of his arms, they were gigantic. Every time I hit the ground I groaned out loud to them. No mercy from these mercenaries. We were setup, they were there waiting for us. This was the starting line from Costa the drunk's horrible betrayal.

"Chelsea, Sanko! Carmine! Andrew!" I yelled.

"Shut the fuck up!" A deep voice screamed.

"Fuck you!"

"My stomach." A sick voice that sounded like Sanko said.

A riot had started in here, we were the windows that rocks flew through. We did not stand any chance at all. I thought I was dead. After so many kicks and punches driving into me, I just stopped reacting. The voices of my innocent friends drove into my skull and hurt more than any of the physical damage. I hated the cries and I will never forget them. Andrew had landed a few good swings with a crowbar he had found but it only caused the fighters to beat him harder. Finally he was the last one to go down and we all just took the beating. This was unreal, impossible.

A few ribs had been broken, our lips had all been scraped off the dirty floor and the vicious weapons had badly bruised us or broke some bones. My eyes were wide open looking into the darkness only for my ears to tell me where we all were. We were all breathing deep lying in thin, wet blood with our spit and tears.

"Why, why are you doing this?" I asked, muffled and mumbled.

"Shut up! Shut the fuck up you stupid little fuck!" A familiar voice said.

He pulled out a gun. I heard the one tell him not to fire but he let out five or six shots connecting one into Carmine's arm and another into Sanko's lower back. They had both let out a brutal, terrifying scream that nobody could mistake for death. We were dying and they were finally finished.

"I smell gas, I smell a lot of gas." Chelsea whimpered.

"Chelsea, Chelsea?" I could hear her crying close by. I stuck my arm out to feel her.

The pain was a drug, we had no time to reason with what we were barely saying. My eyes did not move or blink. I focused on where her voice was coming from. I could smell the gas too. They lit the entire building on fire. It lit up in flames and it finally gave us the light we needed. The men were nowhere to be found but we were trapped in a burning building. The smoke damage quickly found its way into our lungs. Coughing was painful and I closed my eyes trying to block it out, when I opened them I could see Chelsea lying in front of me on her side. She looking down at her cuts, she had taken the knife pretty deep. Her legs were all cut up, along with her ribs and it looked like she took a kick right to her face. She and Sanko were not reacting to the smoke, they were nearly dead and were going to accept the hands of death to take them away from me.

Over the old wood crackling I had could sirens coming closer, the gunfire or our screams must have caught their attention long before the fire was sparked. This would be the bust they needed. They would have all found a way to make it seem like we had done this ourselves. We had to get up.

"Get up, get up!" I yelled out loud.

Even I couldn't move. Then I saw Andrew giving it everything he had to stand up. The cracking of our bones matched the old wood. Our reactions were stained into the blood puddles. A boost of adrenaline came through my mind and told me to 'just do it'. An invisible weight stood on my back weighing me down and I struggled to pick myself up. My arms were done for and my head felt like a brick of cement.

"I'm going to get that son of a bitch." I thought.

"I'm going to get that son of a bitch!" I yelled.

A ruthless death by a ruthless drunk? I did not think so.

"Come on, were getting out of here!" Limping to help everyone up, Andrew and I got everyone's attention. We were careful, working as a team being patient. The flames were growing closer and we were running out of time, but hurrying would only cause more worthless pain. With no words being spoken as we lifted and dragged each other out to the fresh air that gave us the edge we needed. We were crying with only a couple tears each rolling down our faces. In a matter of seconds everything had changed, the building was up in flames and people were gathering around the front, we could hear them and we limped down the old train track path that led all through town. Once you got about forty feet in, trees and bushes surrounded you and we had to make a quicker escape.

We were ripping each other's shirts and sweaters to wrap around the cuts and gunshot wounds while we were still running. Every step hurt with the repeating pain. I tried to step differently, a different pattern while holding two of my best friends. We were all holding each other one way or another supporting our wounds and picking each other up every time we fell. We were running for our lives, away from cops, or the guys that would finish us off if they found us.

"I got fucking shot! I'm bleeding, I don't want to die!"

"You're not going to die," Carmine said. "We better stay in these trails until morning."

"They broke my god damn phone, it was Costa!" I yelled again, "It was Costa!"

"Costa betrayed us, where the hell is everybody?"

"Did they all know? Were they all going to just leave us in there?"

"I don't know."

What happened to Tommy? What happened to Kenny, the trucks, everyone that was supposed to be there? The entire town was lit up with the event, I could tell.

We had run all through the night and the sun was just coming out. My favorite time of the day just became my worst, the tempting orange sky and the sun rising. The loss of blood was our resignation.

When I hit the ground I felt a feeling of guilt spill through my backbone, I was in a state of emergency and I still didn't know what had happened. I looked back and forth zoning in and out of conversations, dull and memorized by the moment in stillness. Finally my vision focused back along with my hearing, catching the end of the conversation.

"How long you think before they get here?" Sanko asked me out of breath and hardly moving.

"Who?" I was still confused.

"The cops, man." The words were becoming more and more structured.

"I couldn't tell you, but soon, I would think." The second I said that, I knew we had failed, I really thought it was the end for us. I started having faint visions of somebody's dark face kicking me while I was down and us all screaming for help.

"I can hear the sirens coming, man. It's a pretty scary sound if you think about it." He finished.

A brief moment fell between them and me that morning, everything had gone so wrong, the cops were coming and they knew exactly who they were coming for, and why.

My memories were haunting me. I couldn't see straight and my hands were shaking, and we all just sat there, bleeding all over the walls and ground, waiting for a miracle.

"Hey, do you think we can still run?"

"Not a chance." Our wounds were stiffening.

Andrew still had the crowbar he found tightened in his hands hitting his head off the dirty wall we sat against, and was sitting right next to me trying to be tough like always, but when he tried to laugh he started spitting out blood.

"Hey, isn't this that same building?" He asked, referring to something we all knew. I looked behind myself and saw the mark I had spray painted so many months ago, my signature tattooed onto the wall.

"Yeah, it is." I could barely say to Andrew. I was so still surprised to see him but I wish he had stayed in the hospital.

"That's kind of funny man." He finished, he always was a tough one, one year younger than us, but when he wasn't training he made everything a contest and never liked to talk about anything negative. He just liked to have fun. We should have been more like him.

Carmine, who supposed to be on lookout, remained silent. I think he was angry that he had fallen into this trap with us. I felt guilty bringing him into all this because he never liked to be a part of anybody other than us directly. He hated the others, like Costa. He could always see right through him, he was smart, dedicated to school and his knowledge for computers. I wouldn't have blamed him if he was upset with me, but I think he was enraged at Costa, like he knew it was him that set up this little charade. Nothing was making sense, I couldn't remember what had even happened, but it obvious that we didn't do this to each other. It was a giant mystery, but I felt even worse and freaked out at the fact of where we had ended up, this was it. So many thoughts raced through my head at once, a cold feeling shook my hands again. "I never thought we'd end up like this guys, I'm so sorry."

"We came into this with our eyes wide open, Alex. It's not your fault."

The war I had been trying to figure out this entire time, was myself against Costa. He was not the leader of anybody. It was just my belief and stupidity that followed his orders. There are no leaders in this game we played. Only fear tells you to listen to a so-called higher power. That fear as you know it, may not be known until you realize that you told yourself what position he was in. He was a fool, a fool with a lot of money, and money talks. I had nothing to fear but fear itself now, because I now knew that he had lost his mind and would stop at nothing to see me dead.

I heard the sound of a car coming up to the back of the building, it was for sure a cop car. It was the supervisors four door SUV, and without a doubt good old Officer Roy was driving the thing. A miracle in police clothing was here to save us.

"Oh my god you kids, I thought you were left for dead! Quick, get in!" He kept repeating to himself how horrible we looked. The fresh and stained blood mixed with dirt and stonewashed clothes made us look like we just survived an all-out war. He picked us up one by one and dragged us to the truck. He took us to the hospital, giving his detailed report of what he saw. He told the story to the best I could explain on the way. Another officer had found and arrested two of the men that were fleeing the scene while the third got away, that damn familiar voice. The hospital staff remembered Andrew and me right away and took us into the emergency.

The twist to Roy's story was that we had broken into the place for a place to drink that night, when these guys thought it would fun to burn us alive, a pointless attack.

Without question and two of the suspects already arrested, we were free after we were treated in the hospital. Chelsea, Sanko and Carmine all had to spend an extra few days in the hospital while we were released after two nights in intensive care and two full days of recovery. Andrew and I were had to get some stitches, a brace around my stomach, a lot of medication, and I had a small cast on my left arm. Walking was hard and painful, we cracked our necks almost every hour and it was hard to go from standing, to sitting to lying down.

For some unknown reason Tommy knew we were walking out back into the world. He was waiting for us away from his car, happy but disordered. He lifted my spirits by not making us walk all the way home. Somewhere in the fire I had lost my wallet, leaving me no money to call a taxi and without my phone, I could not find anybody's number. I had no idea who I could trust anymore anyway.

"Are you okay?" He asked.

"That's a pretty stupid question." I replied.

"Costa has disappeared."

"Where the hell were you?" Going back to that night and during my entire stay in the hospital.

"I have been trying to find Costa."

"Why in God's name didn't you think that we were being set up?"

"Who the hell could?" He yelled.

"Tommy, we almost died."

"I know that! As soon as we saw the fire from across town I knew it."

"That's bullshit, look at us!"

"I'm sorry! You know I would have helped! I'm so sorry, kid. I did everything I could."

"That coward, he almost got me killed!" Referring to Costa, and believing Tommy.

Andrew sat in silence, while I swore up and down aimlessly at Tommy. I acted like an animal, bouncing back and forth, punching and kicking things. I had run for hours that night wondering if I was going to have to watch one of my friends die. The noise I had created grabbed the attention of the most annoying people. I heard a small crowd of people behind me almost running trying to harass us.

I had shown my beaten face reflecting from the sun, a small white bandage on the top of my head with my eyes squinting. With more pain, I saw a newscast and a few cameras with a reporter asking me all sorts of stupid questions. I was angry at the scars that would be left in and on my head already. These questions did not have my answer.

"What the hell is this?"

"Hey you guys!" A causal voice said.

"What?"

"Could I ask you some questions?"

Tommy hated this. He had walked away to his car, "Come on you two." Without answering his previous question we started to walk away as he kept following us.

"How does it feel to know you're alive?"

"Why were you in there? What drove you to go into that private property?"

We did not answer but he kept on us like a fly.

"Why didn't you go to the authority's right away young man?"

I turned around and looked right into the camera. "I was running for my fucking life! I was found on the ground half-dead!" He didn't even listen to me, he just kept asking more questions. His brown suit and slick hair started to really get on my nerves. Tommy had gotten into his car calling out at us, like he was used to this. We took off leaving the reporter with no story.

I stared out the window as we drove off, thinking of my own questions. There were too many loopholes in our system that I had just started to figure out. People would start asking questions. Our lies and stories would not add up if anybody did the math. Thank God I was leaving this damned town, but I just hoped I got out in time.

Everybody turned out okay and all had their own story of some kind of betrayal. Costa's plan was to shut us all up and get out of here along with his father, a plan from the get-go. When we looked at his facts it all started to make sense, the new faces and new drugs, mad amounts of money mostly being given to him. His mood swings were the number one clue that we all should have taken seriously. Funny how you don't see things this coming until they punch you right in the face.

Eventually, I started to forget the entire dialog we all had. We were mad, angry, and had to get it all out on that traitor. I knew it was better for me to just let it go, pack up my bags and leave, but it was so much harder than that. Every day and every time somebody had brought it up I grew even more furious. The fact that somebody so low was laughing at us just got him what he wanted. We had no idea where he was, what he was doing, or what his plan was.

I thought it was my stupidity that would allow him to make his move and I did not need to take matters into my own hands. One night I was walking home when I saw him driving with Marc, I was two houses down from mine getting out my keys when I saw a familiar car way up the road speeding. It blew past me without a single look from either one of them, they were talking and I know for a fact it was the two of them.

Something inside me snapped, I became something new. The phase I had been through helped me adapt to this odd culture. I was losing my temper at almost every corner. I saw those two drive by without a care in the world, I didn't say anything, but my mind was racing. I stomped up my stairs not caring about the week old wounds and bruises. I could feel them bounce in and out of place, seven months of pain had been coming and rushing through my veins. I wanted to kill that son of a bitch.

The more I thought about it the more I realized it must have been Marc, he was the one that was kicking us while we were down, shot at us and lit the damn lighter! How could somebody live in such disarray? It's pathetic. I don't care if you have a billion dollars, that is just sad. Betrayed by people I looked up to, I felt untrue to myself, I thought I knew better. With no phone to call anybody I walked back and forth yelling at myself and trying to put this mess together.

I hoped and prayed that anybody would pull up to my house, I wanted to chase down Costa. I had to suck it up, and hardly slept that night. I thought listening to my music would help me, but every time I saw car go by or heard an odd thump I had to pause it and listen a little more. I sat up realizing I was alone, listening for a knock on the door, the air stood stiff and I mouth was open, and nothing else happened.

When I woke up the next morning I saw that it was a beautiful new day. It was hot, and I had finally heard that knock I waited all night for. I ran to the door still in my underwear with my hair a mess, it was Tommy.

"You look like shit." Before I could get a word in.

"I just woke up."

"You're bandage is gone."

"What?" It must have fallen off when I was sleeping.

He came in and made himself at home while I went into the bathroom to get ready. I didn't want to take the time to have a complete shower. It hurt enough getting soap in the cuts and wasted too much time. He was yelling from my living room as I washed my hair in the sink.

"So I drove around for long time last night."

"The hell were you doing, you should have come here!"

"Why?" the water was running next to my ear so I couldn't hear him.

"What?"

"I said, why?"

"I saw Costa last night, and you'll never believe who I saw him with."

"That's what I wanted to talk about."

"What?"

"I said that's what I wanted to talk to you about!"

"Man! I can't hear you!" I yelled from the bathroom door.

I could hear his footsteps coming toward me. I didn't even rinse out my hair yet. I was dripping like I had just gotten out of a pool.

"He's still in town, he's hiding." He said simply, leaning against the frame.

I went back to the sink and finished putting on another shirt, drying my head off.

"Where is he?" I asked.

"I don't know."

"How do you know he's here?" He scratched his nose not knowing what to say.

"I'd rather not say." He said with a funny smile.

"I don't even want to know."

"Who did you see him with?"

"Him and Marc drove past me last night."

"Did they see you?" He seemed shocked.

"No, but I know Marc was one of the guys that did this." Pointing to the cut on my head.

I finished drying my hands off on the towel and just stood there looking at Tommy. We were normal, casual, somewhere in both our hearts we knew we had to save the anger for when we saw him. We had to find him tonight.

Tonight, we seek our revenge.

CHAPTER XX

—ooo◦❖◦ooo—

A Man and His Bottle

(September 14th, - Less than 24 hours left)

Everyone had stayed outside today because of its nice weather, but at the same time they were moving trying to figure out where Costa had gone to hide. A lot of people talked about killing him. With everyone Tommy and I had run into, we heard nothing except how much they wanted to get their hands on him. He had become our target, and I seemed to be getting a lot more respect from people than I ever had before. Although a lot of them were blaming each other and a lot of trust was lost, the group of us that were in the fire was put aside because without a doubt we were not traitors. They knew I was weak, and just followed what I was told to do. They could see that I was getting stronger and knew how to play the game. The book I was writing got noticed and the few that read it said they could not wait until it was finished. This alone had a lot to do with my trust, but as much as I was happy the day was hot and long.

I could smell normal families having barbeques, or washing their cars. I watched kids go swimming as their summer had ended. Costa would only be a fool to show his face today. All my new and old friends were scattered all through town, all outside with many cell phones ready to call everybody if they saw the two faced mess. It was as if a small army was patrolling the streets waiting for the enemy.

I was walking in a friend's backyard while everyone was enjoying a fire and a late lunch. In the background I heard one of my favorite bands playing so it lifted my spirits. Somebody had offered me a beer and I passed on it considering I knew tonight I would find Costa. They all looked more like Tommy's fathers friends. I had no idea where I was, but I fit in.

It was very strange how everything started to connect, as much as the day dreaded on like a nightmare. This is what my awakening had become, another phase. I was bonding with these people, I was relating to my own stories now and made some of them laugh. They liked what I had to say, they even asked questions about my book. They had heard about what happened and why we were looking for Costa and they gave me their input.

"No honor in that guy, he deserves to get shot." These guys were the exact same as us when we were younger, whatever they had to say was worth listening to. They were professionally retired, while still doing something on the side to make ends meet.

Their names will never be mentioned, only but their appearance might be visible. The five of them were all stocky and they must have been in there forties. They've all bonded since they were kids, and told me stories about recent and past events. They taught me that somewhere any story is worth telling.

When Tommy and I began mine, I talked and talked and talked, time flew by as I explained this very story. The more I talked the more I started to realize that I never had to worry. It was good to be concerned. People all around the world are doing things of greater fear. I even said that it was better to talk and get it out than to bottle it all up inside, thinking too much would have killed me, or at least drove me insane.

While I was here having this conversation, I later found out what my friends had been up to. Chelsea had finally been released out of the hospital and doing some research on where to find the drunken traitor. Sanko of course, didn't have a care in the world, he was still alive and he just went home most likely to smoke himself stupid.

Andrew had teamed up with Chelsea and went everywhere telling everybody about his or her side of the fire. Some people took it very seriously considering the size of Chelsea and how bad she was beaten. Chelsea had known some of these people before I even knew they existed. She had a lot more people on the lookout now. She was always so much more dedicated and determined when she set her mind on something.

We all had our own endings to the same story, Andrew's being that he eventually found happiness in a girl. Again, these names will never be mentioned but she was a friend with one of the girls from Costa's drug party, Nadine or Melissa. To be honest I was kind of jealous, but I was proud. A little known secret about why Andrew is quiet is because his last girlfriend was his first, and she ripped his heart right from his chest and played a lot of games with it.

We were all working together to find our worst enemy, all to ask why he sold us out. The three of us had become a small crew. I loved Sanko and Carmine as brothers, but Chelsea, Andrew and I were a good team. Andrew and I always knew that he was always a better muscle, while I was the one with all the answers now. Chelsea was the good-looking temptress that could fool anybody and had her own ways to get any sort of information. A lot had changed, but it was time to stop dwelling in the past. The tables had turned, but we were accepted and gained all the respect I had wanted from the beginning. Now, I was used to it.

We all had our traits, our perks and different style. Today too much anger was around making it impossible to hide somebody's true self and words. I went everywhere in town today. I was so eager to find him after I heard the good news from Chelsea getting out of the hospital that Tommy and I must have driven past his house over ten times, waiting to see some kind of movement. We checked all the windows and walked around the property the first time, and then we just stayed close surrounding the block for a good hour.

I never felt doing something so repetitive would keep me focused. Normally I would be bored and would have given up. Something in-between the anger, the tears, the frustration, between my smiles and just everything that had happened, I just wanted it to end.

"It may take a long time, but if you keep at it, there is an ending."

My feet hurt but I still wanted to keep looking. Suddenly our beautiful day turned gray, it made the day end much quicker. In the evening it grew colder and I had only grabbed a t-shirt, the few drops all over the sidewalks made it obvious that I should go home and grab a sweater. I figured I'd keep on the lookout as long as I could. Keeping both my arms sheltered in my t-shirt, rubbing both arms for some kind of heat. Finally it was close to eleven when I had given up, I went home.

"I'm gonna come and pick you up tomorrow morning, he's around somewhere." Tommy said.

"Chelsea might be able to come up with something, tomorrow is a new day." I calmly shut the door walking up to my steps.

Tommy had left with a bad feeling, I could see it in his eyes, my heart felt like something was wrong. It must have been nothing because there was no answer, I must have just been tired. All the lights were off in my house and I walked up to the front door as it started to pour rain all over the streets. I looked up and laughed a little seeing my front porch's roof.

Thinking it was Tommy turning around, I heard a car screech down my road. I walked back to the steps looking over the black railing to see Costa speeding down my road again. This time I had to make sure he saw me. I walked into the rain holding my key chain tightened in my hand. He flew by me, again not noticing. Within the second I saw him I could tell he was high on his favorite drug.

"Costa! Costa!" I screamed. My neighbors must have heard me.

I ran down that road with my feet griping on the pavement. My steps pushed me a little further as I kept screaming. I got nervous when he slammed on the breaks, but something else came over me, where I knew I could at least protect myself. After all that he had done, I must have had the upper hand.

The bright red lights signaling his complete stop shined off the dark road. Rain was coming down pretty hard and I was already soaked. He stayed in the car for a second but I knew it was him. I stopped running and started speed walking to his car. If he didn't open the door, I would have ripped him out.

Somewhere in my head when he opened the door I thought he might have a gun, so I slowed down. But he didn't, he was trying to act normal. I got up and almost towered over me as I got to the rear end of his car. Instead of his temper coming over him, giving him the chance to hit me he looked stiff and still. One of us had to say something, and who knows what he was thinking, but I stated to scream at him.

"What the fuck is your problem man, you almost got me fucking killed!"

"What are you talking about kid?" He said trying to make me look stupid.

I walked up to him and pushed him into his car and we fought a little bit, a fist was thrown but it didn't connect with me. I pushed him again.

"You sold us out! You lied to us, you fucking lied to us!"

"I don't know what you're talking about."

"Admit it! Admit it!" I yelled, pushing him more.

I almost slipped pushing him, I struggled to keep him away.

"Is that what your instinct is telling you?" He said like a damn psycho.

"My instinct?" I asked.

"Yeah." He reminded me of Shawn all drugged out in his dirty living room.

"At least I fucking have one, everybody knows what you did!" He cut me off by laughing.

"Did what, kid?"

"I saw you with Marc last night! You drove right past my fucking house!"

He looked over where I had run from, and just smiled with cocaine in his eyes.

"Oh, that's your new place?" I tried to push him again but threw me to the ground.

"Your instinct is society, Costa. You'll do anything to be at the top." I mumbled, referring to his betrayal as a normal thing. He followed whatever society was throwing at him, the best offer. People to impress.

"What the hell does that mean?" I don't know what happened, but I just lost it on him. I snapped.

It was the last thing from the ending to a Hollywood movie. I just swung my arms in complete anger, hitting him in the face and I did not stop. I grunted and yelled at him as I hit him harder and harder. I could feel his nose smash apart as he kept spitting his own blood in my face. I just kept getting even madder. I fought back and his smile had turned into his bloody teeth grinding on each other trying to get me off of him.

He threw me off and started to kick me while I was down lying on the ground. My wounds were not fully recovered, and it was like he knew exactly where to kick. With no phone to call anybody, I thought I would lose this fight again.

I fought for no reason but myself this time, and I rolled over getting back up quickly. I hated watching movies where in-between every round of fighting the fighters would have a conversation. That's not how it works. I just kept my arms up as we circled each other. With families upon families in every house, somebody would surely call the police. We had no time to talk anymore.

I knew the drugs in his system would help him to throw the first punch, I was not much of a fighter, but I knew how to dodge pretty well. My hand-eye coordination was a good match too. I just had to wait. A fight seems a lot longer as you're fighting, but it goes by pretty quick. He gave me a beating, but I did not feel it. I knew I would the next morning but my adrenaline was pouring through my veins just like the rain hitting my face. Energy had won my fight, he swung at me and missed as I caught his side.

Endlessly I punched him fast and hard, I could not think tactics. I just ruined his face. I just kept swinging and connecting with him. I took him to the sidewalk and just beat him senseless. I'm not sure if I knocked him out cold, or what he was doing. All I know is that he did not get back up. I had broken my right hand hitting his face. I walked over to his car kicked the door in.

"Get out of here, or I *will* kill you." I swore it to myself in that moment. I said it, and walked away.

I'll never know if I beat some fear into him or if this was even close to an end for him and me. I did know that all together there was no happy ending. I walked back home, sliding my feet, proud of myself. In some sense I felt bad for doing some of things he had asked me to do, but I could not dwell anymore. At least I knew he was not allowed to come back into our town, we had overrun him.

I walked away, shut my eyes and let the rain poor down my head. With my eyes closed I could feel comfort drive into my skull, I was walking on heaven as I heard the rain hit the road. It sounded like God's drum roll as I got used to it, eyes still shut. I felt tricked into a game I never wanted to play, but now I felt comfortable putting an end to a large amount stress.

I was awake. I was filled with new life. I promised myself I would not tell any of the others what happened, I just let him suffer. Somewhere along the lies and lines I would see a happy moment, but life goes on without any ending. I left him there to bleed and never told the story. The next morning I had gotten up early and had to go for another walk. I ended up sitting at a bench liking the view this town and canal had given me. This unique town had given me a story, and this chapter had been complete.

I was so shocked to find when I got home the night before I just fell onto my bed and slept. No worries, nothing. It all could have been mind over matter, but the thing that

I find that counts is that I had a bright smile across my face. Finally things were changing and I was little more ready for what was coming at me next. My fifteen seconds of fame was over. I had lost so much, but I redeemed myself in a truthful sense so I gained a part of myself back. It's funny, because after wanting to change the world for the better, and how much I had gone through, I was just a little existence. A mere, invaluable dent in the giant world, but I felt good because I know I tried.

A couple of lessons I had learned is that a lot of things will change. The few things that don't, are the things we as people should value and hang onto. Happiness is hard to find today, especially in the long run. That is why these things that stay the same in our lives are true to us. Don't love what you want to love, love what you already know you love.

Life is what we make it, and it does not have an answer. If it did, every soul would be the same without change. This gives us the upper hand to make our choices, wrong or right. It's a path that we will always be able to choose. Always go with your heart because most of the time it's what you really want.

Along with endings, you cannot find a new beginning without creation. We will always carry our past with us and as long as we continue to exist our past will as well. Whether we were to remember it or not, it did in fact happen. A new beginning can be created, but not for the sake of ourselves, therefore leaving only beginnings with its own creation.

Memories and stories make up who we are and how we tell them is different. Now that this story has been told there is only five more months until my lesson and death. The next story waits.

THE END

Edward Alex Smith dabbled in writing before, but A Little Existence is his first book revised from its original title, Trudemption and hopes to make a career out of writing, other art forms and entertainment.